A PIECE OF THE ACTION

Another bead
Stacks' red face, r
dropped to sizzle ⌐⌐ ⌐⌐⌐ ⌐⌐ tne 1200
horsepower diesel generator set he was
making adjustments to. Joe was 61 years
old, the last 35 he had spent working on
oilrigs as he was doing now. The
temperature was 114^{0}F with a humidity of 85
per cent inside the engine compound. At
present the oil rig was jacked up some 20
miles offshore in the Arabian Gulf. Joe's
diseased heart beat wildly trying to keep up
with the demands made on it. The last ten
years of his life had been of constant strain.
Previously living in Beirut with a pretty
Lebanese wife, he had a small business and
commuted to the Arabian Gulf to work on
oilrigs. The advent of the Lebanese civil war
had changed everything.

The shop run by his wife was the first
to go, burnt to the ground in an orgy of
violence. A year later his wife was hit in the
head by a stray bullet, living just another
three days. Joe quit Beirut and rented a villa
on the outskirts of Larnaca in Cyprus,
married his late wife's niece who was only 26

1

and was now finding it impossible to satisfy both his new wife's appetite for material possessions and in bed. To Joe it felt as though a giant hand was squeezing his heart, he gasped desperately for air, then slowly, almost lazily toppled over to hit the deck 7 feet below him. He was dead before he reached it. The heavy pipe wrench he had been clutching slid from his nerveless fingers striking and fracturing a small oil feed line. A thin jet of oil spurted out to hit the glowing hot turbocharger, with a hiss it vaporized into blue smoke and then burst into flames.

Asleep in his narrow bed in another part of the rig Al Jenkins had been having a troubled night, dreams reoccurring flashing back to his former time spent serving as a Royal Marine Commando. Of course there had been good times but these seemed to be a compilation of the bad days. Right through times spent in the ever damp and dangerous jungles of Asia to the fear filled and dirty streets of Aden. At the moment though the dream entered on an incident, which had taken place during Al's last tour in the land of so many stupidly lost lives, the province of Northern Ireland. Corporal Al Jenkins and his section of 8 marines were sitting and dozing around the 2-army land rovers in the forecourt of the disused factory on the outskirts of Belfast, which was home for 6 months for the 120 men of Mike Company. It was a star filled and warm September night and Al's section as the immediate reaction force had had a quiet night. One more hour and they could all turn in.

The operations room door flew open and threw a shaft of light across the darkened forecourt. Across it strode the tall thin form of second lieutenant Williamson, troop commander and just six months out of training.

The words came out in a rush. "Corporal Jenkins, just had a call from the RUC, a car bomb has just gone off outside O'Malley's bar in the New Lodge Road, we have to proceed immediately to the scene and assist in the rescue operation, it seems there are several casualties, Brigade are sending ambulance pigs". He paused and gave his arse a quick scratch.

Looking up he went on "We have to be careful on this one, there could well be a secondary bomb waiting for us all to arrive, any quesions?

Marine Thomas, the section joker spoke up from the darkness "Sir, is there any truth in the rumour that the Milk Marketing Board are behind this recent spate of pub bombings?" "What are you talking about Thomas?" The irritation rising in Williamson's voice. "Well Sir, it has been said that if they shut down all the pubs they reckon on selling a lot more milk!"

Williamson leaned closer towards his corporal "How is it that they can joke at a time like this?"

A smile hovered around Al Jenkins' lips. "Sir, you'll find in this job a sense of humour is just as important as the section machine gun or radio or we'll end up walking around like depressive zombies". Jenkins turned to face the men, he said crisply "o.k, mount up, let's go".

The bar was blazing fiercely as the two land rovers approached, every now and then a blackened wooden support would crash down sending up a shower of sparks into the night sky to mingle with the stars already there.

They pulled up sharply, everyone leaping off the rovers to take up defensive positions. Al stared towards the fire, a man had crawled out to one side, his hair reduced to a few tuffs, dragging one leg, blood poured from two wounds in his shoulder. Two medics rushed towards him from the ambulance, which had its bell ringing. Al remembered the noise, all around him there were different bells ringing, the explosion had set off several burglar alarms, the fire appliances were arriving, bells and sirens adding to the din.

Al Jenkins woke with a start in his small cabin on the rig, throwing back the bedclothes he sat up and swore. "What the bloody hell is going on?" He could hear the fire bells vibrating all over the rig, continuously and ominously. He flicked on the light switch and cast a quick look at his Rolex, 2.30 in the morning. It certainly was no drill. He went to the washbasin and splashed some cold water over his face.

Grabbing his hard hat he crossed the room and quickly pulled his work clothes on. He heard the shuffle of boots outside in the corridor, a bang on the thin cabin door was quickly followed by the appearance of 'Tug' Wilson, tall and thickset, noticeable by the two missing fingers on his left hand, he was American and also the senior supervisor on the night shift. "Come on Al, you're the Safety Officer aboard this rig, we need your help, the whole engine room is a god dam inferno. We can't find Joe either, I don't know where the hell he is, probably sleeping some place". Al was surprised to hear the slight tremble in normally tough Tug's voice; this had to be one bitch of a fire. Grabbling a flashlight he followed Tug out through the door. "Tug, did you close off the fuel lines to the engines?" Tug answered over his shoulder as he began to climb a steep set of steps up to the deck above. "Sure I did, but what worries the shit out of me is that 5000 gallon day tank of diesel in the engine room, it's getting real hot and if that son of a bitch blows we might be all taking a swim in the Gulf".

As they stepped out onto the deck, the heat of the fire, intense, hit them radiating, almost a tangible wall that had to be walked through. A glance told Al that it was going to be very hard to save the ageing rig, as at any time the remaining engine would falter to a stop, which would mean complete loss of power except emergency lighting.

Despite his recommendations for an independent fire pump system the cost conscious company had been dragging their feet over the project, Al reflected bitterly.

The crew fighting the raging fire had sealed off all doors leading into the engine room and were directing streams of water against the steaming steel walls in the hope of containing it. The reassuring thump of the remaining diesel faltered to a stop, and so did all the lights over the 4,000 ton rig. The electrically driven motors ground to a halt, most significantly the two 80 horsepower fire pump motors. The water which had been jetting out of the swollen hoses at 60 pounds per square inch suddenly dropped to a few miserable trickles. The noise of the fire was by now much more noticeable, much more ominous, parts of the engine room walls were beginning to glow with heat, the shouts of alarm by some of the men filled the air. Hugh McDonald, crane operator and foreman of the roustabout crew was a very likeable if dour faced Scot. At the moment though, it was hard to tell what expression he wore though the layers of grime and sweat running down his face as he glanced over.

The now useless fire hose dangled from his hand. With a shout of disgust he threw it down, the brass nozzle making a clatter as it struck the deck. He glanced over towards Al, his aluminium safety hat reflecting the glare of the flames.

"So what the hell do we do now to put this fire out, piss on it!" Al grinned, "There's just one thing we could try, swing your crane round to the chopper deck with a cargo box, I'll go up there and load it up with the large dry chemical extinguishers we keep there for fighting helicopter fires, it's our only chance, so we are going to have to be damn quick".

Al turned and ran for the long flight of steps leading up to the chopper deck. At the foot of the steps he skidded to a halt, Tug, looking weary and grim was moving towards him out of the gloom. On his back he wore a fire blackened breathing set. There was despair in his voice as he spoke. "Just been down in the pump room under the engine compound, the fire has spread

down there and it's gaining, we can't even flood it as we are sitting 60 feet above the god damn sea!" He smashed his fist against the steel bulkhead next to him.

"O.k. Tug, can you grab two of your men and follow me up to the chopper deck, I'll explain when we get there." Grabbing the handrail Al launched himself up the steps, three at a time, his boots ringing on the steel steps.

On reaching the top he raced over to where the large wheeled dry chemical and CO_2 extinguishers were kept, grabbing one he started dragging it towards the centre of the deck. He was half way there, sweating heavily when Tug followed by two floor men rushed over to join him. "Thanks lads, the sooner we get this lot down to where it's needed the better. Hugh is swinging the crane round to pick them up, there's just another three to get over here, so let's get moving."

Al paused just long enough to wipe the sweat off his forehead with the back of his hand. Strangely enough, it felt cold to him. Was it just the heat and exertion that was making him perspire so freely or was it in part fear he wondered. The thought of the flames licking around the fuel tank below him sent an icy chill down his spine. He rushed over to join the three oilmen dragging the next appliance. Usually a talkative and jocular bunch, they were strangely silent, heads down, intent only on the job they had to do. Al whispered urgently to Tug "do they realise about the day tank?" Tug nodded his head in response.

Although the fire was contained within the engine room it was not dying out. High up on one of the bulkheads an air intake fan had been left open, this was feeding the fire, greedy for oxygen. Flames at the bottom of the diesel tank had done nothing except to warm it up a little, but now they had reached up to the full height of the deck head above. It was there that the breathing vents of the tank were located, where the highly inflammable gases were accumulated. With a dull boom the gases inside the tank exploded, expanding with great force to peel the shell of the tank open like a banana skin, like some adolescent's boils, the containing doors to the engine room were ripped off their hinges to be sent flying across the deck to rip great gouges in the steel plating. The noise of the first explosion was quickly drowned by a massive blast as 5000 gallons of diesel fuel ignited in a roar that ripped the engine room roof completely off. The rig resounded to the smashing of glass and falling debris, rivers of fire poured through hatchway combings, a giant puff of black smoke rose above the fiercely burning rig.

Al had been leaning over the handrail looking towards the crane. In his right hand he held the torch guiding the long boom of the crane towards the assembled extinguishers when the first explosion had occurred. Realising it for what it was, he had taken a single step back and half turned away before the blast and shockwave of the secondary explosion lifted him off his feet. A blaze of flashing red stars seemed to obscure his vision as he was sent

crashing across the chopper deck, then he remembered he was falling. This had to be a dream; surely he was wrapped up in his bunk on the rig. But it wasn't a dream, the blast had propelled him right over the edge of the chopper deck, he was falling some 80 feet into the dark sea below. He managed to hit it feet first, but even so it was a numbing, jarring shock and he just seemed to keep going down and down. Luckily, he was wearing slip on safety boots and kicking them off he began propelling himself up through the water to break through the surface at about the same time a large black square object crashed into the sea just 10 feet away. Al looked up at the rig above, the four steel supporting legs seemed to disappear into the darkness, but they were close to the deck and they were reflecting an eerie red glow from the spreading fire. He could see small figures swimming around; several splashes under the rig showed where they were launching the life rafts. It wasn't much help to him though as he was drifting away from the blazing structure.

The black object that had dropped into the sea previously and nearly been his demise was floating nearby. With a few strokes he managed to reach and support himself on it, on the large wooden board the stencilled letters stared back at him ironically "Welcome to Rig Hercules, 243 days without a lost time accident".

The tide was carrying him away from the rig, the water was warm and he felt too tired to worry about the sharks he had seen the day before. They were small he mused. Supporting himself on the wooden board, he let the tide take him and dozed. With a start Al was awake, something was nibbling the sock on his right foot, jerking his foot away he glanced around just in time to see the brightly coloured parrotfish dart away. Over the eastern horizon the edge of the sun was making its appearance, announcing the start of a new day, a day he thought in which he would not be taking a part in. But he was alive and drifting slowly towards the low-lying shape of Jalul Island. He recognised it from previous stopovers on the island oil complex on his way to the rig. He gazed into the water looking at his reflection. He noticed the 38 years of his life, wild and often dangerous at times, the years spent in hot and inhospitable climates were reflected in the deep tan, the small lines edging away from the eyes, the blonde hair beginning to thin. But the eyes were still clear and blue with a slight flecking of grey, the demands of his present job keeping his broad, hair covered chest and flat stomach without an ounce of surplus fat. His 5ft 10 inch, 170 pound frame however was not flawless, on his left arm from the wrist to the elbow ran a vivid white scar, a constant reminder of the night he and his drinking pal Terry North, while both in the Marines had gone ashore in a seedier part of Manila.

It was after midnight and about eight pints of San Miguel as they staggered back to the ship when the machete welding mugger had stepped from the shadows, the first blow had been aimed at Terry's neck, at the time Al had put his arm around it to prevent his pal from falling into one of the roads' numerous potholes, his arm took the full force of the attack, blood spurting over Terry, instinctively Al parried the next downward stoke with his

good arm and brought his left knee crashing up into his attacker's groin. Not exactly as he had been taught, but good enough to leave the opposition gasping and doubled up on the road, fortunately they managed to hail a taxi to get to the local hospital where 36 stitches managed to hold the wound together.

Emotionally Al had a much bigger scar than the visible one on his arm. Two years previously, returning home from a month on the rig, he had arrived to find his wife and two beautiful children had died in a horrific accident the previous day. Driving home late that night the police had informed him the car had gone out of control at the bottom of a hill close to the cliff's edge, it had torn through the old and rusting iron railings to drop 80 feet onto the rocks below, the same rocks where the children had played in the summer.

An hour later his feet touched the sandy bottom of a slightly shelving beach on the uninhabited south shore. Wading out, he walked 10 yards up the beach and then sat exhausted amongst the flotsam and debris of a thousand tides. But it was good to be alive, the sun was warm on his back, he felt the sand between his toes, the wind blowing gently through his hair, like a lover's hand. Every sensation felt as though it was entirely new and it felt good.

The noise of an approaching vehicle interrupted his thoughts. Looking up, he saw a land cruiser brake to a halt above the beach, two men got out carrying a stretcher and made their way towards him. Al stood up and shouted "It's o.k. Fellas, I'm still in one piece, don't seem to have lost any vital equipment. But what about the rest of the guys left on the rig"? They did not need to reply; their expressions told him that it was not good news.

CHAPTER 2

Al lay on his back and stared at the ceiling above him in the hotel room, it was 2 days since his rescue and now he had just a few more hours to kill before his flight back to the U.K. Outside the midday sun was a blinding glare, with very little movement in the dusty desert town. Inside the only noise was the hum of the air conditioner and the hotel piped music. Going through the events of the last couple of days had brought home to him that not only had he lost three of his closest friends in the rig fire, but also his job. The oil company had been quite clear about that, there was nowhere at the moment where they could relocate him.

A sharp tap on the door jolted him out of his thoughts, crossing the room he opened it to reveal a smartly dressed Arab, although not tall there was an air of influence about the man, his dark eyes gave nothing away and when he spoke there was no accent.

"I believe you are Al Jenkins, I would like to talk to you if I may". He felt slightly cautious, but curiosity was stronger. "Sure, come in, take a seat, I'll get you a glass of water".

When he spoke it was a lot quieter and somehow more sinister. "My name is Yousef. I am an aide to the Ruler Sheik Al-Hasani and I have a proposition for you. Of course this conversation has never happened, I take it I have your confidence". His gaze was unwavering. "Yes, of course, go ahead", Al replied.

He settled himself in his seat, looked down at his manicured fingernails and began. "Not so long ago when the Israelis invaded Beirut as you may recall, they turned their heads aside while the Phlangists shot and killed everyone in sight in the Palestinian refugee camps of Sabra and Chantila".

He looked hard at Al now. "What are your personal feelings about this tragedy?" Al was not quite sure where this was leading but he did remember the horrific scenes on the TV newscast of mutilated bodies lying in dirty alleyways. "To be honest at the time I did think it a tragic waste of life, I still do". Yousef nodded. "Quite right, not only tragic but also it could have been avoided if the Israelis had not turned a blind eye to it. Now as you know, we do check out people who come to our country to work and we have a good idea of your background. The people I work for think you could well be the man for the job". He stopped to take a sip of water. "To come straight to the point Mr Jenkins, we are prepared to indulge in using a little of our oil revenue in ensuring the death of the man we hold ultimately responsible for the loss of all those Arab lives, if you decide you can do it we will pay you two million U.S.dollars. That man is the Israeli Defence Minister Ben Rubenstein".

The enormity of what he said so matter of factly took what seemed an age for Al to assimilate, the adrenalin was pumping. Two million dollars, Al would never have to work again, but the target, surely it was impossible. Even so, to turn down an opportunity such as this, there were so many things to consider.

Yousef was looking at him for an answer, but he had none to give. "I'm not sure that it is even feasible and that I want to do it". Yousef stood up and put a card in his hand. "Call me at the number on the card, you've got two days to decide if you want to take it. Goodbye, Mr Jenkins". He let himself out, leaving just the strong smell of his aftershave in the faded hotel room.

Normally on the night flight back to Heathrow Al would wait for the food to be served, wash it down with a few glasses of white wine and sleep for the rest of the journey, but sleep would not come to him on this flight. First of all, could he kill this man Rubenstein, an unknown face to him, true he had killed before during his service with the Marines, but then it had come automatically, it had been his job so he had just got on with it. Although even now, several years after the event it was still clear in his mind. It had been in Borneo. Sukarno was the Indonesian head of State at that time with very definite Communist tendencies and seemed to think it was going to be an easy job overthrowing the fledgling Malaysian government. As he had made the initial reconnaissance he led the Company on a night march through the jungle to take up positions around a fortified Indonesian Army post close to the border. Although they knew that there were also Chinese Communist Terrorists operating in the area (C.C.T's), during the reconnaissance they had got close to the post so he was able to distinguish the shoulder flashes on their uniforms. They were up against the 201st Silliwangi Division, big men mostly coming from Java, with a reputation for not running away.

They went up close in the dark through the humid jungle and settled down to wait for dawn. As it slowly grew lighter they could make out their objective, a small hill only 150 yards away crowned by the low roofs of rattan leaves over the post, while there were earthworks supported by strong wooden timbers and closer to them slit trenches. A sentry came towards them and pissed on the ground close to their machine gunners position, but failed to see anything in the half-light. At a signal they opened up with everything they had, self repeating rifles, machine guns, grenade launchers, the position erupted in showers of dirt, explosions and flying wood splinters but suddenly the machine gun firing on his right fell silent, it had jammed, they were in danger of losing the fire initiative. Two Indonesians stood up and began firing back. He felt a tug on the sleeve as a bullet came too close, quickly flicking his M16 over to automatic he sent a long burst in their direction, one of the 5.56mm lead slugs travelling at 3,200 feet per second hit one of the Indonesians in the chest, a small entry wound but as he was spun round by the force of the impact there was a huge gaping wound in his back, his body jerked spasmodically as his life's blood drained into the dark earth.

"Another drink Sir?" He looked up to see the fixed smile on the tired face of the air hostess. "No thanks". He really needed to keep a clear head. Also if he took the job, Al had to consider how it could be done. He would definitely need some help. However, he had a good idea who to turn to, that is if they would co-operate. He had no job, his father had been wounded while serving in Palestine just after the war by Jewish terrorists, two million bucks, hell, he had to go for it.

By the time the captain announced they were on their final approach to rain swept Heathrow, he knew whom he had to call first.

Chapter 3

Todd Burrows smashed the telephone handset down on to the cradle with such force that a piece of the plastic base flew off to land in a corner of his small office. His co-director of the small printing firm, which they ran together Jack Swift, turned round from the wall where he had been studying the latest sales figures. "What's up Todd, wife playing you up again?" Todd could have been mistaken quite easily for being 10 years older than his actual 35, his features were grim and drawn, his skin had an unhealthy pallor about it and when he spoke his voice was angry and bitter. "I wish it was the wife Jack, no, those bastards at the bank have called in their loan, we're not getting a penny more on the overdraft, the company will have to go into liquidation. Six years of hard work down the pan!" He thumped the desk sending papers flying.

Jack's chin visibly sagged. "You're sure they won't reconsider". "I'm sure Jack. Look do me a favour, round up the staff and I'll come and talk to them, they will all need to know". Jack let himself out. Todd slumped into the easy chair, it was worse for him, the bank had his house as security and he had his two children to think of as well. The buzz of the telephone interrupted his thoughts. "Hello, heaven here, God speaking". He really did not give a damn who was on the other end of the line.

"Still the same old gags Todd, it's Al here, Al Jenkins". Todd laughed. "Al, you old bastard, you just can't believe how inappropriate a time you have chosen to call, I'm just about to address my staff to let them know they are all out of a job".

He went on briefly to explain the situation. "I'm really very sorry to hear how things have worked out for you Todd". Al paused. "However, as soon as you have tied things up over there I'd like you to drive over to see me at my place, it's still the same, the flat just outside Weybridge. I can't say too much on the phone but there's a lot of money in it for you", here he emphasised the words, "it could be very dangerous, interested?" Todd didn't take long to consider. "What the hell, I've got nothing to lose, shit or bust, I'll get over there as soon as I can, stick a couple of beers in the fridge for me".

Al replaced the phone with a smile on his face. Of the three people he needed to help him, Todd had been the one most likely to opt out. They had met in Aden in 1967 just before the British pullout, and he knew Todd was an expert on communications during the time he had been attached to Al's unit on secondment from the Royal Signals. They had remained firm friends ever since.

He put through the call to Yousef. "Hello Mr Jenkins, good to hear from you". He sounded calm. "I'll call you back, I've got a scrambler on my line".

Al replaced the phone thoughtfully. Was Yousef calling it off? Whereas before in his mind the whole project had seemed scary and maybe ill advised, he now knew he had to go through with it, wanted to go through with it. The two minutes before the phone rang seemed like two hours. "Yousef? the answer is yes, I'll definitely do it". "Good Mr Jenkins, you will do us a very great service if you can achieve what I have asked, and what I have asked is not a terrorist outrage, it is simply to strike a blow for those people who were unable to defend themselves". "Yes", Ed replied, "if the world can see it in that light then there is your story, the death of the man is not important, the reason for him to die is".

"In shah Allah" said Yousef, "it is indeed God's will that you may succeed, all you need to know from me is that there will be one million dollars deposited at the Credit Suisse Bank in Geneva in your name and when you have completed the task the balance will be paid. I don't need to know any details, I just want to read about it in the papers. Good luck Mr Jenkins". The line went dead.

So, it was up to him, well not just him, he flicked open his address book at the letter 'G'. Gedler, Viola Gedler, strangely enough the number was a Geneva number. He quickly tapped it out and waited for the connection. They had met by chance in Singapore, he'd been duty Guard Commander at the barracks one night when Viola rung through to the guardroom asking to speak to a Lance Corporal Miller whom she had been dating, however when he informed her that Miller had been posted to Hong Kong the week before he also suggested cheekily that perhaps they might meet up together, to his surprise she agreed. They had met at a downtown Singapore English style pub, but unlike English pubs the beer was really cold. She was a beauty. Eighteen years old, her father was Swiss, her mother Jewish, the combination giving her a beautiful olive complexion, long limbed and with long tresses of black hair. You always noticed her eyes, very dark but very warm. They became inseparable for eight months, when at her mother's insistence the whole family moved back to Israel. Through the occasional letters he received, occasional because her mother had always objected to her daughter's friendship with a soldier and a gentile to boot, it transpired that Viola had had to do her national service in the Israeli Army which she had hated.

She had begged him to come and join her but it was impossible. A couple of years later she married a junior Israeli diplomat, his work taking him to various countries, while Viola had got the job of translator at the Israeli delegation at the U.N offices in Geneva, their home was there at present.

"Hello", it was still the same voice with the soft Swiss accent from those years before. "Hello Viola, it's Al Jenkins here, remember me and Singapore in 68'?"

"Al", the gasp of astonishment was genuine, "how could I ever forget, I may be married now but I do still have my memories and they were good ones. It's great to talk to you again".

Al felt the warmth of her friendship creep over him. "Yes, it is wonderful to hear your voice again Viola, how would you like it if I were to see you again, I have to go over to Geneva in a couple of days on business". Viola's face creased in a broad smile. "Do you think I could recognise you after all these years?" Al laughed. "The hair's a bit thinner, but otherwise I'm still the same, well I like to think so anyway". "Well, you sound just the same", she said, "but I'll be the judge of how you look when I see you, give me a call when you arrive at the airport".

He worked up to 2 a.m. in the night, going over details, sketching out one plan and then another, it wasn't going to be very easy, there were so many details to be worked out. He gave up and went to bed, but slept fitfully not really getting to sleep until 4. His eyes were still heavy when he looked across at the bedside clock and saw the hands reading 5 to eleven in the morning.

He was eating his second round of brown toast when the doorbell rang. He opened it to reveal Todd looking slightly flustered but expectant, he grasped the proffered hand and shook it warmly. "Well you didn't waste any time getting over here

Todd, but it's really good to see you, you haven't managed to get rid of that office tan yet!" "Al, you oily old bugger, Todd spoke loudly, what the hell have you got up your sleeve this time, and by the way you look lousy, been on the razzle last night?" Al led him through to the kitchen. "No, although I feel as though I have, take a pew and I'll make some fresh coffee".

Todd quickly sat down on one of the bamboo chairs and looked up eagerly towards Al. "Well, come on then, I want to know exactly what it is that I have to do to earn my money, you always did like keeping everybody in suspenders". Al smiled on hearing Todd's last word, because despite the banter he knew underneath Todd was a worried man, it was difficult to hide. He finished pouring out the steaming coffee, drew up a chair and sat opposite Todd. He spoke in a low conspirator whisper. "All I want from you Todd is that you get a pound of plastic explosive, the electrical components to make a remote bomb and put it together with your expertise and connections. It shouldn't be too difficult". Todd was sitting bolt upright now, his coffee forgotten. He had all his attention. Al continued. "After that at the time and place you can assist me in making sure the bomb gets to the right recipient". "And I thought you were going to ask me to do something difficult!" Todd tried to speak lightly, but was betrayed by the great furrows on his brow. "And who may I ask are we planning to kill?"

"A man who has already lived most of his life, he's 71, but by taking his, you stand to enhance yours and mine, so just call it a trade if you like, that man is the Israeli Defence Minister Ben Rubenstein". Al paused to watch Todd's reaction. He was staring at the table gripping it hard, his knuckles white. When he spoke his voice was serious. "It can't be done Al, I mean you of all people must realise the reputation of Mossard, the Israeli Secret Service". Al stirred his coffee and then dropped the spoon in the saucer with a rattle.

"Well, I've already decided that it can, maybe your courage will come back to you when I tell you that you can have one hundred and fifty thousand dollars up front in your grubby little hands in a couple of days". Al leaned back in his chair watching Todd thoughtfully. He knew he was having his own private battle within, whether money would compensate the dangers.

At last Todd spoke. "You're right Al, with that kind of money I can get the company back on its feet, the future for me and my family will be secure, yes I'm your man, count me in". Al reached down and grasped a bucket of ice with a bottle of champagne protruding from it. "That's what I wanted to hear, grab a couple of glasses and we'll drink to our success". They spent the next three hours going over details, and when Todd left for home he had an air of confidence about him that wasn't there before.

Al had gone straight to the phone and called Swissair, yes, they could get him on the 11 a.m. flight to Geneva the next day. Getting himself a stiff drink from the drinks cabinet in the airy lounge, he settled into one of the soft leather chairs. There were butterflies in his stomach as he thought of his impending visit to see Vi again after all these years. But more importantly how she would react to the proposal he had to put to her. However, he knew now there was no turning back, he had to go through with it. One thing was certain, their security had to be watertight; the slightest lapse would be fatal to their chances of succeeding.

Chapter 4

The scream of the reversing jet engines jolted Al awake as the Boeing 737 touched down at Geneva. He watched the airport buildings grow larger as the aircraft taxied towards them. It was July 16th and outside the runway shimmered in the midday heat. It was here that the key lay in whether his plan could go any further. Immigration formalities were soon completed. He had travelled on his own passport, as at this stage there was no necessity to do otherwise. He found an empty telephone kiosk and rang Viola's number, it took her a long time to answer. "Hello Vi, I was just about to give you up, look if I've caught you at a bad time I can get a taxi".

Her voice was slightly breathless. "No, really Al, actually I was just taking a bath and at the moment I'm standing here dripping water on the carpet with just a towel round me". Al laughed softly. "Well, I won't say I can just imagine it as I've not seen you in 10 years, but I'm sure you've still got all the curves in the right places". Her voice was slightly husky, "I see you haven't forgotten how to turn on the charm, you no good rascal. Look, I'll be there in fifteen minutes, wait outside for me, ciao".

The black BMW cruised to a stop 10 feet from him the door opened and he found himself looking at the smiling familiar face of Viola, still the same warm eyes, the long black hair, maybe her figure was just slightly fuller than before but otherwise she was still the wonderful girl he had fallen in love with all those years before.

There was a pull at his heart at the thought of what might have been, she at the time had mentioned marriage, but he had not been sure then, putting it down to her immaturity. "Well you great pillock, what are you staring at, how about a kiss on the cheek at least", she laughed. He embraced her then stood back. "Vi, the years have been very good to you, wonderful to see you again, it really is, and you look great". She did as well, wearing a white silk blouse with lace trim around the neck accentuating her femininity, with a small black bow tie and matching coloured skirt.

"You don't look so bad yourself Al, but to what do I owe the honour of you dropping in to see me after all this time? I didn't know you had any business in Geneva". She led him around to the passenger side of the car. "Would you believe dropping in to see about my local bank account", he said tauntingly.

"Actually I would," she said as she slipped the car into gear and pulled smoothly away from the kerb. "You always were a devious bastard, what are you getting up to these days?" Al smiled. "Nothing exciting, I work as an engineer for various oil companies". "Sounds pretty good" she nudged him playfully in the ribs, "but, don't forget I know you of old, I remember that time in Singapore when I went to see you at your flat, two hours I spent in small

talk with your flatmate while you were dead drunk hiding out in the loo. Of course your pal said you were ill and of course I believed him".

"We've grown up a lot since then Vi". Al became more serious. "And I think it's better all round to bring the truth out in the first place, which is why I would like to take you out to dinner tonight to discuss something important with you, in fact I am going to ask a great favour of you". "A-ha", she said smugly. "I thought you might have an ulterior motive for coming over to see me, by the way where are you staying?"

"You can drop off at the Meridian. Well, do we have a date?" Vi adjusted the sunglasses on her pert nose. "Well, hubby is out of town for a couple of days, yes o.k. I'll come by at 8, I know a nice out of the way restaurant but it's your turn to pay". Al squeezed her on the shoulder. "It's a deal, I'll put on my best bib and tucker". Ten minutes later he was booking into the hotel. After cleaning up and a fresh change of clothes he made his way to the Credit Bank Suisse and withdrew the money he needed to pay Todd plus a substantial amount more, there were going to be a lot of expenses.

It was a lovely intimate Italian restaurant overlooking Lake Geneva. Viola looked stunning in a long black dress with a lot of cleavage showing. Throughout the meal they had been engrossed with each other, reliving old memories. They had been good times but Vi had indicated that it was the past and her present life was a happy one.

Al waited until the last of the dishes had been cleared away before speaking to her about what was uppermost in his mind. "Vi, would you be prepared to get me some information from inside the Israeli mission?" A guarded expression came over her face. "So that's what this is all about, you know I have been trying to figure out all evening what exactly you were going to ask me to do". Al tried unsuccessfully to sound casual. "I don't really want to know very much, but you could help me a great deal, it's nothing really important", he ended lamely.

"Let me be the judge of that", she said, "just what sort of information do you want?" He bit his lip not knowing how she would react. "All I would like from you Vi is to get me the itinerary of the Defence Minister over the next month, obviously don't let anyone know about it. It shouldn't be too difficult for you to obtain." She stared at him thoughtfully for a moment. "Yes, I think I could get that, but why Al, why do you want to know his movements?" Al paused while the waiter placed a coffee in front of each of them. "I really think it is better that you don't know, there will be no comeback to you. I mean I know you don't like the old bastard after your time in the Army. You may also know that he was a wanted terrorist by the British in 1947". She ran her fingers through her long black hair and spoke quietly. "I'll have to think about it". Al knew she was wavering. It was time for him to play his ace. "Look, if you get the information, meet me outside here by the lakeside at seven tomorrow night. If you get it I'll give you in return $30,000 in cash".

Her eyes widened, she nervously sipped at her coffee. "O.k., I'll certainly give it some more thought. You're still a devious bastard but I know I shall always care about you". He gave her hand a squeeze. "I wish you weren't married Vi", he spoke softly, "but you know I'll always have a candle burning for you". He wanted to ask her back to his hotel, wanted to feel her warmth up close beside him, to kiss those sensual lips and he was sure that she would agree. But also in his heart he knew they would both regret it the next day. He called for the bill.

July 17th was another scorcher. Al spent the morning in and out of the hotel swimming pool and then had a light lunch. The day was dragging, seven that night seemed a long way off. Would she show? After lunch he took a stroll outside the hotel until he found an unoccupied telephone booth and called Todd. Yes, it seemed Todd had located most of the electrical components he would need for the bomb, but then came the bad news. "Al", he could only just hear Todd over the static on the line. "I'm afraid I've drawn a blank on the P.E (plastic explosive), just can't get it, so hope you have some ideas when you get back". Todd rang off. Al didn't at the moment. He was going to have to think hard and long, maybe they would even have to change their plan. All of a sudden the doubts and fears in the back of his mind came crowding forward. They were confirmed when at seven that night he failed to see the welcoming figure of Vi come towards him. He nervously waited by the lakeside until 8.30. Like the spectacular fountain in the lake which jetted up into the night sky, it must just as surely fall back to earth, just as his plans had been so convincing, his dreams of a financial future, so secure it seemed, they were doomed to failure. He took a taxi back to the hotel and called Vi, there was no reply.

Vi had worked quite hard that day, after taking the previous afternoon off to meet Al. When she arrived in the morning her in tray had contained a pile of formidable looking documents. So it was no surprise to her boss when he came through from his office at five to find her still working and would be another hour before she finished, or so she told him. In fact she had completed the work she needed to.

In the now deserted offices, apart from the security on the ground floor she had time to go through the files in her boss's office looking for the information that seemed to be so vital to her old flame. Although in her heart she was beginning to feel more reluctant to say anything to him, if word got out it would mean her job. The sound of approaching footsteps came clearly to her from the outside corridor. She quickly darted over to her desk, sat down and began writing. The guard poked his head around the corner. "Still working Mrs Gedler". She glanced over to him. "Yes, I'll be finished in half an hour". He nodded and disappeared from view. She waited a few minutes and then went back to resume her search.

After another fifteen minutes of fruitless searching she was about to give up when her eyes fell on the small black diary at the bottom of one of the

desk drawers. She quickly flipped through it. Yes, there were two occasions when Rubenstein was leaving the country in the next month or so. In a week's time he was arriving in Rome to meet with the Italian Foreign Minister and then on the 11th of August he was going to the Canary Islands to promote the sale of Israeli small arms to the Spanish Military. As she put the book back carefully into the drawer and made her way out, she failed to notice the small glass eye of the security camera duly recording her movements. She hadn't known about it as it had been installed only the previous weekend.

It had not gone unnoticed in the security room downstairs. Since he had returned from his rounds the guard had observed her on the small screen for the past five minutes. He quickly tapped out seven digits and spoke urgently on the phone. He replaced it as Viola came down the stairs. "Good night Mrs Gedler". She replied and made her way out to her car.

On the way home she finally made her decision that she would meet with Al but would not tell him what she had found out. There was something sinister behind the query, something that did not smell right. Besides she would have done it for nothing. Al was being extremely generous. Why?

It was nearly six thirty by the time she arrived home at her apartment. She was going to have to hurry to keep her appointment with Al. After a quick change of clothes she was making her face up when the doorbell rang.

She opened it to reveal a man whom she had seen previously around the Israeli mission. His name she didn't know but his occupation she did. He was a member of

Mossard, the Israeli Secret Police. When he spoke he did so with an air of menace. "Mrs Gedler, I would like to come in to talk to you. I'm from the mission as you probably already know. I deal with security". She led him through to her spotless lounge. She could feel her heart pounding against her ribs. What did they know? She sat down. He took a seat opposite her, observing with his small close set brown eyes.

"You can call me Mo. Yes, perhaps you can tell me why you left the mission so late tonight?" She felt slightly relieved. Maybe it was just a routine enquiry. "Oh that, I had to work late catching up on yesterday as I took the afternoon off". "You just worked at your desk and didn't go anywhere else?" They couldn't possibly know she had gone through her boss's desk, could they? "Why, yes of course". She tried to keep her voice as calm as possible. He raised his voice an octave. The words came out flat and hard. "Well, I happen to know that you did. You were observed going through papers in the Head of Mission's office." She fought desperately to keep her voice level. "Oh yes, I forgot there were some details I wanted to know about a delegation meeting next week".

"These details would normally be kept in his in tray, is that correct?" he asked. She felt trapped. He must know she had also looked in the desk drawers. "Normally yes". He leaned closer to her, "I'm afraid you have not

convinced me, now I want you to tell me exactly what you were looking for in that office and I don't want to hear any lies". "I was just looking for papers in connection with my work", she said sharply. For a rotund and slightly dumpy figure Mo was very fast. His right hand came up in a blur and struck her across the cheek. She could feel a slight trickle of blood rend its way down from her nose to her lips and taste the saltiness in it. "How dare you", she sobbed. "Is that the way you are taught to interrogate people? I have nothing else to tell you". Mo flexed his fingers. "You will tell me and I am prepared to wait for just as long as it takes". She turned away from his gaze. She knew it was no good complaining to her boss. Where security was concerned it was paramount. But she could feel her anger and resentment rising against the treatment she had received. If only they had just ignored it, she had already decided not to pass on the information. But after what had just transpired she was now determined to get the information to Al. Would she be in time? He had indicated his stay was only two days and tonight was obviously out of the question. It was rather risky and foolish to call through the hotel switchboard and she would undoubtedly be followed if she tried to see him. No, she could try to slip away during tomorrow's lunch break. After a further hour of questioning Mo suddenly stood up. "O.k. so you have nothing further to say. Perhaps we may be able to believe your story". Although by the look in his eyes, she was pretty sure he did not. He let himself out of the flat.

Vi only had half an hour of her lunchtime left the next day. By the time she arrived at the Meridian she had doubled up and down several streets before arriving. If there was someone following, she was pretty sure she had lost them.

She found Al relaxing by the side of the sparkling swimming pool, his body still gleaming wet from the swim he'd just taken. "Pretty good life for the idle rich", she smiled as she spoke. Al's face split into a broad grin. "Vi, I'd given you up, no, I'm just getting some practice in as I hope to be rich one day". Vi's face took on a more serious look. "I'll have to be quick as I've got to get back, but I have those details you asked for". She sat down next to him and whispered the times and dates he so badly needed to know.

He grasped her hand. "Vi, I can't thank you enough. Wait here and I'll get you the money I promised". She squeezed his hand in return. "No Al, just promise me that you will take care of yourself. I may have problems explaining away all that cash". Her voice took on a more resigned tone. "You know I don't wish to hear what you have planned, but I just hope this problem between the Jews and Arabs could finish once and for all. Although I'm half Jewish I would not mind if Israel gave the West Bank to the Palestinians. I mean after all we did take it from Jordan in the '67' war. If they had their own state that would be the end of it".

Al nodded his head slowly. "You're so right, it really is such a tragic waste of life and resources". The hotel piped music was playing 'A whiter shade of Pale' by the Procul Harem, a song both of them knew and loved. It

had been their song when they had first met and now they both knew they might never meet again. No words were needed, no words could explain how they both felt. "Goodbye my love". Al rose and embraced her. "Let's not say goodbye", she said. "Au revoir sounds so much better". He stood and watched her walk quickly towards the hotel door. She paused just briefly before she entered to turn and smile at him, a contradiction as there were tears streaming down her face. The door swung closed behind her, she was gone. Al slowly sat down and rested his head in his hands. How could he have asked someone so close to him to risk all to help? Deep feelings of guilt welled up inside but because of what she had done he knew now he must go through with it, otherwise it was all for nothing. There was something he'd noticed about Vi, she had seemed to be afraid, he had thought for him but no, she was afraid for herself. Was it possible she had been detected?

He suddenly stood up, grabbed his towel and made for the changing room. He couldn't discount the possibility that she had been followed. It was time to get back to England.

From his vantage point on the first floor balcony of the hotel, Mo watched him stride in. He turned to his Mossad colleague next to him. "Well she told him something, but what? And who is he? I want you to find

out everything you can about him". The man
nodded and strode purposely away.

Chapter 5

On the journey back home Al had been going over the two occasions when Rubenstein was out of the country. There was no doubt Rome was out of the question. It was too dangerous and the time far too short to properly implement any plan. It had already been decided not to plan any attack in Israel; the chances of getting out were far too thin, which left them just the one chance on the 11th of August in the Canary Islands. It was their one shot.

He moved restlessly in his chair back at the flat. It was almost midnight and tomorrow would be the 19th July, there were just 23 days in which to plan and carry it out.

He called Todd's number. There was a grumpy reply from the other end. "What time do you think this is to call?" "I don't know, I'm not the speaking clock", Al laughed down the line. "It's important Todd", his voice taking on a more serious note. "I must see you tomorrow, things are beginning to move. I'll meet you tomorrow at midday. Remember the Windmill pub on the Thames near Walton? See you there. Give my love to the family".

There was no windmill any more near the pub from whence it got its name but it did have an imposing beer garden at the rear next to the slowly flowing river, there were ancient willow trees at the water's edge, droning, swaying leaves kissing the surface. Al made his way through the plastic topped tables clutching a pint of shandy and occupied a table close by the river. It was 11.45, the lunchtime rush was yet to come. A quick glance showed just two other tables in use, one was occupied by a young couple, their heads nearly meeting, engaged in an intimate conversation, while at the other a burly thickset fellow was devouring a Cornish pasty, interspersed with gulps of beer from his pint mug.

Al leaned back in his chair and took in the scenery. The sun came out from behind the scudding clouds to transform the river into sparkles of light where the current eddied trees throwing shadows that danced and weaved over the surface. The tranquillity of the scene was in marked contrast to his thoughts, namely planning the demise of the Israeli Defence Minister.

He glanced at his watch. Ten past twelve, however as he did so the tall gangling figure of Todd Burrows came through the swung doors. He looked irritated. He came over and plonked himself down opposite Al, the steel chair legs screeching across the concrete floor as he pulled his chair up close.

"That damn M25 motorway. I think everybody is driving round and round not knowing when to get off", he complained. "Don't worry", laughed Al,

"go and get yourself a drink, you'll feel better for it". Todd stood up. "O.k., you don't need a refill do you, as your glass is still half full?" Al prodded him towards the bar. "Half full, I'd call it half empty, no, but you are right, no more for me thanks". Todd was back in two minutes clutching a pint of beer in one hand and an oversized sandwich in the other. As he sat down Al pushed across the table a bulging brown envelope towards him. "That will keep you in sandwiches for some time to come", Al paused, "now, let me know how far you have got with our little device". Todd leant closer in order not be overheard.

Across from them the young couple carried on their conversation. "O.k. Helga, it looks like the man Jenkins is going to be here for a while. You know what you have been paid to do. Go now and look over his apartment. As soon as it looks as though he is about to leave I'll drive ahead, so get out as soon as you hear my horn". The slim attractive girl nodded and quickly made her way out to the car park.

Todd was worried. Building the device was going ahead well thanks to contacts, except for the vital component without which it was useless, the plastic explosive.

"What hasn't helped, he said, "is all this recent IRA activity, it seems almost impossible to get hold of the stuff without a lot of questions being asked". Al stared hard at his now empty beer glass. "Time is getting short, he said, and we don't have a lot of it to spend obtaining P.E especially in this country. You're right, we can't afford to leave any sort of trail which could lead back to us".

"So what do you suggest?" There was despair in Todd's voice. "I really don't have any contacts overseas". It was a full two minutes before Al replied. He had been sifting through the files in his mind, of people he knew both past and present who might, just might be able to help them out. "I can think of only one person who might be able to get his hands on what we are after".

The frown creasing Todd's forehead eased slightly. "Who have you got in mind, the Red Brigade?" Al grinned. "The trouble with you Todd is that you have no faith. Do you remember an American I have spoken to you about on previous occasions by the name of John Brooks?" "Wasn't he the U.S. Marine Corps Officer you knew during your time out East", Todd replied. "The very one, and I happen to know here he is at the present time. I got a postcard last month from a seedier part of Bangkok. He is an adviser to the Thai Government". Todd looked doubtful. "Advising on what? Where to direct American tourists to get the best lays!" Al grinned. "That's sacrilegious Todd. Mind you he is probably pretty qualified in that field as I remember".

Al did remember too, back to when he had first met John or JB as he used to call him after they became friend. It was 1967, Al had just come back from a six-month stint in Borneo and had been assigned to the Jungle Warfare School in the south Malay state of Johore as an instructor. John was one of a batch of three recently graduated officers from the States assigned to his care to learn basic jungle skills before heading off to the conflict in Vietnam. They had struck an instant rapport whereas some of the officers on those courses were inclined to be patronising, feeling that mere N.C.O's were not worthy to impart any skills to them. John was different. Firstly both of them being in the Marines, but mainly due to the respect they held each other in. He would absorb every piece of information that was fed to him, either in lectures or practical lessons in the jungle, sign reading, tracking, booby traps, plant identification.

He thanked Al before leaving Vietnam saying they must get together one day over a few beers. Al didn't expect to hear from him again, so it came as a surprise when he did.

Al received a card from Bangkok six months later. J.B was staying there for his R&R. Could he come up? Al had some leave due so what the hell, he took the overcrowded and hot night train to the City of Angels as the Thais called it.

He stayed with J.B at this father's house. His father, an imposing man, was an ex-Colonel of the U.S.A.F and was now running trips into Laos for Air America on covert missions for the C.I.A.

After an evening barbecue, J.B and Al headed into town. The place was swarming with American G.I's and sailors on

R&R. However, they managed to find a quiet little bar where they could have a chat. It wasn't the same J.B Al knew before he left for his tour of duty. He was very intense, relating his experiences in the jungle, but seeming to get more depressed. After two hours Al thought it was time to call a halt, the evening was becoming too morbid.

"J.B, there's a real good looking couple of girls over there giving you the eye, how about it?" He shook his head. "I don't think I'm in the mood right now". Then he winked, "Tell you what, let's have a couple more beers and I'll review the situation". They laughed and called the waiter over. "We'll have a couple more cool Singha beers khoop kun mak". In fact they had four more before J.B suddenly threw up his hands. "Tell you what", he said, "never mind those two by the bar, I've got a better idea". "My dad said if I ever felt the urge, to go to this place". He indicated the card. "There's a great choice and they are all clean, don't want to carry an lasting souvenirs with me back to the States". He laughed as he staggered to his feet. Al followed him to the exit, the room seeming to swim slightly before his eyes. They grabbed hold of each other for mutual support before emerging out to a stifling hot tropical night. That and the roar of the traffic brought them back to reality, well almost.

The taxi dropped them off fifteen minutes later at an address in the suburbs, the street was deserted. The only sounds were those of the distant hum of traffic while closer at hand a radio was blaring out a popular Thai song. The iron grill gate creaked as they entered into the driveway of the low roofed bungalow at whose door stood a powerfully built young man. He beckoned them in. The light was dazzling after being out in the dark empty night, the air heavy with the smell of incense. "Sawadi Krap". The traditional Thai greeting came from a middle aged colourfully dressed Thai lady whom they took to be the madam of the House. "Come this way and choose one of our beautiful ladies to make you happy. You must pay first please. Very high class ladies".

She led them over to a large window, through which they could see half a dozen scantily clad girls of varying beauty, some sitting down and talking while two of them were standing opposite them, combing their flowing long black hair, then it struck them it was a one-way mirror. They could not see through. "I've seen the one I like pal, what a way to go eh?" J.B slapped Al across the back and turned towards the Madam.

"That little beauty sitting at the side of the room will do me, yes Sir". She led him away. Al had been studying the girl standing almost opposite him. She seemed to be trying to improve her flawless complexion, rubbing at an imaginary spot, her raven hair sweeping down to frame the delicate features. Her tiny graceful hands fluttering like little birds as she smoothed down the figure hugging black dress. The way she looked would have made most people happy but there was a sad look in her eyes, that is what made Al choose her.

Five minutes later she took his big hand as they walked into the small room she used, a low wattage bulb threw light over the bed, a chair and a small dressing table, the only furniture in the room.

"You American G.I, yes?" There was softness in her voice, which matched her features. "I suppose you could call me an English G.I. I'm from England". She looked surprised. "Not often we see Englishman here, why you come?" She slid out of her dress and undid her bra. "I've come to see you of course". Her face smiled but her eyes stayed sad. "Englishman like to make joke, quick, you must take off clothes". He obliged and sat beside her on the soft bed. "What do you want to do to me, anything special?" She said it as if there was a menu in front of him. He gave her a big smile. "No, sweet thing, a massage would be wonderful to start with". Her hands may have looked dainty but they felt very powerful as she eased his aches and pains away with an expertise that only the Orientals seemed to possess. She told him her name was Tina and that she had come from a poor fishing village in the South, her income was supporting her entire family. The combination of massage and alcohol running through his veins was too much and he fell asleep.

The next thing he knew was a rough hand shaking him by the shoulder. "Come on Al, I reckon you've been overdoing it, you randy bastard". He looked up to see the broad grin on J.B's face. "Your friend Tina here called me to wake you up, I guess it's about time we got back". He dressed hurriedly, but before he left he arranged to meet Tina the next day, that is,

before she started work. He still felt a great desire for her, but also to find out the person behind the façade she put up. J.B and Al really lived it up that week, but before Al returned to work he managed to meet Tina on several occasions during the afternoon.

They would meet up and go to a small Thai eating-house, spend an hour or so in a hotel swimming pool before going upstairs to make love in the afternoon. Torrid days with Tina, he promised to see her again, but he knew he probably never would. Shaking hands with J.B at the station before heading back, even after all these years the memories had not faded. Al even recalled that Tina had told him her real name was Anya, she loved him she said and gave him a small Buddha to protect him.

"Come on Al, stop daydreaming. Where do we go from here?" Todd's voice brought Al back to the present. "Sorry Todd, yes you're right we had better get things moving. I've got a call to make". He pushed his chair back and stood up. "I'll let you know as soon as I've got some news". Todd walked with him to the car park. "Let's just hope that it's good news", he said. "We've only got three weeks left".

Chapter 6

Helga was good at her job. It wasn't the first time she and Jack had been asked to turn over a particular premises. The swarthy looking man who hired them always paid good money. Getting in to Jenkins' flat had been no problem, but she knew that he could arrive back at any time, so she had to find out as much as she could about the man. Those were her instructions. But up to now she had drawn a blank. Going through the desk drawers had revealed nothing but bills, personal letters from friends and other assorted paperwork. She had been told in particular to look out for anything concerning Israel or the Arab States, but it seemed there was nothing of interest that would indicate Jenkins was other than an engineer working for an oil company, although from what she had seen he had also served previously with the Armed forces. There was a framed citation on the wall above his desk. She made sure everything was back in its proper place and slid shut the last of the drawers.

Sometimes it was the person's clothes that hid the clues. Keeping her ears open for any sound of Jenkins' arrival, she opened the wardrobe doors and quickly started going through the suit and jacket pockets. Her nimble fingers soon found the navy blue British passport. Flicking through the pages revealed several entry and exit stamps from Arab countries but otherwise nothing. She looked up sharply from her browsing at the slam of a car door close by, followed almost immediately by the sound of Jack's horn. Helga quickly went to put the passport back. In her haste it slipped from her fingers. Bending down to retrieve it she noticed the small business card that had fallen out. There was an Arabic lettering as well as English written on it. As she slipped it into her pocket the sound of a key turning in the lock of the front door reached her ears. Her long legs propelled her towards the door counting on surprise to get past Jenkins as his framed filled the doorway. She lunged past but just was not quick enough to avoid his outstretched leg to send her flying onto the path outside. She clawed desperately at the gravel to get up but felt his weight pressing her down. "You bitch, you're going to be sorry you tried to rob my flat". He was leaning close over her shouting the words so he did not see the man step up behind him, the small heavy cosh coming down in a blur to strike Jenkins close to the temple. Helga pushed the now unconscious body from her and stood up. " You bloody idiot Jack, why the hell didn't you give me more warning?" she said angrily. "Come on, let's get out of here, I'll tell you in the car", Jack said as he strode quickly away.

They were a mile down the road before Jack turned to her. "We were all sitting down at the pub when all of a sudden this guy Jenkins suddenly gets up and the two of them made off to the car park, so I could hardly rush in front of them". He changed down a gear as they approached a set of traffic lights. "Anyway", he continued, "On the way down here the traffic was so bad I just

didn't get a chance to overtake him". She didn't look convinced. "Well, you're going to have to smarten up your act you know. He must have got a good look at me". Jack said reassuringly, "Well, I don't think he will be going to the Police somehow". Then added, "So what have you got for our benefactor in London?" She told him about the passport and then handed him the small card she had picked up. Jack turned it over in his hand. "Is that it? Well, let's hope it's enough for us to get paid."

Forty minutes later they kept their appointment with the man who had hired them. The designated spot was a bench in central Hyde Park. He listened impassively as Helga related the details on what she had seen in Jenkins' flat. He studied the business card with the same detachment. However, behind the dark glasses there was a flicker of interest. He passed over an envelope containing fifteen £20 notes. His tone was dismissive when he spoke. "Thanks for the job. I'll be in touch if I should need you again". He adjusted his glasses, turned away from them and made off in the direction of Princes Gate.

Mo Jacobs turned round from the window where he had been surveying the lunch time traffic on the busy Geneva street, walked over and took his place at the head of the oval shaped table. Three men dressed in dark suits looked up from the files they had been studying.

"Gentlemen", he began, "I take it that you have read the report from our operative in London, well to me it leaves a nasty taste in the mouth". There was a general nodding of heads. He tapped the file in front of him. "O.k. so what have we got, one of our employees was observed going through the Chief's desk, not much there I grant you. However, the next day she meets up with this Al Jenkins, again nothing really out of the ordinary. But just to be on the safe side we get our man in London to check up on him". Mo paused to light a small cheroot and dropped the match into the ashtray. "It seems that Jenkins is carrying the calling card of Yousef Hamedi, who as we all know is the Chief Paymaster for Sheik Al-Hasani, channelling funds into the PLO and other organisations.

There was a brief silence as the four Mossard men weighed up the implications. Harry Reynolds, a tall man with a sharp pointed face and cropped grey hair was the first to break it. "As Jenkins has a military background, it could be that he has been hired to procure weapons for the Arabs." "It is possible", Mo said, "but I just have this gut feeling there is more to it than that. I have spoken to Superintendent Bill Scott of the Yards Anti-Terrorist Squad, they have run a check on the computer and have come up with nothing".

Reynolds said with a wave of his arm. "So maybe we have nothing to worry about, you could be overreacting Mo". A look of anger crossed Mo's face. "No, I've had these feelings before and I've invariably been proved   right.

I think we ought to continue surveillance for the time being". "O.k.", Reynolds replied sourly, "but I'm sure that you will find it is probably a waste of time and resources". Reynolds and Jacobs had been rivals for years, both wanted the top post in the organisation; therefore they usually disagreed even on trivial details in order to steal a march on the other. There was a sharp tap on the door, one of the men sitting nearest it got up and opened it to reveal a middle aged woman clasping a sheet of paper.

"Excuse me, but I've got a telex here for Mr Jacobs". The man passed it across to Mo. The slow ticking of the clock suddenly seemed quite loud in the wood panelled room as they waited for Mo to reveal the contents of the message. "It seems", he paused to look at this watch, "that our Mr Jenkins has just caught a flight out of Heathrow, destination Bangkok. It left half an hour ago". Harry Reynolds sat back in his chair, a smug expression on his face.

"Well, we don't have anybody out there to watch him, so we will just have to wait for his return".

Mo stubbed out his cheroot viciously in the ashtray. "Damn it, I just know this guy is up to something but what?" He stared hard at the table as if it would give him inspiration.

The small dapper man on Mo's right said quietly, "We may not have a man in Bangkok but we do have Richards in Australia. If we gave him a call now he could be in Bangkok before Jenkins arrives, depending on available flights of course". Mo rounded on him, his voice full of enthusiasm. "That's a great idea, yes let's do it, we can fax Jenkins' picture and flight details immediately". "Well, it's your decision Mo", Reynolds said sourly, "You can explain to the General why you may have sent Richards on a wild goose chase." "I'll take that chance", said Mo brusquely. He picked up the phone and began barking orders down it.

Chapter 7

To Al Jenkins it felt as though he were crawling along a dark tunnel, it was painful to crawl but he thought he could just see light at the end of it. He forced himself harder, his eyes flickered open, and he was staring at the sky. It took him a minute to realise where he was, he sat up and saw the half open door to his flat and it all came flooding back.

He remembered opening his door, the flying form of the female charging past whom he just managed to trip, he had been trying to restrain her when the blow had come from behind. He reached up slowly to touch the side of his head; there was a huge lump there, which still seemed to be growing.

He got slowly to his feet and made his way inside the flat, a deep throbbing pain running through his head with each jarring step. He took some ice cubes out of the fridge and carefully wrapped them in a towel; with it pressed against the side of his head he conducted a check around the flat but could find nothing missing. "Strange", he mused. However, he could have disturbed her before she had a chance to take anything. There was something else that was puzzling him. He could have sworn he'd seen the woman before, but where?

He suddenly recalled the reason for his coming home at this time. He put through a call to the Thai Embassy in London and managed to speak to the Assistant Military Attaché.

Yes they could confirm John Brooks was acting for the Thai Government in an advisory capacity but no they could not provide any home or address details. However, they did give the name of the Government Department to contact in Thailand.

Al sat down in one of the comfortable chairs to ease the pain in his head and went over the options open to him. Really he knew there were no grey areas, it was a case of calling it off or proceeding with the plan, but now that plan seemed so difficult to execute. Also, there were doubts in his mind in his conviction that he could live with his conscience if the plot ran its full course. He knew in his heart that he had agreed to do the job in the first place mainly out of desperation, without too many thoughts for the consequences. If it were up to him he knew he would call it off, but he had his partner to consider, Todd Burrows may not be of the same opinion. He reached for the phone and dialled Todd's number. "Hello Al, I've just walked through the door", he sounded breathless. "Have you come up with anything?" "Absolutely zilch," Al said. "I get home to find my flat being robbed, I get hit across the head by someone else and the Embassy can't provide me with JB's address". "It doesn't sound as though it's your   day".

Todd said it lightly but he could not hide the concern in his voice. "Not only that, but I think maybe it's better if we didn't go ahead. I've had time to think that perhaps I was too impetuous, too hasty in making that decision. I was feeling very low when the approach was made".

There was a stunned silence from the other end of the line. "Are you still there Todd?" "Yes, what the hell are you talking about, you really can't be serious". Al shifted uncomfortably. "I'm afraid I am, it's been on my mind a lot these last few days". It had as well, when Yousef had presented himself he was very depressed, the trauma of getting off the blazing rig on which several of his best friends had died, his job had gone down with the rig. Having to come home to an empty flat, with only the memory of his dead wife and children he had grasped at the chance to secure his future. After the misery that had been his lot what would the loss of one more life mean? That had been then, now that he was that much closer to carrying it out he knew that he had failed at the first obstacle in his path, but perhaps that was because he had not even tried to surmount it.

He could hear Todd's voice shouting down the line. "I think that maybe you are suffering from that knock on the head, you just can't do this to me". Suddenly the anger was gone from his voice and it took a tone of pleading. "Al, you threw a lifeline to me just when I was in danger of sinking into a morass with no escape, because what you don't know is that the wife had made it quite plain that if the business collapses I have to sell the house, she is leaving me". "I'm sorry Todd, I had no idea". The shock in Al's voice was genuine. "Also", Todd continued, "have you thought about the money we have already spent on this project. I don't think the Arab is going to be very happy about us calling it off, he is going to want his money back". That was true. Al thought carefully. If Yousef did not receive all the money back he would be furious. He knew how these people operated. There would be a contract put out on him. The realisation came to him that he had already stepped into the abyss, there was no turning back, he was beyond the brink, somehow, someway they had to carry it through. He made his decision.

"O.k. Todd, if this plan has any chance of succeeding I have to try and obtain what we need most, which means I'll have to get the first obtainable flight to Bangkok and try and make contact with John Brooks". The relief in Todd's voice was undisguised.

"I do think that is our only option, however while you are away I'll keep looking, maybe I'll come up with something".

"Yes", said Al, "I think that's just as well, the best of luck, I'll be in contact as soon as I have something". He replaced the receiver and stared out of the window. The fine summer day had disappeared, it was growing dark, and the rose bushes outside were bending over from the force of wind, which heralded the approaching rainstorm. The first drops of rain sputtered against the glass and ran slowly down.

Chapter 8

Simon Richards took a last look at the home he loved, making sure everything was secure. The bungalow was situated at Burleigh Heights on Australia's Gold Coast.

Surrounded by blue gum trees with a panoramic view over the sea he had spent a lot of time improving it since he purchased the home six years ago. He was loathe to leave it, in fact he had already told the Agency as they liked to call themselves that he would not be doing any more jobs for them. He had not wanted to do this one, but the money was hard to refuse.

He opened the door to his gleaming new Nissan Pulsar Hatch, one reason why he needed the money; he still owed a large percentage to the finance company. Putting the car in gear he settled down for the forty-minute drive to Brisbane International Airport. The first thing one would notice about Simon Richards was the piercing blue eyes set under the curly blond hair; a broken nose lent him a somewhat piratical appearance. Nine years spent in the Australian Special Air Service had certainly given him an air of self-confidence plus those special talents, which were needed on several of his assignments. However, he mused this particular mission would appear pretty straightforward, basically a watch and report job. He had received the details only twenty minutes previously.

He had the name and photograph of one Al Jenkins. All he had to do was observe and report back. His flight from Brisbane was due to arrive just ninety minutes ahead of Jenkins from London.

It took Al Jenkins an hour to complete the customs and immigration formalities in bustling Don Mueag airport before he caught a cab to town. It wasn't air conditioned so he wound down the window and let the warm tropical evening steal in. The sounds and smells took him back to those years when he first met Anya. The thought brought a smile to his face.

As they sped along the highway into downtown Bangkok he was amazed at the changes that had taken place. Huge towering blocks of apartments and offices seemed to have mushroomed up everywhere. Unfortunately, it seemed the road system had not kept pace. Their speed slowed to a crawl while they were still three miles from the hotel, which gave Al time to look around at his new surroundings. He noticed but gave no further thought to the airport taxi two cars behind him, it contained a single passenger, a tough looking blonde headed man. After a further fifteen minutes Al arrived at his destination, the Imperial Hotel just off Sukumvit Road. It was a modest place but ideally situated in the centre of town, although he had arrived too late to make any enquiries today. Despite the tiring journey, after a cold shower he felt fit enough to take a stroll downstairs

to the large lobby. Sitting in one of the comfortable chairs he ordered a coffee and observed the Thai Wedding party that was in progress in the adjacent dining room. It was a lively affair with loud music, clinking glasses and raucous laughter. How totally different he thought, as he reflected on the purpose of his visit to this particular hotel. Their marriage union would bring new life into the world while his mission was ultimately to end one.

Draining his cup he stood up and made his way out into the street outside. The heat was tolerable but very sticky. He didn't know where he was going, all he knew was that he just wanted to walk to clear his head. After a good half-mile though the sweat was beginning to run down his face, damp patches forming around his armpits.

He stopped to survey the brightly lit façade of a cocktail bar. In large letters at the entrance he read the proclamation "Our Hostesses are the prettiest girls in town". It wasn't that though, more the thought of an ice-cold beer that made him turn towards the entrance. It took a while in the dimly lit bar for him to get his bearings. He charted a course towards the bar. It was a long but not wide room with a small stage at one end on which a three man band were trying to put across a poor rendition of 'Raindrops keep falling on my head'. They had a lot of competition. In one of the several booths that lined the walls were a couple of loud American businessmen surrounded by several hostesses. It seemed that they had already been bought several drinks, there were squeals of laughter from the girls as they pretended to understand the loud jokes. He hitched himself up on a bar stool and ordered a singha beer. He emptied half the glass before putting it back on the bar. As he did so he felt a touch on the arm. "You buy me drink Johnny". He turned to look at the slightly built girl who spoke to him, she couldn't have been more than eighteen but her low cut dress with the slit up the side revealed she had all the assets of a woman.

He knew he should have said no but she had such a cheeky little face and he felt the need to speak to someone, especially one as pretty as her. "O.k. but just the one drink you understand, I have to go back to my hotel room". Her face split into a broad grin. "No sweat darling, we can have a nice talk then maybe you feel better, you look worried". There was a nice lilt to her voice, which almost made him forget she did this for a living. The bartender pushed across a filled glass to her almost before she had time to signal him. "Choop Dee", she said, raising her glass to him. "And good luck to you", he said, getting an eyeful of her proud bosoms over the edge of his glass.

They chatted for a while. Her name was unpronounceable so he called her 'Cheeky'. She didn't seem to mind. It suddenly occurred to him that she could be useful in his quest to find John Brooks. He needed someone who spoke Thai and knew their way around. The level of liquid in her glass had disappeared at an astonishing rate. He succumbed and bought her one more. "That's it, no more for you tonight Cheeky, but how do you fell about making some money tomorrow morning". She looked at him quizzing, cocking her head to one side. "Tomorrow morning? We go shopping   yes?"

"No, we don't", he laughed. "I want you to show me around some places". She smiled mischievously. "Where you stay then?" "The Imperial. You can meet me in the lobby at 10 a.m." "No problem", she said, "I know everywhere in Bangkok". He turned round on his stool as the volume of noise from the party in the booth increased. One of the Americans was arguing loudly. It seemed he had caught one of the girls tipping her drinks into the nearest potted plant. He shouted at her. He reached for a full glass and emptied the contents over her head. Uproar followed, shrieks and screams, as the other girls picked up their glasses and threw their drinks at the Americans. Al thought it was as good a time as any to leave. He said goodbye to Cheeky and threaded his way out between the combatants. As he left he noticed a blonde curly headed fellow sitting hunched over a drink in a corner, somehow he seemed vaguely familiar.

He strode briskly along, jet lag was catching up on him and he wanted to be fresh for the morning, time to get some beauty sleep. Half way to the hotel there was a stretch of darkness where the streetlights were out, the tall apartment blocks threw deep shadows over the street.

He looked cautiously about him as he headed towards the hotel, his footsteps ringing out eerily. He didn't observe however the four men in dirty t-shirts and shorts, who stood close to the wall, but they were studying him, in particular what caught their attention was the gleam of gold from his wristwatch.

For people who got by on a dollar a day, it was well worth the risk in trying to obtain it. Al sensed rather than saw his four assailants as they rushed him. He quickly dropped into a crouch, taking the first man by surprise as his fist swung through the empty air where Al had stood a second before. He was also committed. Al thrust out both hands horizontally to grasp him firmly by the ankles, stood up quickly taking the man with him to send him flying over his back. He landed with a dull thud as the top of his head connected with the road. He was too late though to stop the second man landing a jarring blow against his ribs. He kicked him in the balls as the man doubled over Al, brought his right knee up to smash in the groaning man's face. An arm grabbed him from behind, squeezing his windpipe. Al desperately struggled to get free, he could see the fourth man coming towards him with what looked like a broken off chair leg in his hand. He was beginning to black out with the pressure cutting off his air supply, almost as if in slow motion he could see the club descending on him. There was no mistaking the determination in the man's eyes; he was mouthing some obscenity when the muscled hairy arm reached out from the darkness to arrest the descent of the club. The pressure came off his windpipe as the sweating man behind him released him and bolted up the road. Through the mist covering his eyes Al saw his rescuer dispatch the remaining would be robber with a sharp karate chop to the neck.

"Thought you could do with a bit of help there mate". The accent was unmistakably Australian. Al stared up at the powerful frame of the man opposite him, the piercing eyes topped by the sun-bleached hair.   It   was   the

same man he had seen earlier in the bar. Al's breath was still coming in gasps as he recovered. "I've got to say you did choose a good time to turn up, mind you I could probably have handled them alright". The Australian laughed. "It didn't look that way to me". He stuck out a huge hand. "Simon Richards, I'm over here for a couple of weeks to take a break from life's drudgery". Al shook the proffered hand warmly. "Al Jenkins, I'm in town to look up an old friend, seems like I've found a new one". They started walking back down the now deserted road towards the hotel.

Richards said with a hint of admiration in his voice, "I was impressed with the way you took out those first two. Where did you learn to fight like that?" "I think it was more of a reaction than training," said Al, "although it's true I spent several years in the Marines". He could have bit his tongue as he said it. He'd just met this Aussie, he'd have to be very careful what information he let slip; there again maybe he was being just too cautious. He changed the subject. "I'm staying at the Imperial, are they putting you up as well?" "Yep, I've stayed there before", Richards lied, "and I find it pretty comfortable for the money". They had arrived at the hotel's entrance. Richards opened the door for Al. "Fancy a beer in the hotel bar before turning in". Al smiled warmly, "No thanks Simon, I've had enough excitement for one night, but don't think that I don't appreciate what you did earlier, so I'll buy you a drink tomorrow night at eight if that's o.k. with you". "Yeah, that's fine by me Al". Simon gave him a wave as he turned and headed off in the direction of the bar. Al got back to his room and closed the door on the world. After a quick shower he climbed stiffly into bed. He was asleep almost before his head touched the pillow.

It was almost nine by the time he took the elevator down to the ground floor. He had a big breakfast of scrambled eggs and sausage at the hotel coffee room while reading the early edition of the English Language Bangkok Post. The date was the 21st July, a reminder that time waited for no man. The 11th August seemed ominously close. There was one news item that caught his eye. It seemed there was quite a lot of Communist activity in Thailand's southern province bordering Malaysia. Several men had been killed yesterday while others were missing from a Thai reconnaissance patrol. He knew it to be the area where John Brooks was working.

"Hello Al, can I have coffee with you, yes?" He looked up to see Cheeky grinning broadly at him. She looked entirely different from the girl he met last night. She was wearing tight faded blue jeans and a loose fitting light coloured blouse while on her face there was not a trace of makeup. "Yes, of course Cheeky, you look very nice this morning". She slid in the seat opposite him. "Maybe you will take me somewhere nice?" Al signalled to the waiter over before replying. "Well I don't think you are going to find it too exciting unless of course you like walking around Government Departments". She pulled a face. "But", he held up his hand before she could say anything. "If we finish early I'll take you shopping and buy you the best dress you'd care to have". She squealed with delight. "O.k. we can go now, yes". "Yes", said Al, "why not?"

The heat was oppressive outside and unfortunately the taxi had no air-conditioning. By the time they arrived at the Ministry of Defence the sweat was streaming down Al's face, he could feel it trickling down his back to make a mockery of his freshly ironed shirt. Cheeky proved her worth as they waded through a bureaucratic jungle until finally they arrived at the office of a Colonel whose job was liaison between the small contingent of American advisers and the Thai Army. He gestured towards a chair as they were shown in. "Take a seat Mr Jenkins". He spoke in a slight American accent; he'd probably received part of his training there. A shaft of sunlight fell across the brown friendly face, his immaculate uniform contained three rows of decorations. He shuffled through some papers on his desk before looking up. "Why do you wish to meet Major Brooks, it's an unusual request". Al explained about their past friendship and about the fact he was only in Thailand for a few days. The Colonel listened intently and then seemed to make his mind up. He spoke slowly. "When you walked in here I was going to tell you that you would be unable to get permission to visit the area where Major Brooks is currently based, but I have decided I will allow you to go, you can't take the girl with you though". He rested his hand on his chin and continued. "I served in Vietnam with the Thai division and so I do have a soft spot for someone who even indirectly helped us. If you would care to wait outside I'll have a pass made out for you". The meeting was at an end. Al stood up and thanked him profusely.

Ten minutes later they were both standing outside the Government Building. Al slapped Cheeky playfully across the blue denim that covered her rump. "Well my girl, I think you've earned yourself a new dress. Let's go and find you one". After what seemed an age of travelling from one shop to another, Cheeky finally decided she had found the one she wanted. It was three in the afternoon by the time they arrived back at his hotel. Al stepped out of the taxi with Cheeky following him. He turned to her. "I thought you wanted to take this taxi home". She said coyly. "Can I come to your room to try the dress on one more time to make sure it is right for me?" He looked into her soft brown eyes. Could there possibly be another reason for her wanting to come up? Whatever it was it could not be bad. It was good to get back in to the air-conditioned room. He quickly stripped off, wrapped a soft towel about him and made for the bathroom.

"Try your dress on while I take a shower". Al emerged ten minutes later, refreshed after washing off the day's grime. He found Cheeky lying stretched out on the bed, wearing just a bra and skimpy knickers. Her youthful skin shone with health. She turned towards him and beckoned him across the bed. He sat beside her and ran his fingers through her long silky hair. " I will make you happy", she said very simply. "You already have", he said, as she deftly peeled the towel from around him. He sank into her embrace as she helped him remove her lacy bra, revealing her perfectly formed breasts. She moaned as he caressed, teased and licked her nipples. Wriggling out of her knickers she wrapped her legs about his, thrusting her body hard against his. The tension of the past few days slid from him as he moved together with her supple body, groaning as they reached the summit together. She turned on her side and in no time was sleeping soundly. He smiled and gently drew the bed cover over her.

He woke her up at six. She still had time to get home before going to work that night. "You promise to come and see me before you go home to England", she said as she kissed him goodbye. "Yes, of course, how could I possibly forget", he replied, although he had a feeling it was a promise that probably he would not be able to keep. "Take care of yourself", he said, as he closed the door behind her. He turned to look at the now empty room. For a few hours she had filled his life but now was gone like so many before her since his wife had died. A sudden sense of loneliness came over him. If he could fulfil the task ahead of him he knew that he would look for Anya. They were such happy days that they had spent together but now they were lost in the mists of time. If he could just find her again and of course if she was not married, so many ifs. He fingered the small bronze Buddha she had given him, which he still wore around his neck.

He felt annoyed with himself. This was no time for daydreaming. He had to get the first flight south tomorrow. Taking the lift down to the ground floor he made his way to the hotel's travel desk. "Yes, it can be arranged", said the smiling, efficient good-looking travel courier. "We could get you on a domestic flight to Pattani, its as far South as they go". Al consulted the map she held up for him to study. It was still quite a distance from Betong where John Brooks was based, however he would have to find some alternative transport from there. He was quite looking forward to the surprise he knew JB would show when he turned up. It was little before eight by the time he had concluded his travel arrangements. He thanked the girl and made his way into the bar. The subdued lighting together with music coming from the piano in the corner gave the place a restful air. There were few patrons and as yet it seemed Simon Richards wasn't amongst them.

He took a seat next to the wall from where he could observe the entrance. A sleek waitress with flowing black hair glided up and took his order. The giant frame of Richards suddenly filled the doorway, his eyes peering into the interior. Al gave a wave. "Over here, Simon" He ambled across and spoke when he was ten feet away. "Strew'th, bloody hard to see you in all this murk". Al smiled as he sat down. He couldn't help liking the easy going Aussie. "What's it going to be Simon, I've just ordered". Richards didn't take long to make his mind up. "Make mine a four X, I reckon the local brew is a weak as gnats piss". Al laughed. "Maybe that's why I drink it, gives me a clear head". "You've got a point", the large Aussie replied, "it reminds me of when I was in 'Nam' with the Aussie contingent. We were based outside a large town and several of the guys had gone in to town one night, well" he paused as they were served their drinks. "Two of them came back so blind drunk they couldn't find the camp entrance, so they just fell asleep against the coils of barbed wire on the perimeter. When we saw them in the morning we were sure that they were dead. Of course, when they sobered up they wouldn't believe they had slept there all night". He took a large gulp of his beer.

Al leaned back in his chair. "Yep, you're right, drink certainly makes you do some strange things. In Singapore we would have trishaw races, we would tell the drivers to take a back seat, pay them and pedal like mad to the nearest brothel or bar". Simon grinned at him from across the top of his beer glass. "That sounds like fun" he said. "Not really" Al replied. "By the time we got there we were too bloody knackered to do much". They continued their banter, the jokes grew coarser and the laughter louder as the night wore on. Al drained his glass and put it down belching loudly. "Well, that's me Simon, I've got a busy day ahead of me tomorrow". Simon glanced at his watch.

"Hell", he said, "it's only just after 10.30, I'm sure you can handle a couple more beers". Al pushed the glass towards the centre of the table in a gesture of finality. "No, sorry pal, but I've managed to locate my friend in the South and I'll be flying there tomorrow". Simon looked thoughtful. "You know what", he said. "I've always hankered to try out a few of those southern beaches, they reckon some are pretty spectacular. What about if I come along with you, you're not bad company for a Pommie!"

Al stared at the ceiling for several seconds. This guy had been pretty good to him, in fact had done him a great favour, to refuse such a simple request surely would be totally out of character. Besides, it would only be as far as the airport. "Well o.k, if you want to tag along that's fine, but once I get to Pattani I'm heading inland, so I'll leave it to you to suss out the beaches. You can tell me all about it when I get back". Simon looked pleased. "That's great, I'll see about getting on the same flight as you in the morning".

Al called the waitress over for the cheque. As she came back with it Simon dug deep into his pocket. Al raised his hand. "Oh no you don't, these drinks are on me for last night. I don't forget that easily". Was it really only 24 hours since that encounter in the street? They parted in the lobby, Simon heading for the coffee shop while Al took the lift up to his room. He called the hotel desk and booked a phone call to England. They came back to him half an hour later. "Your number's ringing Sir". There was a series of clicks on the line and then after a few more seconds the unmistakable voice of Todd Burrows. He gave his number. "Todd, it's Al. Thought you would like to know I've located JB, I hope to see him tomorrow. How are things your end?" Todd sounded downcast. "Not too good. No joy I'm afraid, reference the merchandise we are after". Al sounded grim. "That's bad news, I just hope I can come up with something tomorrow otherwise we just may have to pack it all in". Todd's voice was faint on the line. "I'm sorry Al, I don't have any better news for you. I guess it is all up to you now if we are to have any chance". "Don't worry", Al spoke with more reassurance than actually felt. "I'm sure I should turn up something over here, I'll let you know how things turn out". Some of the lightness came back to Todd's voice. "That's great, right, talk to you later. By the way, watch out for those girls over there if you know what I mean, wink, wink!" He put the receiver down before Al could give him a suitably rude reply.

Al stripped off and climbed into bed. He was going to have to think carefully how he should approach John Brooks with his request. Whereas JB could probably know how to get this hands on some military explosive, it was still doubtful as to whether he would accede to a demand, friends notwithstanding. There was also the problem of getting the stuff out of the country and shipped to the Canary Islands. By the time he fell asleep he knew how he could move the stuff out, at least he thought it stood at least a fifty percent chance. It was a simple plan, strange that it had never occurred to him before. He slept well that night.

Chapter 9

More than 500 miles to the South from where Jenkins was sleeping soundly, Major John Brooks, United States Marines Corps was woken up at four in the morning. The orderly who had called him also brought a steaming hot cup of black coffee. He took large gulps and rubbed the sleep out of his eyes. He had completed 18 months of a 2-year tour of duty on secondment to the Thai Army. There were very few Americans still doing the same job. The Thais were becoming very adept at Jungle Warfare so he viewed his appointment as probably more political than military. However, he knew it had been a good stepping-stone to further his career. It had only been last week that he had received the news that his next post would be a staff position in Washington with the rank of Lieutenant Colonel, providing of course that he left this job with a good record. He was at present attached to the Headquarters staff of the Thai Army Brigade, which was stationed at Betong close to the Thai-Malaysian Border. There had been an upsurge recently in Communist Guerrilla activity in the area and only yesterday four men on patrol had been killed in an ambush while a further two had been reported missing. There had probably been a more recent development, which would explain his early summons.

He quickly donned his jungle green fatigues over his lean body and ran a comb through his close-cropped hair, slightly turning to grey over the temples. By the time he arrived at the Headquarters building it was a blaze of lights with figures scurrying to and fro. He returned the salute of the sentry at the entrance and made his way up the stairs to the Brigade briefing room. The Brigade Intelligence Officer, a Thai Army Captain who spoke excellent English, met him. "Good morning, Major", he said, "Sorry about the early call but I thought you would like to be in on this one".

The Captain led the way over to a large wall map of the area. He picked up a thin bamboo stick and indicated an area of the map. He spoke quickly. "We have just received a report from one of our foreward patrols at this point", he tapped on the map, "that they have found the camp which was used by the terrorists who carried out yesterday's ambush". JB interrupted. "Did they find anyone there?" "Unfortunately no", the Captain continued, "no sign of our two missing men either, but it has been decided to launch an immediate follow up operation at first light. They are getting the choppers ready on the landing zone now, we are sending in two companies". He turned from the wall map to face Major Brooks and continued. "Obviously it is vital to pick up their trail before it runs cold, with the experience that you have it's quite possible you may notice something we may have overlooked". JB gave a disarming smile. "You can count on it Captain. I must admit I'm pretty wise to most of the tricks these Gooks try to pull". The Captain nodded. "Right Major, you will get a further briefing at the forward landing zone. I've informed your orderly to pack the gear that you will be needing at the other end". He quickly glanced at the large clock on the wall. "I think you've just enough time to get an early breakfast, your orderly has the details of your aircraft allocation and departure time which should be in about an hour's time. Right, I've got to get the Colonel's map". He saluted and rushed away.

The sky was just beginning to lighten in the East as John Brooks waited by the side of the landing zone. All available helicopters were already in the air, taking the two infantry companies to the foreward-landing zone to secure the area. He had fifteen minutes wait before one would return to pick him and his men up. He cast a glance towards the distant tree line where the jungle crept down the hillside; already patches of white mist were beginning to form around the treetops. There were another five men from Brigade HQ assigned to his aircraft, engineers and signallers. They complained loudly about the loads they had to carry. The distinctive sound of the thudding rotor blades of the approaching helicopter came clearly to the ears of the waiting men. It swept in to land 70 feet away from them. After a thumb up from the grim faced pilot they boarded and were soon sweeping low across the thick jungle beneath them, leading towards a range of hills close to the Malaysian border. JB peered down at the jungle canopy, reflecting sombrely on the fact that it would take a man an hour to travel a thousand yards through the dense growth.

A smoke flare had been set off in the foreward landing zone as they approached in order to give the pilot better identification and wind direction. He needed it. The landing pad seemed tiny as they came into a hover, tall trees surrounding it on all sides. The pilot decided not to trust the unknown surface, letting the aircraft hover two feet above the ground, they piled out quickly and headed for the cover of the trees where they were met by sweating guides who led them into a secured area.

"Hello John, good to see you got here alright". John Brooks turned round to see one of the two Company Commanders striding towards him. He'd known Major Malee for quite some time, having worked together previously on the border close to Kampuchea. Unusually tall for a Thai, very intelligent and tipped to become a high-ranking Officer in the future. JB grinned at him as he swung the heavy pack off his back. "Yeah, Mal, it looks like we are going to earn our pay for the next few days". They went and sat on the trunk of a long dead tree. Major Malee pulled a map from his trouser pocket and spread it across his knees after first flicking off the ants, which crawled up his legs. "Well John", he said, "it seems at first indications that there were about 15 to 20 commies in the camp. We are going through it now with the help of the Engineers that you brought with you to check first for booby traps, then we'll see if we can turn anything up that may help us". He went on to explain that while his company was engaged in this task and guarding the area, the other company had gone ahead further up the hill following what they thought was the trail taken by the escaping Communists. JB did not agree and told him so. "I know it makes sense that they would want to head into the hills, away from any inhabited areas, but these people are cunning. The jungle is their home, they would guess that you would go straight up the hill after them". Major Malee nodded. "That's right John, they would but I still think they would head that way". There was no conviction in his voice however. "Besides, I've already committed my forces, I don't want to call them back at this stage". He spread out his hands in a gesture of fait accompli.

JB stared hard at the map as if it would provide some sort of clue as to which direction their quarry lay. "O.k. Mal", he said, "you could well be right but if you can let me have the use of a chopper for about an hour I'd like to go on a recce further down the hill, there's a lot more open ground down there and if they have headed that way it's just possible we could spot them". "Yes, that sounds pretty reasonable". As Malee spoke, he signalled his radio operator to approach him. He spoke rapidly in Thai and then turned back to John. "I've just got to get clearance from the Colonel but I don't think there will be any problem". Just as he finished speaking there was a muffled explosion from the direction of the camp up the hill. He reached over and took the handset from the radio operator. After a short conversation he came back over to John. "There's going to be a delay before you get your chopper I'm afraid, as we will have to use it first for a casualty evacuation. Somebody was a bit careless and stood on a jumping jack mine, he's still alive but we will have to get him back now if he's to have any chance". JB knew well enough about what a jumping jack mine was; he had good cause to remember them after his experiences in Vietnam. A small anti-personnel mine once trodden on as soon as the foot was lifted it would spring into the air and explode at waist height causing severe injuries, sometimes fatal. He noticed the Thai soldiers around him suddenly taking a new interest in their surroundings as they were told the reason for the explosion.

Major Malee had disappeared in the direction of the camp, shouting orders. He was angry that one of his men had failed to be just that little more vigilant; the difference between life and death lay just beneath the rotting covering of dead leaves on the jungle floor. The brought the casualty down on a stretcher ten minutes later. He was somehow still conscious despite the huge gaping hole in his stomach, crudely bandaged over with field dressings. The blood was still seeping through, turning them red while in contrast his face was white as a sheet. JB's own stomach turned over at the sight even though he had seen it often before in Vietnam. He knew he had not reached the stage where he could be callous about it. His vision was suddenly obscured by the form of his orderly who handed him a mess can of coffee. "Thought you might like this Sir". "Thank you Sirapon". JB sipped at the scalding liquid. "Fancy a trip in a chopper?" The orderly looked pleased. He hated being in the jungle; it was the reason why he had volunteered to work in the Officer's Mess.

They were airborne within the hour, heading back down the hill. JB pressed the rubber eyepieces of the binoculars against his eyes and studied the terrain below him, relaying instructions to the pilot through his headset. The dark green jungle canopy was almost impenetrable but every now and again there were large areas of cleared ground planted with young rice, dotted amongst them were several of the local houses built entirely of wood and bamboo with their roofs constructed of rattan leaves. There were some people in the fields, their upturned faces peered at them as they flew over while others stayed with bent backs working in the paddy or walked behind the slowly plodding buffalo just as their forefathers had done hundreds of years before them.

They were approaching a smaller clearing, just a few neglected areas of rice fields with about four houses ground closely together on one side. They swept low over it. JB noticed movement amongst them. He ordered the pilot to go back for a second look, he wasn't quite sure of what he had seen but in the back of his mind he knew there had been something to arouse his suspicions. The aircraft banked steeply coming around in a 180^0 turn and slowed as they went back the way they had just come. He stared hard at the tranquil scene. What had he seen? As they got closer there wasn't a sign of life, nothing stirred down there. He felt the hair raising on the back of his neck just as he shouted to the pilot to gain height. He saw them. At first they just seemed to float lazily up towards them, a line of orange coloured spots until with a series of ear splitting cracks the tracer bullets homed in on them.

It wasn't just the tracer as between each one were another four high velocity bullets. That first burst had crashed into the side of the chopper above his head, the bullets ripping through the flimsy metal airframe to gouge great chunks out of the growling turbine. He heard the shouts of alarm over his headset as the pilot fought desperately to keep control of the aircraft.

The door gunner managed to get off a long burst in the direction of the firing before a tracer caught him in the chest throwing him violently across the floor of the chopper, the glowing phosphorous burning for several seconds, the stench of burning flesh filled the cabin. They were losing altitude rapidly, too rapidly, falling towards the water filled rice field below them. He felt the impact as several more heavy calibre rounds ripped through the fuselage; there was scream of pain from Sirapon his orderly. He clutched at his right arm, which was hanging limply at his side; blood was oozing between his fingers. To JB it felt as though his stomach had gone through the deck of the chopper, he wanted to throw up but couldn't. There was just this complete sense of helplessness, were these to be the last moments of his life?

The chopper hit the water of the rice field, which was 2 to 3 feet deep in places. It was probably that which saved his life; it helped reduce the impact as they crashed in. It came slowly to a halt and then began tilting over, the dirty brown water of the paddy came rushing through the door, the rotor blades first hit the water and then the ground underneath. As they did so, they disintegrated, pieces of blade flew through the air with ear piercing whistles. Opposite the door was an emergency escape window, he quickly kicked it out and scrambled through to drop in water up to his waist. "Major, help me, my arm, I can't get out ". He turned round to see Sirapon's head framed in the window he had just left. He knew the danger he was in, the smell of aviation fuel was strong in the air. He grabbed hold of Sirapon's good arm and pulled him through to land in the water beside him. Supporting him around the shoulder they waded through the water and dragged themselves up onto a dry bank. It was at this point that the helicopter exploded with a white flash. Debris rained down to splash in the water close beside them.

Sirapon gave a loud groan and slid down the bank. JB scrambled down and began pulling him back up. It was then that he noticed the five-inch piece of shrapnel sticking out of the centre of his back. Pulling it out he gently turned Sirapon over and rested his head in the cradle of his arms. The eyes of a dead man stared back at him. Almost reluctantly he felt the man's artery at the side of the neck as though he knew he would feel no life giving pulse beneath his fingers. He sat with his dead orderly's head in his arms and stared at the fiercely burning chopper. His mind was numb with grief. He knew he should be away from this spot, the Commies were bound to be heading this way and they would not be carrying any stretchers.

He laid Sirapon out and took from his pocket a piece of blue parachute silk, he had carried it ever since he had obtained it back in Vietnam, it had been at Khe Sann when the airstrip had been closed due to the constant bombardment from the hills. He had taken it from one of the resupply parachutes. He had always felt it to be an omen of good luck.

Sirapon had often asked if he may have it but JB had never granted him that wish. He did so now, gently placing the silk over the upturned face. He heard them before they were in sight. They were coming up the bank opposite him, scrabbling up the muddy surface, their laboured breathing clearly audible. He clawed desperately at the Browning automatic pistol strapped to his side, it had just cleared the holster when the first heads appeared at the top of the bank. There were four of them, the red stars on the forage caps they wore clearly visible. He quickly squeezed off a shot at them. In his haste he missed but the heads disappeared rapidly. He thought desperately, the adrenalin pumping. If he kept to this side of the bank he might just make it to the tree line if he could just keep their heads down. He began slowly edging his way back towards relative safety when suddenly all four of them appeared, they had spaced themselves out this time, knowing he would lose a fraction of time before deciding who to aim at first. He saw the black barrels of the Klasnikov assault rifles swinging up, looked down the nuzzles from where he knew death would come as he pulled the trigger of his automatic, there was just a click as the gun jammed.

The second man from the right who appeared to be the leader rapped out a sharp order. They lowered their rifles as they came towards him. There seemed no point in running, his only reward would probably be a bullet in the back. Screaming, he ran at them using his pistol as a club, he swung down viciously just missing the head of the nearest one, but the foresight of his gun ripped open the man's cheek, leaving a diagonal red line. He never saw the rifle butt which hit him just above the hairline. It felt as if his skull had been caved in, a brilliant white flash and he knew he was going down. He fell to his knees when he felt another painful blow to his left side. He ended up face down in the dirt, just before he lost consciousness.

It suddenly came to him what had first raised his suspicions as they flew over. What he had seen was a woman, nothing wrong with that, but it was what she was doing. She had been hastily collecting clothes, which had been spread out, on the grass to dry; the clothes were all jungle green uniforms. The leader of the group with his foot rolled JB over onto his back. "American swine", he snarled, "we should get some money for this one, also some information, bring him back with us".

Chapter 10

Al woke refreshed; he had slept soundly that night with the thought of meeting JB once more. Things were at last beginning to move in the right direction. He settled his hotel account and turned round to see Simon standing behind him. "Guess what, you old bastard" he said as his face split in a broad grin. "I have managed to get on the same flight as you". "Nothing surprises me where you are concerned" Al replied as he lifted up his travel bag. "Right, let's make tracks for the airport, fate awaits us". "As long as she is good looking I don't give a damn" Simon guffawed.

The flight to Pattani was uneventful despite the moans from his companion about the lack of drinks of the alcoholic type. It was nearly two in the afternoon by the time the aircraft touched down, after having their passports checked they both met up again outside the airport building. "What are your plans Al?" "I am going to get myself a decent hire car or jeep and head off as soon as possible Simon, I've got a long way to go". Al turned towards a group of taxi drivers, signalled one across after a lengthy explanation of his destination in town, and climbed into the front passenger seat.

Simon was still standing at the kerb; he seemed hesitant when he spoke. "I'll take a lift with you Al to this car hire place if that's o.k. with you, I'll make my own way from there."

Within half an hour the taxi dropped them outside a two storey gaudily painted building, loudly proclaiming the benefits of their own particular car hire. Al was lucky, they had one four wheel drive Suzuki jeep which was just what he wanted, he had a pretty good idea of some of the roads he may have to travel over. After completing the paperwork, he bade goodbye to Simon, who had been standing to one side of the dingy office drinking Chinese tea. "Saving yourself for the hard stuff later on Simon?" The big Aussie put on a show of outrage. "There you go, you Pommies reckon all we do down under is knock the booze back all-night and lie in the sun all day". Al laughed and then spoke quietly. "Well, I am sure about one thing, I am damn glad you decided to go and have a drink in that Bangkok bar the other night or I might not be here today". Simon grinned and thrust out a large hand. "I am sure you would have handled it even if I had not come along". They shook hands. "O.k. Simon, I'm off now. When I pass back through this place in a couple of days or so, I'll expect a full report on the beaches and birds and not necessarily in that order". "You've got it, keep your powder dry".

Simon Richards watched the jeep disappear up the road, he knew where it was headed so there was no hurry, besides he couldn't afford to get too close now or his cover would be blown. However, he had a feeling that before too long now he would be able to report back exactly what the purpose of Al Jenkins trip to Thailand was all about. He was glad that he had decided that this was definitely his last assignment, because he had taken quite a liking to the guy. No, from now on it would be full time back in the pub with his

partner, no more of this cloak and dagger business. Within 10 minutes they had fixed him up with a battered Toyota Saloon and he was heading south generally along the line of the Pattani River towards the dark menacing hills in the distance. He put his foot down, he knew that it would not take long to overhaul the jeep and there was really only the one road that Jenkins could take. However, it would be stupid to lose him at this stage. Just a couple more days and he could be home, for good this time, he smiled to himself at the thought of sitting back home with a cold beer in his hand, watching a couple of steaks sizzle on the barby.

Further up the winding road Al was pleased with the performance of the Suzuki 4 x 4. He was making good time. With a bit of luck he may just make the army camp JB was stationed at before nightfall. He wanted to drive as little as possible during darkness on the lonely unlit roads which ran through the jungle, many an unwary traveller had fallen victim to bandits in these parts, even buses sometimes had been held up at gunpoint. He stopped briefly in the bustling market town of Yala to fill the tank up and then continued south. He was now seeing very few vehicles on the road, but he knew he was going to pull over as soon as a suitable roadside eating house beckoned to him, his stomach was protesting loudly at the absence of any food over the best part of the day. After a further six miles he pulled in just off the highway to park next to a large wooden building which had what had seemed at first glance some sort of restaurant at the front of the premises, several chickens were running around at the rear, the hard packed earth around the building was dotted with empty coke and can beers. He knew through experience though appearances were deceptive, the food here would most likely be excellent and amazingly cheap. He felt self-conscious as he walked into the brilliantly lit dining area, they certainly did not get too many 'farangs' as the Thais called foreigners, eating here. He soon forgot about being stared at after he was presented with a steaming hot plate of Thai fried rice with an egg on top, together with a large glass of beer. He was feeling on top of the world and eager to continue his journey.

Simon Richards was cursing his luck; he had trailed the jeep successfully through Yala and beyond, however on turning the last corner the straight open road had stretched out ahead of him with no sign of the jeep. He put his foot down, a half-mile on and he had just noticed out of the corner of his eye a jeep parked up next to a Thai eating-house. There was no point going back and getting too close, so he chose a convenient spot further up the road to stop and wait. He backed the car up into the dense undergrowth making it invisible from the road and settled down to wait. He thought enviously of the food that no doubt Jenkins was getting stuck into and also a nice cold beer. He could really murder one after the long hot trek. It was hot and humid inside the car, even with the windows open, he slapped angrily at the buzzing mosquitoes but he needed the windows open to hear the approaching jeep. After half an hour he was beginning to feel drowsy in the heat but knew he must keep awake. He stepped out of the car to stretch his legs.

He found himself facing two evil looking unkempt wiry looking men, one of whom had in his right hand a long vicious looking machete, the other was carrying a crude shotgun. He was well aware of what they wanted but even if he gave them all the money he had, it was no guarantee of his safety. He decided to act throwing himself to one side as he saw the barrel of a shotgun come up, he lunged towards them, there was a loud blast as one of the barrels was discharged, there was a horrible numbing pain to his left arm, using his good right arm he swept the gun up just at it fired for the second time, the smell of gunpowder was in his nostrils. They grappled together, the big Aussie forcing him back until his foot caught in a protruding root, they both crashed to the ground heavily by the side of the road. Simon wrenched the shotgun free and smashed the butt into the man's face, he was still getting to his feet when he felt it, he realised he was screaming, the pain was so intense. He looked stupidly at the point of the machete, it had been driven right through his body, and the blade was sticking out of his stomach. Through a red mist of pain he saw the jeep approaching along the road and heard his assailant crashing through the growth as he made his escape. Like a giant oak tree he slowly toppled over onto his side.

Al had enjoyed his meal, made even more enjoyable when he saw how little it had cost. He gave the waiter a large tip. After having checked the Suzuki over he drove off, a couple more hours on the road should get him to his destination. He had not been on the road for more than a couple of minutes when he saw them, there were two men struggling together on the verge and one of them looked like Simon Richards. But that surely was impossible, Richards was supposed to be back in Pattani. It was him! He accelerated, he saw another man step up behind Richards and drive something deep into his back, he looked up at the approach of Al's vehicle and then turned and ran. He brought the jeep to a shuddering halt next to where Richards now lay groaning in the grass. He could see at once that Simon was going to bleed to death if he did not get him to a hospital immediately; blood was oozing out into the reddish brown earth in a thick stream. He gently lifted the man's head to make him more comfortable. Simon's pain filled eyes stared at him; there was a flicker of recognition. "Hang on, old pal", he reassured him, "you are going to make it all right, but first I'm going to have to extract that bloody great knife sticking out of your back and I'm going to pull it out slowly, can't afford to risk cutting anything else".

Simon nodded with just the slightest movement of the head. Al looked quickly around and noticed the car parked up. He went through the bag inside and selected two large clean shirts, ripping them into lengths as he went back to Simon's side. He gave a piece to Simon to bite on and then slowly began easing the machete out taking care to remove it at the exact angle. The big Aussie gave a muffled groan, his hands digging deep into the ground as he tried to blot out the pain, as the blade came clear his whole body relaxed, he had passed out.

With the weapon now out he worked feverishly to wrap the makeshift bandages around the wounds, he knew only too well if he could not stem the bleeding he would have a corpse on his hands before arriving at any hospital.

He desperately needed help, it was going to be a struggle to get he large man into the back of the jeep but there was not a sign of a passing vehicle. Grasping the now bloody handle of the machete he quickly hacked down several straight bamboo poles and trimmed them to his satisfaction; he then laid them on the tailgate of the jeep so that they formed a gentle slope. Even so he found it hard pulling Richards into the back, he made him as comfortable as he could, wedging him between the seats to restrict his movement. 'Al', he only just heard the whisper before starting the engine. He turned around to see Simon just lifting his head. "Hold on Simon, I'll head back to Yala, there's a hospital there, should not take long". But he then realised that the man's pale lips were forming words he could not hear. He cut the engine and leant over. He could just make out the words. "I may not make it, so please listen". Simon gave a gurgling cough and spat blood from his mouth. "I want you to know that when you first saw me in Bangkok it was no accident, I was sent to spy on you and the people behind it are Mossard, they are the paymasters".

Simon started coughing again, blood coming up with each rasp from the throat. Al spoke into the stricken man's ear. "Don't talk anymore, I've got to get you to hospital right now". He turned the jeep around and accelerated fast back down the road to Yala, it didn't take him long to find one. He screeched to a halt outside the main doors.

He had to shout before he got anyone's attention. Two weary looking male nurses made their way over to him. Luckily one of them spoke reasonable English, he explained the circumstances of the wounding while the other went to fetch a stretcher, he didn't want them thinking he was responsible. Even so, after he watched them carry Simon in, he drove off, he couldn't afford to spend hours in some sweltering police station explaining all he knew. He desperately hoped that the big Aussie would pull through even after his revelation that he had been sent to keep tabs on his own movements.

Looking back over the past couple of days, it all made sense. Of course while he had been keeping his eyes open for any sort of surveillance, he had not thought for a moment of suspecting Richards, the guy had been so natural. Strangely enough though he bore no malice towards the man, it was disturbing to think that Mossad were running a check on him, he must have been spotted with Viola in Geneva. How much did they know? He was pretty confident they were not aware of his plan or by now they would have taken some sort of action against him and now with Richards in a hospital bed there was no way of them finding out the true purpose of his visit to Thailand. He glanced outside at the countryside flashing past. Although it would be dark before he reached the army base, the night was closing in quickly now as the jeep began climbing up the low range of hills, the jungle seeming to encroach upon him as lines of trees merged into a black blur. The clock on the dash showed nearly ten o'clock by the time his headlights finally picked out the red and white pole that barred his way to the army base.

He showed his pass to the roused Corporal at the gate, who directed him to report to the Officers Mess although he added that several of the Officers had flown out that morning on a follow up operation.

A junior Officer who spoke a little English met him on the steps of the Mess. He turned the pass over in his hands as he listened to Al's request to meet Major Brooks. He then disappeared for several minutes before coming back with an orderly at his side. "I'm sorry Mr Jenkins" he spoke slowly as if unsure of his words, "but Major Brooks was of those Officers who flew out this morning, at the moment we don't know when he will be back, you can stay here tonight, tomorrow maybe there will be news". The Officer glanced at the orderly standing next to him. "This man will show you to the room where you will stay. I will talk to you in the morning". He turned around and walked down the empty corridor, his footsteps ringing out. Al reached down, grabbed his bag and followed the soldier in front of him down the featureless wall. He was shown a small room with a single bunk; a large ceiling fan revolved slowly disturbing the muggy air. "Everything o.k." The orderly spoke, pleased at knowing a couple of English words. Al reciprocated in Thai, "Dee Maak, khop khun maak, krap". The orderly smiled as he turned and left closing the door quietly behind him.

He woke with a start; the strange surrounding of the barrack room confused him for a split second as to where he was. Outside the sky was just beginning to shed some of its darkness. He felt optimistic and stepped into the shower, the icy cold water sharpening his senses. At last today there was a good chance of getting closer to his objectives. He dried himself off quickly, dressed even faster, eager to find out when JB would be returning. However, a quick search of the building revealed that he was one of the first ones up, so a quick breakfast would kill some of the time. He had finished and was on his second cup of coffee when the Officer who had spoken to him last night came through the canteen doors. Even before he spoke Al knew it wasn't going to be good news, the way he stopped in front of him pausing for quite some time before first giving him the traditional Thai greeting. Al reciprocated and waited. The young Thai Officer searched for the right words. "Yesterday, your friend Major Brooks, he was flying in one of the helicopters, we have received a message to say that he was shot down and I am afraid to say that he is missing".

To Al it was as if someone had squeezed his heart. No JB to meet. In fact, his friend could be lying out there dead, entombed in a burnt out helicopter. The coffee tasted bitter in his mouth and it had nothing to do with the way it was made. "What other information do you have about the chopper?" He stared hard at the man, hoping just hoping they may know something that gave JB a chance of survival. But the man just spread his hands out. "That is the only message we have received, but as soon as there is any more news we will let you know". He turned as if to go then added quietly, "I'm sorry Mr Jenkins". Al clenched his hands tightly, turning the knuckles white and felt the despair well up deep inside him; there must be something he could do, but what?

Chapter 11

Through the red mists of pain JB slowly and methodically checked each one of his limbs, just tensing each arm or limb at a time. Without opening his eyes he could feel the ropes that bound him prisoner, but he was moving, they had tied him to a stretcher. Except for the throbbing pain in his head, it seemed he had escaped injury. It might be better at this stage to remain playing possum, as having to carry him was bound to slow them down. The temptation to open his eyes was great, but even with them closed he had a good idea of the route they were taking, by the noise they made it had to be thick jungle and it was an uphill gradient which meant they aimed to escape by getting into the hills, perhaps even to cross into Malaysia to throw off any pursuit. Although they stopped occasionally for a short break, the jolting journey seemed to carry on for hours and hours until he was dumped unceremoniously on the ground. He was shook roughly by the shoulder. "Wake up American", came the voice in his ear, "or I'll stick a knife in your arse to see if you really are dead". JB thought it was wise to maybe return to the land of the living. The first thing that struck him when he opened his eyes was the fact that it was already nearly dark. He indicated with his bound hands that he was in dire need to attend to the call of nature. With a grunt his captor released him from his bonds and marched him just to the perimeter of the small camp they were setting up.

As he squatted in the undergrowth he could see there were 11 communists including 2 women, assuming they must have at least 2 on watch, a total of 13. While in the centre with a man watching them were the 2 missing Thai soldiers from yesterday's patrol. It was a surprise to see they were both alive, but of course they would have used them to carry the stretcher. Above his head the tall creeper covered trees, almost blocking out the sky completely. Surrounding them on all sides, the thick jungle undergrowth seemed impenetrable. Thoughts of escape were dismissed almost as soon as he thought of it. In daylight he might take a chance, but now with darkness upon them under the jungle canopy it would be blacker than a raven's wing. From his own experience he knew well the only light they might see would be the ghostly fluttering of fireflies or pale phosphorous showing on upturned leaves. To run or even to walk through that blackness courted disaster spikes, razor blade thorns and aptly named wait-a-whiles could cut and slash a person to ribbons while small ravines, tree roots and head high vines remained unseen until it was too late. JB snapped off a couple of leaves to complete his ablutions, as he did so hoping there was nothing live or furry on them. They sat upright against a tree, tying his hands behind after feeding him with some cold rice and dried fish. About 10 yards away in what seemed the leader's bivouac, three of them sat round a small fire talking amongst themselves and gesturing his way every now and then, he knew his fate was being decided.

After some time one of the trio detached himself and came over to JB, squatting on his hunches in front of him. By the dim light of the fire JB could see the prematurely aged face of what appeared to be a man of Chinese-Thai origin. Two thin scars ran down the left hand side of his face. "So major, you have had a ride today but tomorrow you will be doing a lot of walking". There as an ominous tone to his voice. "However you have tonight to have a rest and it also gives you time to think over exactly all the information that I shall want to hear tomorrow". "All I can give you is my name and number", replied JB, returning the other man's stare. "We shall see about that". The man stood up. "I think your Embassy in Bangkok will be willing to pay a large amount of money for you". He turned and began walking back towards his tent. "I wouldn't count on it" JB threw back.

He tried to make himself comfortable but with his back against the tree it wasn't easy. The whole area was now in total darkness and the mosquitoes were out in force droning around him and biting him at their leisure. His clothes were still sodden with sweat due to the high humidity; his head throbbed as he eventually fell asleep almost entirely due to sheer exhaustion.

It was the pre-dawn chorus of insects and animals in the surrounding jungle that woke him eventually, he felt as though he had just gone ten rounds in the ring and he had been on the losing side. A quick look around showed that he was not the first one to awake, several of the Communists were already up and about, packing their few possessions or cleaning their weapons, they were eager to be away from this place in order to press on into deeper jungle. The guard came over and cut the jungle wire restraining him, he also placed some cold rice before him. Using his hands he indicated to JB to eat. The guard returned a minute later carrying a large bulky pack, which he deposited on the ground next to JB. "This will carry you all day, you understand", he said. Before long they were all assembled ready to move out into the jungle. The scar-faced leader took a final look around the campsite making sure there was nothing left to betray their presence. From long experience they were good, only a trained tracker would possibly recognise the site for what it was.

They moved off in single file up the hill, the guard immediately behind him while the two captured Thai soldiers were further towards the back. Although it was early morning and still relatively cool, after an hour's trek JB's jungle green fatigues were once more sodden with sweat, he had forgotten just how difficult and strenuous it was this marching through thick jungle with a heavy pack. His captors seemed unaffected by the conditions, moving through the undergrowth with ease, saying nothing, using hand signals to communicate all commands. As the day wore on the small column moved further along the ridges into deep primary jungle, here there were no signs of human habitation as they moved ever closer towards the Malaysian border. Once a helicopter flew over but it did not return. JB assumed they had not been seen.

Some time after noon they came into a small clearing where the leader called a halt. JB collapsed onto the ground accepting gratefully the little water that was offered to him. He looked around and saw the two Thai soldiers equally exhausted; they were carrying even heavier loads than him.

Sitting there he knew he had to work out a plan to escape and it had to be soon. Of course the reasons he had not been pressed for information last night was all part of their strategy. Whereas the previous evening they were aware he was still strong and resilient, they also knew a few more days of continual trekking through the jungle would bring him almost to breaking point on the meagre rations they provided. If he were to attempt to get free, it had to be today while he still had some strength left and preferably just before sunset, that way it wouldn't give them much time to find him before nightfall. The scar-faced Communist leader walked over, poking him with the barrel of his Klasnikov assault rifle in the chest. "How do you like our little walk", he said with a sarcastic grin. "I have been on better ones", replied JB, trying to appear unperturbed. "Well, we have a long way to go, so you better be up to it". He paused. "Right, on you feet, we are moving off again".

Towards late afternoon with the sun descending in the west, they began climbing steeper hills, the tall trees towering above them with very few shafts of sunlight penetrating down. There was the constant hum of insects while in the distance a group of Gibbon monkeys could be heard chattering. The straps of JB's pack bit hard into his shoulders, he kept looking for a spot to make a break for it and also to slow down the pace but the guard behind fixed a bayonet to the end of his rifle, he knew what would happen if he tried to slow and at this moment he could do without any further pain. About an hour before dusk they came to a halt, JB eased off his pack and sat on it. A short distance away the leader and two of his comrades were in a huddle, obviously discussing whether to progress any further before night set in. They were on a ridgeline which stretched up further, it was still heavily forested. However, on one side of the ridge close to where he sat, the ground dropped away sharply, impossible to climb easily, it was a mixture of red brown earth and small scrub bushes. There was just a chance maybe, he thought, if he did something they didn't expect. The element of surprise might be enough for him to get away with it; on the other hand he also risked breaking his neck. He watched the guard as he had on previous stops, knowing that in a minute or two he would lay his weapon down in order to take out his tobacco pouch, it would only be for a few seconds.

Leaning forward JB placed his head in his hands, observing out of the corner of his eye the man a few feet from him. As though taking this for a signal, the guard placed his weapon down and reached for his smokes. Standing up, the tall American reached down to the pack with both hands as if to rearrange it, grasping it tightly he suddenly took one, two, three quick strides and launched himself into space over the side of the ridge, even with the pack held in front when he hit the loose earth it sent a bone jarring shudder through his body. But the pack did as he hoped it would, acting as a makeshift sledge he hurtled down the steep slope towards the comparative safety of scrub bushes and rattan grass, it was as if he could almost feel the gun sight being lined up on his back. He was right. The guard, after his initial surprise, had followed the American to the edge and quickly drew a bead on the fleeing man below him, carefully judging his shot he squeezed the trigger. A shower of dirt erupted just behind his intended victim; he shook his head at how he had missed. Then the realisation came; he had forgotten the bayonet on the end of his rifle, which would automatically drop his shot by 6 inches. He cursed as he re-aimed, as he looked along the rifle he was just in time to see the man's heels disappear into the scrub. JB head the crack of the rifle and felt the impact behind him, then he was crashing through clumps of grass and small bushes, which tore at his face and hands until he was brought to a sudden halt by a small tree, which barred his way. Shots were still being fired from the ridge above but now there was nothing for them to aim at, he was completely screened by the undergrowth. Still, taking no chances he crawled further on down the hill until reaching dead ground. He came up into a crouch, saw what looked like a small track and ran, heart beating wildly, hands flailing at the obstructing greenery. It was a full quarter of a mile before he came to a stop, chest heaving, listening intently for any pursuit. There was none that he could hear but that did not mean he was not being followed.

Stepping off the path he made his way slowly into the thick jungle to his right, being careful to leave little evidence of his passing. It would be dark in half an hour so there was a good chance of not being discovered. After a further fifteen minutes travel, he came upon a couple of large moss covered boulders sticking out of the jungle floor. They formed a natural shelter; it would be as good a place as any to spend the night.

Before he could settle for the night he must try to find water. Living without food for a few days was possible, without water he couldn't last long. A quick search of the area revealed none and light was fading fast as it did in this latitude. What was it he recalled that Al had shown him all those years ago when they had been at the Jungle Warfare School? Of course, there was a particular jungle vine that produced pure water in its stem; it had to be the right one as others could be deadly poisonous. After casting around he found what he thought was a small vine of the correct sort, breaking it open he placed a tiny drop of the fluid on the inside of his lip as he remembered being taught to gauge first if it were harmful. It passed. With relief JB held up the vine vertically to let the life giving drops of water cool his parched throat, it was only half a cup but he was fortunate and thankful for finding it. A long night lay ahead. He slept in fits and starts, sleeping a little and then waking up at every unusual sound in the dark eerie forest that surrounded him. He stared long and hard at the nearby undergrowth, wondering if there were men out there or just nocturnal animals. It was with a sense of relief almost when he detected the approach of a new day. As soon as it was light enough he would be on his way, but which way?

Up here close to the Malaysian border on the hills human habitation was very sparse. He was lost in the midst of an ocean of trees with no horizon to see. His friend Al (where was he now he wondered) had told him that when completely lost in the jungle, just take a course which led downhill or head for the nearest gully or valley, sooner or later that way he must come across a small stream. There were two reasons for this. First, he would need the water and secondly if he were to continue to follow the course of the stream he must eventually come across habitation. Even so, that still may take a couple of days and he had to remember to travel at least 50 yards from the water source, to blindly follow a stream would mean having to make progress through the thickest part of the undergrowth. It was also a likely area for ambushes. It was quite possible there were other guerrillas in the area. Tearing a strip of material from the bottom of his shirt, he wrapped it tightly about his head; it would help keep the sweat out of his eyes but not the apprehension he felt as once more he stepped forward into the unknown.

Judging by the sun, it must have been about ten in the morning when the first rattle of shots rang out through the jungle. Instinctively crouching down he realised the gunfire interspersed with the dull thumps of grenades was coming from the direction he had previously travelled. It could be that the Thai forces had caught up with his previous captors, but he wasn't about to take any chances. Increasing his pace, oblivious to the extra noise that was created by his passage, he aimed to put as much distance between him and the conflict going on behind. The lack of water was affecting him now, causing a loss of co-ordination, the heat and humidity sapping his strength. Every now and then his head would spin with dizziness, and would trip over one of the myriad tree roots with increasing frequency. A large fallen tree barred his way. He had to rest. Sinking down to the ground the stench of his sweat soaked clothes came to him. The stubble on his face itched and his hair was unkempt and tangled. He longed for a hot bath, the comfort of a clean warm bed, the softness of a pillow on which to lay his head. He sat back and leaned against the unyielding surface of the tree. He felt he could sleep for a week, his eyelids dropped and he fell into a doze. His last thoughts were the need to keep moving but his weariness overcame and his chin sank unto his chest. He never saw the stealthy figure approaching him, a man who leaned over to stare at his face. He would have been surprised at the expression on the man's features. He was smiling.

Chapter 12

Al had returned to his room in the barracks, the news he had received over breakfast had left him feeling numb, almost as though his brain refused to accept what he had heard. Sitting on the narrow bed he stared vacantly through the dust-streaked window at the wooded hills in the distance. Somewhere out there his friend lay, was he dead or alive? Would the authorities accede to his request to join any search party that was sent? Each passing day he knew lessened his chances of completing the mission, the 11th of August seemed to be coming up fast but his heart held him here, he would wait to find out.

It was close to midday before there was a soft knock on the door. An officer whom he hadn't seen previously entered, followed by an army private who was carrying a bundle of jungle green clothing and boots. Shaking hands and pointing at the uniform the officer spoke, "I'm surprised but it seems that you have been given permission to travel to the forward base camp, if you could change into these clothes, there is a chopper leaving in an hour". Al grasped the clothes as if they were some sort of lifeline. "I'll do anything to help and try to keep out of your way. Thanks for the chance", he said. Within an hour and a half the Bell helicopter carrying him swept into land on a cleared landing zone deep in the jungle. It was as though he had gone back through time, bringing back all those memories from his previous service days, some good, some bad. But he had a strange feeling of belonging, of being as one with the jungle. It was also comforting to blend in wearing his new uniform, there were less curious looks as he was led towards a large tent than he had experienced upon his arrival at the barracks.

Inside the tent several officers were gathered around a map table in the centre, carrying on a conversation in Thai. One of them detached himself from the group and came over to greet Al. Tall, his jungle green fatigues streaked with sweat; he shook Al's hand with genuine warmth. "Welcome to our forward operations base Mr Jenkins. I'm Major Malee". "I appreciate being given the opportunity to assist in any way I can to help find my friend Major", Al replied. "He's mentioned you to me several times and with some regard", the Thai officer added, "and I'm amazed that you should show up at this precise time". Al smiled. "Don't believe everything he's told you about me". His voice took a more serious note. "Do you still think there is a chance of him being found alive?" "A very good chance. His body was not amongst the others at the wreckage of the helicopter and we searched the area thoroughly. If he had been hiding nearby he would have shown himself once we arrived", the Major paused. "No, I feel sure that he is a captive. He's out there somewhere". Seeing the look of concern on Al's face, he hastened to reassure him, "We are doing all we can, there are several patrols out looking, in fact a squad is going out by chopper in half an hour. They are dropping in further up in the hills". Al grasped the officer's arm gently. "Let me go with them, I've spent a lot of time in this kind of country, I won't get in the way and it will be one more pair of eyes". "When I said they were going to be dropped in, the helicopter will not be landing, the men are going to abseil in due to the terrain up there, so I don't think that it will be possible for you to go". "You're wrong there Major, I was born to abseil. O.k. that's not quite true, but I have had quite a lot of experience at it". Major Malee gave a wry smile. "Rather you than me. Still, if you are determined to get yourself killed I'll let you go, but as you probably already know I will not accept any responsibility for your welfare". Al's face broke into a wide grin. "Major, you have a friend for life". Malee returned the smile. "Let's hope it is not a short one and I hope we are successful as JB is a good friend of mine also and as I said, I don't accept that he is dead". The Sergeant in charge of the squad does not speak a great deal of English, however I will brief him before you set off". Al thanked him and watched him make his way back to the group at the table.

Ten minutes later he was introduced to the Sergeant. A thick set man with arms which would not have been out of place on an orang-utan, while his face was more akin to a ruptured football. "You crazy farang", the Sergeant said laughing, "like to go with us into jungle?" If the Sergeant's English was lacking, his expertise in his job was not. He deftly showed Al the way he was expected to hook up prior to abseiling from the helicopter. Leaving him to go and check his men and equipment, Al felt a brief moment of panic. He had seen men before who had lost control on an abseil and the injuries were normally horrific as it was the legs that hit the ground first, and on most occasions there would be multiple compound fractures. The Sergeant was waving at him; time to board the chopper, too late to have second thoughts now, he would have to go through with it.

After a fifteen minute flight the aircraft came into a hover over tall towering trees. It seemed impenetrable. Staying in a hover the chopper descended slowly until the downdraft from the swirling rotor blades created an opening. At a signal from the pilot, the first man launched himself out of the aircraft. Wearing the special gloves provided, Al pulled up the rope strap around his waist and snapped on the steel carabineer, he made his way to the aircraft exit where the dispatcher stood waiting to attach the thick strong yet flexible nylon tape. He could feel the heat coming through the gloves in the 200-foot descent. Ten feet from the ground he savagely whipped the tape to the left with his right hand, braking his speed until his feet touched the jungle floor. Running over, he joined the other crouching figures, to be joined quickly by the last man. Above them they heard the sound of the helicopter receding until the stillness of the jungle crept over them.

Using hand signals only the Sergeant led them off in single file, weapons at the ready, the two leading men searching for any sign. They crept on through the afternoon up a winding hill track, stopping frequently to cast around for clues to show if the guerrillas had passed this way recently. On one such stop they came upon a 20-foot python. The snake made no effort to evade them but just stared, its tiny eyes watching; halfway down the snake's body was a huge bulge. The Sergeant explained it was common for a snake of this size having taken a large meal (probably a monkey) to just lie and digest. The light was already beginning to fade when the two leading scouts began to point excitedly at something they had noticed up front. After a brief huddle with the Sergeant he returned down the line to say that they had picked up a trail, from now on they would have to be extra vigilant. He intended to follow it just as long as the light lasted, he did not know who it was they were following.

It was a long and miserable night. Al was asked to do his share of the guard duties, which meant three hours lying on his stomach in a shallow body pit observing the path they were following. A green length of cord ran from his right foot to the Sergeant in the centre of the squad, if he were to observe the slightest movement he could alert the sleeping soldiers without a word being spoken. The only attack that night came from the ever-present mosquitoes, biting through the thin material of jungle shirt and trousers. Even before it was light they began to advance cautiously further up the track. At nine in the morning their progress was halted at a signal from the front. While the men went into firing positions, the Sergeant called Al forward. They were on a ridgeline, which on one side dropped sharply away. Even before Al saw any evidence of previous occupants, the area held an air of almost silent menace. One of the soldiers pointed at something with the toe of his boot, there lying on top of dead leaves were a few grains of rice. "How long since they were here Sarge?" Al asked keeping his voice low. "Maybe one or two hours, not more". The reply was confident. "How can you be so sure", Al insisted. "Easy, ants like rice very much, not be long, eat very fast". A quick search round revealed nothing more, however just over the edge of the steep slope there were markings in the soft earth which showed somebody or something had gone down the hill. A radio call was sent to the forward base camp informing them of their find. Instructions were received to press on as fast as it was expedient.

Although at first Major Malee had been reluctant to issue a firearm, he had subsequently relented, something for which Al was grateful as he felt the reassuring weight of the M16 in his arms. The track weaved and turned up the hill in thick jungle. After one such bend the leading Thai scout found himself facing a startled dishevelled looking man. On his head he wore a forage cap and on the cap a red star. Both of them opened up on each other at the same time, the sharp crack of the firearms sending a shower of birds squawking from the trees. The communist dropped to the ground with a cry of pain as the Thai soldier clasped at his leg, blood seeping through his fingers. The unmistakable sound of a machine gun came from the communist position, the bullets sieving through the foliage, splinters of wood flying from the trees as the rounds struck home. With two of the squad Al ran forward to cover the wounded Thai. They dropped to the ground and began returning the fire. It wasn't enough to silence the heavy machine gun, it began to become more accurate, showers of dirt erupted immediately in front. The young soldier next to him gave a groan; a trickle of blood ran down his face. Although Al was aware that the Sergeant behind him together with the rest of the squad had moved off to the right in a flanking movement, they would not be in a position to attack for another couple of minutes. The machine gun had to be silenced if they were to stand a chance of being successful. It was out of grenade throwing distance and to stand up would invite certain death. As it was, his companion was already dead. It was then that he noticed the M69 grenade launcher strapped to the man's back. He quickly slipped it off and at the same time removed three of the high explosive rounds from the ammunition pouch. Breaking it open he loaded it. An easy gun to fire, it worked just like a shotgun but the end result would be far more devastating. Taking a line on where he had seen the muzzle flashes he squeezed the trigger, there was a bright red flash followed by a dull boom. The force of the explosion sheared off small branches and twigs. The machine gun stopped firing but he knew very well that it could just be temporary, reloading he took advantage of the lull to take a more deliberate aim. Just as the launcher kicked at his shoulder bullets whistled over his head once more, only this time before the echoes of the exploding grenade had died away it was followed by screams of pain. He reloaded and fired again; there was no return fire.

There were shouts and cries with a rapid exchange of shots as further up the ridge the Sergeant and his men attacked. Loud explosions and the shouted orders of men but as quick as it had started it was over with just the occasional bark of command, silence settled once more over the vastness of the jungle. Al and the remaining Thai soldier looked at each other and then slowly and warily got to their feet. Reassuring the wounded man they would send back a medic, they advanced with caution towards the machine gun position. The air was still strong with the smell of gun smoke as they came upon a scene of devastation. Three men lay at various angles around the now useless gun. A piece of grenade shrapnel had pierced one man's throat. It would have taken only seconds for him to die while another's fate had been much more cruel, his intestines were spilled on the ground from the split open stomach, already the wounds were covered by big green bottle flies. The third man made just the slightest movement. Was he alive? Quickly feeling his pulse Al detected a feeble pulse, it seemed his only injury was a deep cut on the forehead. He could well be just concussed from the blast of the explosions. Leaving the Thai soldier to watch over him, al made his way further up the ridge where he met up with a heavily sweating Sergeant.

"You do very good job, very glad you come with us" he said, shaking his hand. "Wait a minute, I only helped. I am afraid one of your men is dead while another is wounded back down the track. They did much more than I". Al replied with genuine remorse in his voice. The Sergeant shouted at one of his men to attend the wounded before turning back to Al. "We get one prisoner but others get away when we attack, no matter I already call on radio to HQ, they send helicopters to land men further up hill". He spoke the English slowly with confidence in his voice. "Yes, that should cut them off if they are quick enough", Al paused and then spoke the thought that had been uppermost in his mind. "What about my friend the Major, any news of him?" "Arrh, the American, yes the man we catch say he run away last night at the place where they camp". The Sergeant looked thoughtful. He had a lot to think about, looking at the English man he realised what he was about to ask and so replied first. "No, I am sorry but my Captain has told me I have to stay here, maybe the communists try to come back this way". Al saw the wisdom of that but he also knew he must try to find JB today, for all he knew the man may be lying injured, the jungle was vast and trails soon grew cold.

"Just let me have two of your men Sergeant and I'll go back down the track to see if we can find him, all we need is a few hours". The Sergeant looked doubtful, knowing the farang was his responsibility but he also knew he owed the man a favour after the morning's little battle. "O.k., but come back by 4 hours even if you do not find him or you give me big trouble". Al looked relieved. "Thanks, you can count on it". He waited for the two men detailed to join him. They did not speak English but that was possibly an advantage as sign language would have to be used. With just the three of them they could not afford any unnecessary noise. After first checking his own equipment he made them jump up and down a couple of times to ensure they did not have anything that rattled or made any other noise, that done he led the way retracing their steps. It was not long before they were once more at the site of the previous communist camp. The first thing to check out was the definite marks leading down the steep slope. Slowly and gingerly, inching their way down they followed the trail down until they were once more in dense undergrowth. It seemed as though here the trail finished. They cast around searching until one of the Thai soldiers came over to indicate he had found something. There on the ground almost hidden was an army knapsack, but not the Thai Army standard issue, but why should the guerrillas throw it away? Making sure to check it first for any booby trap they found it contained just rice. Why should they discard food or could it be that JB had in fact escaped this way and dropped the pack in his haste. Al decided to take a chance. If it was the latter they did not have a lot of time and there seemed no other obvious ways in which he may have gone. The two Thais felt sure that someone had gone this way although there were no real signs of anyone passing. There was a small track that led further down the hill, possibly made by animals. It seemed logical to follow.

The heat was oppressive and the adrenalin ran high as the three of them worked their way down the narrow twisting track hemmed in on all sides by the luxuriant foliage, stopping every few feet or so to examine the slightest sign that might indicate someone had passed this way recently. It was only due to this diligence that caused Al to notice just a few scuffed over leaves on one side of the track. Following it further there were definite signs that someone very recently had passed this way. On the underside of several jungle leaves very small hairs would be present, if someone were even to brush against them the hairs would remain pointed in that direction for some time, it was something that only a trained observer would notice, but they did and they knew they were closing in on an unknown person or persons ahead of them. It was not long before they found the huge moss covered rock and beside it the broken vine. Next to the rock was a faint indentation in the ground of a man's body. In their minds there was no doubt they were following just one man, it did not take them long to find the new trail that led away from the rock. Although signs were not frequent, once they established the direction and line of the trail they were able to increase their pace. In fact after some time the signs became more obvious as though the person they were following was becoming more careless in hiding his trail. Their hands gripped the stocks of their rifles tightly, peering intently and with ears strained for the slightest noise they knew soon they must catch sight of their quarry.

Suddenly Al shot his hand forward to restrain the leading Thai soldier. The man looked startled for he had seen nothing to cause alarm and in fact could still not. Drawing his razor sharp machete slowly Al pointed with the tip at something that was level with the man's shoulder. His face visibly paled under the dark skin as he looked into the eyes of a deadly green mamba curled menacingly on the small branch, hardly more than a foot from him. Al's arm was a blur as he brought the machete down cutting off the snake's head and the branch in one swift movement. "Khop Khun maah maak krap" the Thai whispered his thanks profusely. They both knew a bite from the snake could have been fatal. Usually snakes would disappear rapidly on feeling the vibration of men's feet excepting large snakes such as the python they had seen earlier when it was digesting a large meal. There was only one reason a smaller snake such as the mamba would remain as humans approached, it had to be ill, it would not have the strength to leave but its bite would be just as deadly.

They continued following the signs of the unseen man ahead of them knowing now they were almost out of time before they would have to turn back. The two Thais were beginning to show signs of reluctance to continue further. It was now more than two hours since leaving the ridge track high above them. Al made a sign with his hands to indicate that after a further ten minutes they would have to call off the search although he was loathed to do so. A broken jungle fern stem they had just spotted was still weeping sap which would indicate it had happened not much more than half an hour ago. After a further ten minutes the soldiers decided they had gone far enough. They sat down on the trail pointing at their watches. Al knew it was not fair to ask them to go further, they had their orders to follow. He told them to stay there, have a drink and rest while he would just follow the trail a hundred yards before they could return together. They were happy with that, thinking that he was another mad farang. They were convinced by now that their search would be fruitless.

Al left them, slowly picking his way. Once out of sight however although sweating profusely he increased the pace, he knew the two men he had left behind would wait at least five minutes before getting anxious. The jungle seemed to be getting thicker. Although slowing him down the signs of the previous man's passing were easier to spot. Ahead in the murky greenness there appeared also a large fallen tree, which would obstruct him. Could that be a man's form that was lying against it? He slowly advanced, training the muzzle of his rifle on what could now be clearly seen as a man who was either dead or could possibly be asleep. It was then that the recognition came to him. After all these years the lean hard face with the jutting chin surmounted by the close cropped blond hair was still the same, well almost. The hair was beginning to thin and the stubble on his face did not completely conceal the extra lines that ran from his mouth and eyes. It was John Brooks. After all this time he had at last caught up with him, only one question remained, was he alive? He did appear so as Al walked right up close to him he could see the gentle rise and fall of his chest. He smiled down at the incumbent form, reached forward and shook him by the shoulder. The eyes blinked open in alarm, he raised his left arm in front of him in a protective gesture then dropped it as he saw no danger and his eyes took on a look of incredulity. When he spoke there was almost a note of disbelief in his voice. "It just can't be, but it is Al Jenkins". I must be dead and I've woken up in hell, only you have beaten me to it". Al just kept smiling before he replied. "You are one hell of a hard man to find JB but I am glad to see that you are alive and kicking". JB shook his head as though in disbelief. "Yeah, sure I am alive but I am not so sure about the kicking bit". I still cannot believe that I should wake up to see you here. What's that saying? 'Old soldiers never die, they just fade away'.

Al helped the exhausted man to his feet before replying, "It's a long story but before I tell you all about it we have to get back up the track someway, there are two disgruntled Thai soldiers waiting for us, at least I hope they are still there". The other man laughed quietly and followed Al back up the trail. "And there I was thinking that you had come all the way out here by yourself". They rounded a corner coming into view of the surprised looking soldiers before Al replied. "You should be so lucky, the jungle is swarming with Commies, I wasn't about to attempt a one man rescue mission". Although they were behind on their time schedule they made the return journey much quicker, not having the laborious task of trying to find a trail. As they arrived at the scene of the morning's battle the Sergeant had already gathered his men ready to move out back down the hill to base camp. He seemed overjoyed to see them come back with the Major. "Dee maak, die maak", he said using the Thai words to convey very good, he was too excited to think of the English words but he did go on to explain in his halting English that most of the Communists had been either killed or captured further up the hill when they ran into the troops which had been airlifted in by helicopter. Two of the previously captured soldiers had come through unscathed while the third had died in the firefight. Still, the Sergeant was more than happy with the morning's work, he knew it could well mean a promotion for him.

After a debriefing back at base camp, Al and JB were lucky to be put on the same flight back to the barracks. Disembarking, they walked across the grassed area towards the accommodation. Once they had left the howl of the aircrafts turbines behind JB looked across at Al as he spoke, "Well, right now all I want to do is to get out of these filthy clothes, take a long bath and then head over to the Mess to get some good grub". "You took the words right out of my mouth", his companion replied. "I smell like a Turkish wrestler's armpits" "And", JB said, "over the meal we can have a little chat about old times but also I'll be very interested to hear just what brings you to this neck of the woods. I mean, what the fuck are you doing here?

More than an hour and a half later they sat facing each other across the plain mess table. The meal and the small talk was over, they both knew that. Al began "You're quite right of course to realise that I did not come all this way just to visit you and I respect you too much to beat around the bush, so I'll just come straight out with it, I need a favour". JB laid his hands flat on the table in front of him and looked Al straight in the eye as he replied, "After what happened this morning you can ask anything". The expression that JB wore was one of complete sincerity; even so Al was still loath to ask of him something that he knew would put him in a predicament. "Well, first of all of course I want you to help me but you must discount everything that happened this morning, that must not influence your decision". The tall American gave a snort before replying; "There's no way I can forget today, although I know I was a fool to get myself in that position. I should have stayed

146

behind my desk". He raised his hand before Al could interrupt. "You know what I was thinking before you found me, that I had survived two tours in Vietnam, two indelible tours that I shall never forget only to maybe wind up dead in some forgotten piece of jungle miles from anywhere. I know in future to stay away from the field. Waking up this morning to see the barrel of a gun and then your ugly face was something that completely threw me". He lit up a cigarette, leant back in his chair and blew out a cloud of smoke before asking, "So, how can I help?" Al tried to sound nonchalant as he replied, "Not a lot really, just a couple of pounds of P.E and your help in getting it out of the country". He whistled through his teeth, thought for a moment and then said, "It's a pretty tall order, in fact it would be very hard for me to get hold of some without a lot of questions being asked and I take it you don't want any questions". Al nodded. "That's right, I don't want it traced back to you, or to me for that matter".

JB flicked the ash from his cigarette into the ashtray. "Look", he said, "be my guest for a day or two and if I do manage to get hold of some I want you to promise that it is not used against Americans or American interests". "Believe me", said Al, "if that were the case I would not have come to you".

"Sure Al, I ought to have enough faith in you by now, but you know my position. I have a promotion on the way and a good posting to Washington, I don't want to screw up". "I'll make sure that no one hears any of this from me", said Al. JB stubbed his cigarette out and rose slowly to his feet. "Well", he said, "time for me to get some work done and I should be in a position to give you some news tomorrow, but you must be under no illusions. It is doubtful whether I may be able to gain access to it". His voice held a note of uncertainty that was not feigned. Al suddenly realised that even after all the tumultuous events of the last few days, it could still end up with a bit fat zero and that he could well be back at square one. They arranged to meet the following day at the same time when he could give Al a definite answer but what that answer would be, only time would tell.

Chapter 13

Simon Richards was making a good recovery from the injuries he had received at the side of the road. He knew now that when he had first been admitted to the hospital in Yala apparently there had been a great deal of shaking of heads, but to their credit they had achieved in stabilising his scondition before having him moved the next day to the larger and more modern hospital at Pattani. It was here now that he had just managed to convince the doctor that he was fit enough if he used a wheelchair to make a phone call, he had lied saying it was imperative to contact his mother and father. That hadn't been enough at first but when he explained that besides allaying his parents' fears for his safety, he also needed them to send extra money for his medical treatment, that part of the argument had done the trick. That had been forty-five minutes ago, the operator had booked his call to Geneva and warned him at the same time he would have to wait at least half an hour before being connected. At least it gave him time to reflect on events since his arrival in Thailand and what he was going to say to Mo when he eventually managed to speak to him. He knew that he was damn lucky to be alive and mainly due to the intervention of the man he was trailing and yet the irony was if he were to get his full fee for the job, he had to shop the man who had saved his life, not that in his present condition he would be able to find out a great deal more.

He was so deep in his thoughts that when the phone rang, it startled him. "Your call to Geneva Sir", he heard the Thai lady operator saying, "It's ringing for you now". After speaking to the switchboard at the Israeli Mission, Mo came on the line. "Good Morning Mr Richards, nice to hear from you. I was expecting a call from you yesterday, how have you progressed?" There seemed almost an echo on the line. Simon gave it a couple of seconds before replying. "I've found out all I'm going to be able to find out at this stage I'm afraid". The man at the other end seemed almost gruff, there was a certain edge to his voice, "That does not sound like the Simon Richards I know, what makes you so sure that you won't get any more information?" Simon told him of the attack by the roadside and finished by saying "If it were not for the intervention of a passing motorist there is no doubt that I would have been killed". Mo did not ask about the identity of the motorist and Simon was not about to tell him. When Mo spoke next, there was a certain sympathy in his voice. "O.k. Simon, just send any information you do have by the usual means, but there is just one question I need to know now, do you know what our mutual friend is doing out there?" "All I know is that the man was coming out here to visit a friend of his, at least that's what I understood", he said. "Do you know the name of the man he was supposed to see" Mo insisted. "That's a negative", Simon wanted to move away from the area of questioning. "I'm sorry that I've not been able to help more but under the circumstances there's little I can do". "Yes of course", Mo replied. Simon continued, "However, after what I have had to go through I do feel I'm entitled to the full fee for the job". He waited a full three seconds for the response. "I don't really control the purse strings but I will recommend you get the total amount". Simon breathed a sigh of relief away from the mouthpiece before speaking. "And also because of the nature of the wounds I have received I don't feel I'll be up to carrying out any more field trips for you Mo". "That's a damn shame, you've done some good work for us in the past". "I'm sorry mo, but that 's where I want to leave it, in the past". The voice on the other end was resigned. "O.k. Simon, I'll put it to my superiors, but from myself I'll be sorry to lose you, but if you do remember anything else about our man give me a call immediately". Simon replaced the phone with mixed feelings; he knew on the one hand that he had just given up the opportunity to make good money in a short period of time; on the other hand really the scales came down far more heavily. What was money after all, if as had happened on more than one occasion there was the chance of him ending up on some foreign cold mortuary slab? There was still life to be had; he was breathing it, feeling it, even though at the moment he was temporarily incapacitated. Still, what was the name of that pretty Thai nurse, she could help him to his bed.

Mo put the phone down in his office wearing a thoughtful expression on his face. After his conversation with Simon Richards he knew that there was nothing conclusive to be gleaned from it, in fact maybe Harry Reynolds was right in saying he was wasting time and money in pursuing this enquiry. But he was loath to admit it and of course it would enhance Reynolds bid for the top job if it were to be seen that Mo's instincts were failing him. But the trouble was he still had this gut feeling deep inside him that all was not as it seemed on the surface, there was more to it than just a simple visit to Thailand by the man Jenkins. There was just one more ploy that he could use in trying to obtain more information but he would have to do it before Reynolds got wind of the negative details from Thailand, otherwise he knew the investigation would be stopped. It was an underhand trick, something he did not like doing but where the security of the state was concerned, nothing else had more priority. And if it meant getting to Viola Gedler through her husband, then so be it.

She knew her husband was angry the minute he stepped through the door of their luxurious Geneva apartment. He didn't have to say anything, she knew him well enough by now. He was also late. "Bad day at the office, darling?" He did not reply immediately but threw his brief case onto one of the easy chairs. "What I'd like know is two, no make it three fingers of whisky with a bunch of ice", he said sharply. Ever since she had married Greg Gelder it was very rare to see him lose his temper. He was always very calm and methodical so it was all the more surprising and worrying to see him like this now. He had slumped into one of the easy chairs while she busied herself fixing the drinks; she took her time hoping that when it came to talk his temper would have abated somewhat. She took the sparking glass of amber liquid over to him wondering at the same time if he had found out about the visit of her old flame, but surely that was not enough to put him in this mood.

He took the glass without speaking so she broke the silence. "What's troubling you darling? Things are never as bad as they first seem". That seemed to startle him out of his deep thoughts. "Bad? They could not be any worse than they are at the moment. I have just been informed today that I can kiss goodbye to my career". She was more than just surprised by his announcement. "That cannot be", she cried. "I know how highly you are regarded at the mission". "I was ", he replied sourly, "until I was told today that my wife was some kind of security risk". He twisted his face into a grimace as he continued. "You, of all people were the one I had always counted, no, relied on, to always support me".

She was staggered. They were threatening to fire her husband effectively unless she could persuade them otherwise, which of course meant that she would have to tell them all about Al in the hope that it would clear Greg. It was a position that she had hoped could never happen to her, to choose between her husband and ex-lover, though even as the thought passed through her mind, of course there could only be one choice. She would have to support her husband as her children's futures depended on it as well, which meant having to betray Al. It meant never being able to face Al again and it meant never again would those arms of his enfold her. She was going to have to banish all thoughts of how good it was when they had first met up in Singapore. It had been her first true love, only eighteen at the time she could never forget the nights and days of passion spent in those distant climes. She could recall even now laying on the hot sands under a cloudless sky just the two of them, cold drinks in the icebox, the murmur of the seas as they caressed the sparking sand. The distant shouts and calls of others on the beach never intruded upon their own private personal world, a world they lived from day to day believing it could never end.

"I take your silence as an admission of guilt, or are you just trying to think of a suitable response", her husband broke into her thoughts. She stared straight back at him as she replied. "No Greg, I have just decided to tell that little fat man at security everything I know, there won't be any threat to your job, I realise I owe you that". The aggression had gone out of his voice as he replied, "Just what did you do darling, because when it was first brought up at the office I said it was impossible that you were even capable of going against the State and we certainly don't need the money". "There was no money involved, you're right", she said as she re-arranged her long legs on the seat. "What I did was a favour for an old friend, but there is no damage done if I go in tomorrow and explain what I was doing". Greg drained his glass. She stood up and taking his empty went over to the drinks cabinet. "I'll join you in a drink and tell you all about it, but whatever conclusion you draw, remember it is you and the children I love, otherwise I would not take the steps I have to". Greg looked vastly relieved. He swept his arms about her kissing her on the cheek. "Thank you sweetheart, I knew I could rely on you". She laughed in his embrace, raising her eyebrows as she spoke, "Ah, but you weren't so sure half an hour ago". Then in a more serious note, "right let's have our drinks and I'll tell you all about it and after that I'm going to get dead drunk".

Mo looked around impatiently at the gathering round the table, including him there were six of them including Harry Reynolds, all engaged in Mossard activities and working out of Geneva. They were in the same drab office where Al Jenkins' name had first been discussed. Only this time Jenkins' name was almost at the bottom of the agenda, not being considered of sufficient importance to discuss first. Mo smiled inwardly, nothing pleased him better than to deflate the self-important Reynolds and the information he had would do just that. The Chairman of the meeting rustled some papers on the desk in front of him before selecting one. "Item number 9", he said. "Al Jenkins. If you select the file in front of you, you'll se there has been no progress as yet to confirm or deny that this man is in fact working against the Jewish State". He looked at the paper in his hands before continuing, "therefore we have to decide at this meeting whether to continue the investigation or to close the file". Harry Reynolds was on his feet even before Mo had a chance to open his mouth. When he spoke the sarcasm was obvious. "In my mind from the start I felt this was an unnecessary waste of time and money with very little justification or basis for it, and now I think I have been vindicated by the report from our agent in Thailand, as in fact the report tells us nothing". Mo got to his feet. They were all staring at him now knowing that it was he who initiated the investigation at the onset. His reputation was at stake. "Gentlemen, I am afraid that the file in front of you is not entirely up to date, there has been a further development this morning which means that this case should definitely remain open". He had all their attention now. The Chairman was impatient. "Well, come on, don't keep us in suspense, spit it out".

Mo obliged, "this morning I had a visitor, the same woman who originally raised our suspicions as you will know. Anyway, it seems that she has decided to come clean. She told me the reason why she was going through the Mission Chief's desk". He gazed at Reynolds before speaking again. "It seems that this man Jenkins had asked her for the itinerary of the Defence Minister and this she duly gave him, but she insists that only two relevant dates, the visit to Rome and the one to the Canary Islands were the ones he was interested in". Harry Reynolds was the first to speak. "So what conclusion have you drawn from that ". "What I do know, he said, is that a man with Jenkins' background is not interested in getting the man's autograph". Harry was not put out. "Could it be that possibly the man is trying to muscle in on the arms sales market?" The Chairman spoke this time. "I think and I am sure you all agree that it warrants informing the Minister that there may be a possible threat to his life". There was a general nodding of heads. The Chairman continued, "I shall first request the Minister to change the dates of the visits, that should preclude any action being taken against him. However, if he refuses, gentlemen I am afraid we may have a problem". The meeting broke up after a further fifteen minutes. The Chairman called Mo to one side. "I don't know how you got that woman to talk but thanks, it's possible that you have done all of use a great favour in unmasking that man. Let's just hope that the Minister is receptive in changing days". Mo tried hard to keep the smile from his face.

Chapter 14

Al dug his fingernails deep into the palms of his sweating hands as he watched Major John Brooks approach him from the direction of the canteen doors. There was nothing to indicate by the expression on the man's face if he was the bearer of good or bad news. "Hi there Al, don't look so glum". His cheeky voice echoed around the mess hall. He drew up a seat opposite, observing to see there was nobody within earshot of them. Even so, he bent forward to talk. "I've got some good and bad news, what would you like to hear first". Al felt there sounded some hope in his voice; he just hoped he was going to hear the right answer. "Well you're looking perky JB, you better let me have the bad news first, let's get it out of the way". There was a mischievous smile playing around JB's lips. "I'm sorry to say that I was unable to get hold of any P.E for you". Al was aghast. "Bad news, I would call it disastrous". "Hold on, buddy", the Major threw up his hands. "I can however offer you something, how about a couple of Claymore mines, do you think you could use them?" Al did not have to think long; he had used this type of mine previously, on several occasions. Several pounds of high explosive encased in plastic with 700 steel ball bearings embedded in the P.E, it was a devastating device which could be detonated remotely or by wire and with nothing else on offer he could not turn down this chance. "Give me the tools and I shall do the job", he said. The American looked amused. "Yes, I seem to have heard that somewhere before, but if you want the job done, two Claymores will help you.

Before replying Al waited while the Mess orderly placed two steaming bowls of Thai porridge in front of them, hot watery rice with elements of seafood and egg mixed together, it was a common Thai breakfast. "I ordered this for us both", Al said with a smile. "Thanks, but you still haven't answered my question". Al picked up his spoon and began stirring the mixture in the bowl before replying. "I'm sure that you don't really want to know and of course there is still the possibility that it may not be carried out, however if it is I will send you a newspaper cutting". "Yes, maybe you're right if I know nothing about it, by the same token of course I shall expect you never to reveal how and where you obtained the mines". JB's face had grown grim as he spoke. "You can take that for granted". Al paused to take a mouthful of soup. "In fact, I've already thought out a plausible tale as to how I obtained them. I'll say I picked them up in Vietnam from some back street dealer. There were stocks of them left over when the Americans pulled out. JB pulled a face. "You could say that with your hand on your heart, when I think of the amount of material that was left behind, what a waste". Al was sympathetic. "Believe it or not but I do have some idea of how you felt". The Major looked surprised. "You do? I had no idea that you had been in a similar situation". Al scraped at the bottom of his bowl, looked up and gave a sardonic grin. "There you go, and you thought you knew everything". "Well almost", the American laughed back, pushing his half eaten bowl of porridge to one side. "Sorry, I can't handle any more of that. Anyway, tell me about it". Al leant back in his chair; it did not matter if anyone heard this part of the conversation.

"In '67' you may remember we withdrew from Aden, it was basically the same situation there, really all down to politics. We were ordered to leave vast quantities of equipment behind, I imagine in some strange way the politicians thought by doing this the incoming government would be sympathetic to Britain and adopt a democratic system". JB nodded and lit up a cigarette. "Anyway, I was there with others and we knew damn well the locals would not be influenced in the slightest by any such gesture once they were in power". "I can see that", said the American. "The politicians being out of tune with the military". "However", Al continued, "in one instance this insistence on fair play was taken too far, in a neighbouring barracks which was due to be handed over the lads became a little boisterous with the thought of going home and a few windows ended up being smashed". "Don't tell me, they had money docked from their wages". "You guessed it, so by this time we were one of the few units left, we dug in around the airfield when up comes this Arab with a fistful of money offering to buy our excess equipment such as grenades, tents, etc. He didn't seem to be aware that we were going to leave it and we were not about to inform him. JB smiled as he envisaged the situation. "So you took his money". "We did, sending some to the lads who had lost money and keeping the remainder for our unit". The mess orderly came over and cleared away their plates. Al bent forward in his seat again and spoke quietly. "This little gift you have for me, I have already devised a plan for getting it out of the country but I will need your help". "I will do what I can but of course I can't promise anything", said JB.

Al took a sheet of notepaper from his top shirt pocket and passed it over. "On that", he said, "You will see I've listed a possible route with dates by which time I have to have the material". JB studied the paper for some time before looking up and speaking. "You know that is a damn good way you devious bastard, with your luck and my connections you might just be lucky". Al smiled back at him. "I thought if we plan this with some thought we may be able to eliminate the luck side of it". The two of them sat together for another half hour going over the route, after which time JB stood up and pocketed the note. "Look Al, do you think you could stick around for a couple of days while I have time to implement this plan?" "I'm not sure, Al replied, but you're right, maybe I should before flying back home, I may as well know now before raising my hopes too high". "Look, I know that time is against you, so call this number each day and maybe I will sort it out sooner rather than later". He quickly wrote down a number and handed it to Al. "Thanks JB for all you have done, let's hope that it works out. It also gives me time to see a friend of mine who is in hospital at Yala, so I'll give you a call from there tomorrow". They shook hands before departing with JB adding, "don't leave it so long next time and maybe we could have a drink together before you leave even". "Good idea, shades of the past", Al replied as he made his way out through the canteen doors.

It did not take him long to pack the few possessions he had and load them into the back of the Suzuki. In half an hour he was travelling back down the winding road towards Yala. Through the open windows the smells and fragrances of the ever-present jungle came to him. When he was younger he was afraid as though there was a constant menace deep within the brooding green and damp acres, but now he regarded the jungle as his friend, a place where a man could seek refuge, sanctuary and peace. The concrete jungle was just that, concrete and alien to him, overpowering with the mass of humanity, all desperately seeking to earn a living. Out here in the tropical rain forest if one cared to look, there was everything a man could want. He wondered at his feelings. Was it because at some stage in the deep and distant past his forbears had originated from a place such as this or was it the delayed sense of relief at coming out alive, at being able to help a friend, a true friend, one who promised to try to help him even at his own jeopardy. He did not know. He only knew that he was glad to be alive, yes that was it, alive to fulfil what he wished if he so chose.

He pulled over to the side of the road and switched off the noisy engine. Getting out, he walked into the dense undergrowth before coming out into a small clearing surrounded by tall vine covered trees, sunlight filtered down to make spots of light on the leaf covered floor, above monkeys chattered in the high branches, unseen. He walked slowly over to one such spot and sank down to his knees, he swept the leaves away to reveal the dark earth underneath, he reached and grabbed a handful and slowly let it trickle to the ground. The realisation came to him; sooner or later everyone was reduced to this, just a handful of dust. No matter what rank or privilege people had enjoyed in life or how poor and destitute, in death it was all the same. In Earth's life span the life of a human could be measured in the blink of an eye. But he was here now, alive, there was still time left to enjoy life and if his plan were carried through successfully he would have enough money to do just that. The roar of a passing truck on the nearby road brought him out of his thoughts making him realise his vehicle was vulnerable out here. He quickly walked back, got in and drove off in the direction of Yala.

There was just one thing in the back of his mind as he watched the countryside flashing past. Since the death of his wife and children there had been a terrible void in his life, even now if he were to become wealthy it occurred to him that if he had no person to share that wealth with, it still did not amount to much. He was getting on for 40 years old now and although he could still attract the attention of younger women, if they knew his financial status he could never be quite sure of their motives. However, he pushed all negative thoughts to the back of his mind as he entered the outskirts of Yala. After all that had happened, it seemed weeks since being here but of course it had only been a few days, albeit, long and trying days when he had left Simon Richards in a critical condition. He was surprised to find out on his arrival at the small hospital, that they had moved him to Pattani. They said that his condition was stable. Al was pleased that they had not moved him to Bangkok. He could contact JB from Pattani tomorrow. Leaving the hospital he filled up with petrol at a nearby garage and began the journey to Pattani, there was still a lot of the day left. He knew of course every day was precious, to have everything ready by the 11th August in the Canary Islands even now was getting tight, but there was no point in rushing back to the U.K. before clearing up all the loose ends here. In one way he was pleased it meant that there might be an opportunity to see JB one more time before leaving and also, the least he could do was visit Simon Richards. Indirectly he felt responsible for the Aussie being in hospital, although it was not he who had put him there. Why, he wondered, had the big fellow come clean and admitted he had been hired to follow him? Most probably he had thought that perhaps he was about to die. Perhaps he should have been angry when he heard the man pretending to be his friend, was really just digging for information. Still, there was no damage done. He could not possibly know anything about the reason for his visit, so therefore he could not bear the man any malice.

It was with these thoughts in mind that he finally pulled up in the rather small hospital car park in Pattani. The crisp white linen of the nurses' uniforms and the antiseptic smells in the hospital were a welcome change after the dirt and death he had witnessed in the jungle. He was surprised to find that Simon was sitting in a wheelchair on a balcony that ran outside his ward, gazing down at the green hospital grounds below. The nurse who had guided Al told him to stay no longer than half an hour, she turned and left them. The big

Aussie turned his head to see who his visitor was. Al could see that his normally bronzed face was tired and pale, there were swathes of bandages around his middle. "Dreaming of a few cans of beer?" said Al, pulling up a chair to sit close to him. There was surprise written all over his face to see him. "Well, blow me down, you are one person I never expected to see again after what I told you back at the roadside". He reached slowly over to grasp Al's hand. "You know something, you should still be in your bed in your condition". He shook his head. "I know, that's what the nurse keeps telling me, but they allow me to sit out here an hour each day. I just can't stand lying in that bed all the time". "According to the doctor whom I spoke to on the way up here, one reason for your quick recovery is your fitness". Simon gave a short laugh. "That's news to me". He studied Al for a second and then said, "You don't look so sharp yourself, looks as though you've been out in the bush these last couple of days". It was Al's turn to be surprised. "That's a bit of a wild guess". He laughed longer this time. "Hey, you can't fool an old vet but that's your business. Did you get to see your friend you were looking for?" Al was glad he changed the subject. "It took me some time but you could say we eventually met up, a pretty unusual place mind you". "That sounds interesting", he said, "but I don't suppose you are going to tell me where". "You suppose right, but I will tell you one day". "I can't wait, you sly old bastard". Al looked behind him to see the nurse hovering there. She indicated that it was time for her patient to get back into his bed. Simon looked less than pleased at the interruption. "Look Al, get yourself a paper and pen and I'll give you my address in Australia, come over to the Gold Coast some day and I'll buy you a couple of beers". "That's an offer I can't refuse", Al said, searching through his pockets for a bit of paper. "And I hope to see you back on your pins". He gazed for what seemed like minutes out over the balcony before replying. "Yes, and they won't be taking me overseas again unless it's for a holiday. I've made my mind up that it is going to be an easy life for me from now on". The attractive nurse came over and wheeled him back into his ward. He protested but it fell on deaf ears. Al took his details and shook hands once more before leaving with his last remark ringing after him. "Don't forget to look me up or I may have to track you down again". Al made a suitable reply using a hand signal, which was not listed in any Jungle training manual. Al could still hear him chortling as he walked down the corridor.

It was nearly six in the afternoon when he emerged into the still bright sunshine outside the hospital. There was not much he could do with the rest of the day other than to find some reasonable little hotel, check in and try to unwind a little, maybe at the hotel bar. He would call JB early tomorrow and hope that he had managed to fix the details as he had suggested for the shipment of the mines. He found a hotel and although small, it was reasonably clean plus the bar boasted a quite considerable range of drinks, but he was never one to drink alone for any amount of time, so by ten in the evening he abandoned his bar stool and made his way up to his room.

He had barely closed the door behind him when the phone rang. He recognised the voice on the phone as that belonging to a coy looking Thai girl he had seen earlier downstairs in a corner of the bar. She had asked him then if he would like to buy her a drink, he had declined. Now it transpired as she told him in her singsong voice she had just purchased some tasty morsels of Thai food and would he be interested in sharing them with her. She was prepared to bring the food to his room and no doubt as she implied, one thing might lead to another. He wasn't sure about the other, but the company would be welcome, so he asked her up. A few minutes later there was a soft tap on the door. He opened it and sure enough there she was, although this time he could make out her features more clearly than had been possible in the dimly lit bar. In one hand she clutched a couple of bamboo leaf covered parcels of food, the brown eyes were mischievous behind the dark fringe of hair, a tight fitting white dress of mini proportions clung to her slender figure while the brightly coloured blouse highlighted the olive skin with the cute freckle beneath the right eye. "Hello", she said, as though greeting an old friend. "I see you downstairs alone, you like to have food with me?" Without waiting for an answer she breezed into the room. She still bore the traces of a not unpleasant perfume that mingled with the odours emitting from the yet unseen food. "Why not", he said, as though this was an everyday occurrence. "I can't think of anything better to do at this time of night". She gave him a wide infectious smile. "Cheeky boy, maybe you think of something later". She eased herself around the room before settling on the floor, began undoing the little parcels of food, which looked quite appetising. He realised also it was some time since he had eaten.

Squatting down on the floor beside her, as the room boasted one chair, he studied the girl next to him. It was on thing the Thai race seemed to do so much better than others, that ability to make you feel at ease, to be treated as an honoured guest whether or not you were a salesman or a statesman. It was a characteristic they seemed to excel in, although it was fair to say from the many Americans he had met on his travels, they also had this trait. In fact on several occasions after only half an hour of meeting some American stranger in some far flung bar it was a case of "next time you're in Mobile Alabama or Sacramento California etc, drop by and see me", although he always had this feeling in the back of his mind, if he had 'dropped in', on seeing him on the doorstep they would be hard pushed to remember him.

"Kin Khaw". His companion said to him, using the Thai words meaning it was time to eat. He grabbed a succulent looking chicken leg with what seemed a sort of brown sauce on it and found it surprisingly tasty if a little hot and spicy. "Alloy maak", he said and meant it. She looked pleased at his compliment in Thai. "You speak Thai a little". "Yes", he replied, "but only very little". "What you do in Pattani, vacation?" "Something like that", he said absent mindedly as he watched in amazement at the amount of chillies she seemed able to consume without the slightest difficulty. She must have a throat made of asbestos. He stood up and went to the bathroom bringing two glasses of water back, she must surely need one. He knew he certainly did. "Not so many farang come to Pattani for vacation, they like to go to Pattaya and Phuket", she said with an air of someone who should know. "If they find out about you they will all want to come", he said, giving her a playful jab in the ribs. "You like to make joke about me", she said, not understanding. "No, I don't make a joke about you, you are very pretty". She looked pleased, sighed and stretched out her slender legs, she had eaten her fill. "You know", she said, "if you go a little bit to the south of Pattani there is small village and a beautiful beach, nobody go there much, but lovely and quiet". The thought was quite a pleasant one. "That sounds nice, if I get a chance I'll try and make a trip out there". He went and sat on the not too soft bed. "The floor is hard", he said by way of explanation. She said nothing but slowly got up and joined him on the bed. He put an arm around her shoulders; it seemed the most natural thing in the world to do. "Thanks for the food", he said simply. "Mae pen lie", she replied and rested her head against his chest.

After a few moments like this she brought her left hand up and slowly unbuttoned his shirt, then sensuously caressed him until her hand came up against the small Buddha he always wore around his neck. "Where you get this?" she said with a little surprise in her voice. "Quite long ago, I got it in Bangkok". He was not about to tell her it had been given him by another girl, Anya. "I am surprised", she said, because this Buddha is from the temple, this not the kind that farang people buy". He looked at the small object she held in her hand. "I did not know that". She sat up a little and brought her hand back down. Al thought back at the recollection of when Anya had given him the Buddha, they were happy days. But all thoughts of her soon disappeared as the woman next to him slowly began unbuckling his belt. Her name was Wanchai, it was a nice name and she was drop dead gorgeous. This was about living for the moment. They both stood up together and removed the remainder of their clothes. For a few seconds they drank in each other's bodies, then she giggled, "You are a big boy". He took two steps forward, lifted her up and carried her over to the bed. Her giggling turned to moans as he slowly lowered himself on top of her. The hot steamy night was matched only by their passion for each other.

It was quite some time before Al reluctantly swung his legs back on the floor to take a quick shower. When he returned she was sitting by the side of the bed combing her hair. He clasped both her hands in his and spoke softly. "I have to phone my friend in England soon, but stay a little longer and talk to me and before you go I must pay you for the food". She smiled warmly. "O.k., you lovely sexy man. I can talk to you some more". He squeezed her hands, she was naïve but very nice. "Tell me more about this beautiful beach that you know". It was forty minutes later when she kissed him sweetly on the cheeks and let herself out of the room. She was happy. He knew he had given her considerably more than the cost of the food. It was time to call Todd and let him know how events were progressing. The poor guy was probably on tender hooks.

After giving the Operator instructions to try and obtain the number, Al sat down and reflected on the last couple of hours, he wished perhaps it could have been Anya. The telephone rang. Through the crackle on the line he could hear the West Country accent of Todd. "I'm glad you called Al, I was beginning to wonder what you were getting up to out there". "That's a long story Todd", said Al, "but I've been keeping busy you could say". "Yes, I have not been sleeping over here either. I've managed to track down a source of what we need over here in North Wales". "But", he added, "It is going to cost quite a great deal of money". "Hold on there Todd, because you are a day late and a dollar short and I don't want you to commit yourself yet, as I may well have the answer over here". Todd groaned. "You mean I have done all that spadework over here for nothing". Al was quick to reassure him. "Not really, it may still come down to using your source if things don't work out over here". "When will you know for sure? You know the time limit is getting pretty short". There was a note of anxiety in his voice. "Well, I have been told that tomorrow is the day of decision". Al tried to sound positive but was not sure if his conviction carried over 8,000 miles of telephone cable. "Either way I will call you tomorrow and let you know how it works out". There was sadness in Todd's voice when he next spoke. "Just let's hope that it is positive. I had to do something very disdainful yesterday". Al's heart leapt, he was hoping that Todd had not done anything foolish that could jeopardise their mission. All sorts of possibilities raced through his mind. He spoke calmly. "Are you going to tell me about it". As though reading his thoughts, Todd said, "It's o.k. nothing for you to worry about, but I just saw the end result of all my years of hard work, I cleared out my desk and handed over the keys of the business to the bank". "I am really sorry to hear that, I know that nothing I can say will help, but perhaps if anything it will give you some motivation for our project", he replied. "I am really desperate for it to succeed, that money will be enough to get me back on my feet again. I'll be able to look the wife in the eye again". "I'm sure that she does not blame you entirely", Al cut in. "The trouble is she has no one else to blame and as you know her parents always took her side". "That's true". "And of course you are not in a position to say to her, "Look darling, hang on in there just a bit longer as I am going to come into a large sum of money". "Exactly". Todd paused and then laughed. "I can just see her face when I tell her that and then being unable to explain where the money is coming from, somehow I just can't see her believing me". "I guess you're right Todd. Look I'll call you tomorrow about the same time and give you the news". "I won't sleep a wink tonight, you know that you rat!" "You're not paid to sleep". Al laughed and put down the phone before Todd had a chance to reply.

During the conversation Al had been observing a small lizard on the wall opposite. It had been very successful in catching any mosquitoes that came its way; perhaps it was a good omen. He made one more call to the Barracks he had left earlier that day. They were not able to contact JB so he left them his phone number in order for JB to call him in the morning. As he slipped between the covers he heard in the distance the mournful wail of a police siren. It sent a shiver down his spine. Tomorrow would be the 27th July, time was getting short.

Chapter 15

All heads turned as Mo walked into the room and watched him as he drew up a chair and sat down at the table. Overhead the strong lights reflected off his baldhead. He reached up now and scratched it as was his habit before making a statement. "Gentlemen", he began, "I'm afraid to tell you that I was not successful in persuading the Minister to either cancel his trip to the Canary Islands or even to change the date of his visit there". He took a sip of water from the glass on the table in front of him before continuing. "Although this gives us a headache as far as his security is concerned I accept his reasons". "And they are what?" Harry Reynolds interjected. "They are," Mo looked at his questioner with a slight frown. "That with the visit only two weeks away it would be discourteous to our Spanish hosts who have already made arrangements". "Bearing in mind the object of this visit is not only goodwill but to get them possibly to purchase Israeli arms". "Well", and here Mo spread out his arms to emphasis the point, "it would be just like scoring an own goal, it would defeat our purpose". One of the men on the other side of the polished table spoke.

"How about sending a junior Minister in his place", he suggested. "No, to downgrade the visit would imply that we were not serious about selling the weapons". Mo stood up from the table and added. "It seems the die is cast, possibly Jenkins is still in Thailand or there again he may not be but if we are unable to run him down before the visit we have to prepare for any eventuality that may occur in the Canaries". He began walking towards the door. "Gentlemen, if you follow me in the room next door, I have had a scale model made of the area where the Minister is most at risk". Mo was secretly pleased at the way he had pre-empted any difficult questions at how Jenkins' trail had been lost, in particular from Reynolds.

They filed in behind him to gather around a raised table in the centre of the room on which had been built the model. "As we know", Mo began, "the visit of the Foreign Minister to the Canary Islands is primarily to improve relations between our two countries. Having said that it is also a good opportunity to promote our arms sales at the same time which is why the Minister accompanied by the Spanish Defence Secretary will be observing the demonstration being put on by our men". "Yes, yes we know all that", Reynolds said sourly. "Let's get to the point". "This is it",

Mo replied, picking up a thin wooden stick and pointing with it toward' s the model. "The only time the Minister is vulnerable is at the firearms display. I am positive that would be the ideal time for any assassin to strike, besides the only other meetings he has are behind closed doors". He paused as he watched them take in his statement. One of the group standing at the table spoke up. "I must admit it would seem logical bearing in mind that it would be obviously noisy and it would be a tremendous blow against our country in full view of foreigners". "Exactly", said Mo. He seemed pleased with himself. "And that is why I had this model made up. It is an exact replica of the area where the weapons display will take place. I think between us we should be able to pinpoint all areas from where a possible attack could be mounted". There was a general nodding of heads. "Therefore", he continued, "if we can identify those locations we should be able to take precautions in order to neutralise any threat". Harry Reynolds spoke up. "What about Spanish security. You don't think it will be adequate?" Mo smiled wanly. "I feel that they won't be over jealous. There has never been a terrorist incident in the Canaries to my knowledge and at this stage I think it would be more prudent not to inform them of any threat on the Minister's life". "Why on earth not?" There was a hint of indignation in Reynolds' voice. The man standing next to Mo replied. "I agree with that. If the Spanish are informed there will be added security which can only help us". Mo gave his companion a friendly pat on the shoulder. "You're right, however I would prefer to keep this under wraps because if Jenkins and his associates get wind of it they are going to be that extra bit cautious. At the moment we have the edge, surprise will be on our side and I want to keep it that way". "Perhaps you're right". The man next to him conceded. "So let's go over the ground". Mo pointed with his stick again at the model which lay before them. "As you can see the area of the range is this barren rock strewn valley, with on one side of it a few range buildings. Immediately in front of those buildings a raised dais will be built which will command a view over the whole valley. It is on this dais the Minister will be sitting along with other senior officers". Mo stopped his narrative to light up a small cigarillo, after taking a deep draw he blew out the smoke in the direction of the valley. "Of course", he said, "what will be obvious to all of you is that just as he is able to view the whole area, anyone in the valley can likewise see him". They murmured in accord. "However", Mo continued, "there are several options open to a would be assassin so I think if we start going through all the possibilities we can begin working out the counter measures we may need". Harry Reynolds spoke first. "O.k., let's discuss security at the entry point to the firing range first".

Meanwhile in another part of the Mission building Viola Gedler contemplated the paperwork on her desk, only her mind was not on the task in front of her, it was miles away agonising over her decision to inform the Security Service about Al Jenkins' interest in the Defence Minister. Of course it was too late now to go back and she was sure she had made the right decision in safeguarding Greg and the children but why did she feel so guilty. Of course she knew the reason, really there was no point pretending. It was though she had stabbed Al in the back. He was out there somewhere unaware that there could be people lining up to get a shot at him. Of one thing she was sure, his life would definitely be in danger. She had to do something but what? She had to warn him but how. He had left her no phone number or address. She did not want to hear he had been killed. They had shared so many good memories together. She thought fondly back to one occasion when after an evening together at a Singapore nightclub they had emerged drenched in sweat after dancing together nearly all night and that was despite the club being air-conditioned. "Let's go for a drive to cool down" Al had suggested. They had driven out of the hustle and bustle of Singapore across the causeway into a neighbouring deserted beach. It was a beautiful clear still night in complete contrast to the noisy crowded dance floor they had just left. They had sat together looking across at the lights of Singapore with just the faint noise of the sea lapping the beach. She could even now recall his words to her as he had turned and spoke, slipping his arm protectively about her shoulders. "See how the moon shines down upon the sea, it is making a path of silver light that leads directly to us". She remembered replying. "Why don't we go down to it, see if we can step on it". It had all seemed so natural. They walked hand in hand down to the waters edge, discarded all their clothes and dived into the sea together. It had been wonderful, she had felt so free. With the water dripping off them they had returned to the beach and lay down on the sand. It was still warm from the day's sun. Her body ached with desire and they were drawn into each other with no thought for the consequences. It had been the first time they had made love together.

"Vi, are you alright?" She heard the concern in the voice of Ruth, one of the women who worked in the office with her.

They were good friends and sent their sons to the same school. Vi quickly dabbed at the tear that had begun to roll down her cheek. "It's o.k. but I think I may have something in my eye". If Ruth thought otherwise she did not say so. "Why don't you go and get it seen to". "You're right, maybe I will do". Vi grabbed the paperwork on her desk and thrust it into one of the drawers. She knew she must get out of this place to think, she had to do something. "Inform the Boss for me will you Ruth, thanks".

She left the building and walked out to her car but did not drive off immediately. Instead she leant forward with her head in her hands against the steering wheel going over in her mind everything that Al had spoken about during his brief visit to Geneva. It was no good, there was nothing she could think of that would enable her to contact him. She drove off. Getting home early would give her more time to herself which is what she needed right now. Her neighbour always picked up the children from school so she would let the arrangement continue today. Her driving was erratic, two other motorists hooted their horns at her but she found it hard to concentrate. It was with some relief when she finally pulled into the parking lot beneath her apartment.

She had just applied the hand brake when it came to her. She hit the steering wheel with some force, feeling stupid at the realisation. The knowledge had been there all the time. Of course it was right that he had said nothing to give himself away on his visit, but when he had called her the first time from England one of the first things she had asked him was what job was he doing at the time. He had said he was working in the oilfield and not only that but had mentioned the name of the company. What was it now? An easy name to remember. World, no, Wide World Drilling, that was it. She hurriedly parked the car and went upstairs feeling sure that his company must have an office in London. After a few enquiries the telephone operator was able to supply the information she wanted. It was an address and phone number in the West End of London. With some trepidation she lifted the receiver and put the call through. A girl with a cockney accent replied. She asked to be put through to personnel. "Yes, how can I help you"? The well-spoken voice came clearly over to her. "A friend of mind works for your company but unfortunately I have misplaced his address. I wondered if you would be kind enough to give me the details". "I am sorry but it is our Company's policy not to give out information about our

Employees over the phone". The blood froze in her veins as she saw her last hopes being dashed. There was no other way she could possibly contact Al. She asked the girl if she could possibly make an exception but the answer was no. She put the phone down with a heavy heart.

The children arrived home soon after. They questioned her why she had come home early that day. When she replied that it was due to her being unwell and that she was trying to find an old friend's address that had been lost they said something that really made her think. "Why don't you just go to visit your friend if you can remember where the house was. I'm sure that Dad won't mind". There was something in what they said which made sense. Why didn't she just take a couple of days off and fly over to England. She thought hard and long until satisfied there was a way in which she could wheedle the address out of Al's company. She could present herself as Al's sister Jessica whom she knew lived over in the United States and very seldom came over to visit her brother in England. It was very possible they had never set eyes on her before.

When Greg arrived home she told him that taking a couple of days off on a visit to

England would do her a power of good if he didn't object too much. To her surprise he was all in favour of it. "After the way you stood by me and I know it was not an easy decision to take, you've earned the right to take a break. Go on; enjoy yourself for a few days. I can look after the kids here". She made arrangements to fly out the next day and booked herself a hotel in London that was in the middle price range. Despite being the end of July when she flew the next day it was overcast with the threat of rain but she did not allow this to dampen her spirits, at leas she was doing something positive and there was this feeling of being closer to the man she had once loved so much. "Where to love?" The cheeky looking man at the taxi rank hailed her. "The Palace Hotel in Bayswater Road. If you could drop me there please". Another reason she had chosen that particular hotel was because it was only a short distance from the office of Al's company. While not being opulent she like the clean and comfortable room and quickly hung up her clothes. After spending five minutes in front of the mirror practising a slight American accent she felt prepared to venture forth. Even so it was still with some apprehension as she approached the company office, adjusting the camera over her shoulder to try and fit in with the image of a visiting relative.

The receptionist was a model of efficiency, leading her to a seat and asking if she would care for a coffee, while relaying Vi's request to see someone from the personnel department. It was five minutes later that a middle-aged rather pompous looking woman put her head round the door to announce. "I'm afraid that if you are looking for a job there are none at present". Hiding her dislike for the woman, Vi replied in a friendly tone. "That's not what I am here for. I'm the sister of one of your employees and I wish to see someone about his current address if you don't mind". The woman drummed her fingers on the doorjamb obviously unprepared for that reply. "I think in that case you had better see our personnel director Mr Atherton. Could you give me your name please"? "The name is Jessica Jenkins".

It wasn't long before the intercom bleeped on the receptionist's desk. She answered and then spoke to Vi. "Mr Atherton will see you now, if you follow me I will show you where his office is". Vi followed her along a narrow corridor just a short distance before coming to a plywood door with the brass nameplate J Atherton. The receptionist left. Vi knocked and walked into a large bright and airy room in the centre of which stood a large desktop computer. Sitting behind the desk in a swivel chair was a bearded man wearing gold-framed glasses. In contrast to the woman she had first seen from personnel, he wore a welcoming smile. "Take a seat Miss Jenkins and let's see if I can help you".

Vi sat down demurely in the seat indicated, crossing her long shapely legs in front of her. "Yes, well I came over from the States a couple of days ago, one reason being to visit my brother. However, he was not at the address he had given me so I thought perhaps he may have moved as it is several years since I have seen him". Atherton adjusted his glasses. "You say that your brother is an employee of our company?" Vi nodded. "Yes that's right, the name is Al Jenkins". The man gave her an engaging smile, picked up a disc and inserted it in the computer. "Well that won't take a minute", he said tapping the code into the keyboard. He stared at the screen and then turned round to her. "That's strange", he said, "but your brother's name has not come up on the screen. Can you think of any reason why?" Vi thought furiously. She was sure that Al had told her Wide World was the name of the company but wait a minute, what was it he said, he had been working for them, so maybe he had already left. Atherton was still looking at her, waiting for an answer. "You know", she began, "I am positive that this is the company he used to work for, but maybe that is it, perhaps he has already left. Does that mean you don't have his record any longer?" "Hell no, we keep records of our past employees for several years, only of course that is kept on a separate file". She watched with interest as he removed one disk from the computer and inserted another. It did not take long but it seemed a lifetime to her before he pointed at the screen and said. "Ah, yes it seems your brother was made redundant a couple of years ago but I would not be surprised if he would be required again in the near future". He pushed a notepad and pen across the desk to her. "I'll read out the address and phone number if you want to get them down". She quickly jotted it down and tore off the page, standing up she leaned across the desk to shake hands with him. "Mr Atherton, I am very grateful to you, after coming all this way and not meeting my brother would have been a tragedy". He seemed surprised at the warmth of her thanks. "I'm very pleased I could help and I hope that you have a pleasant stay over here".

She walked quickly down the street away from the office with a spring in her step. Passers by may have wondered why she was smiling; she cared not but only knew that now at last she had the means to contact Al once more. She never felt happy after saying goodbye to him at the hotel in Geneva and even more desperately sad after having to give his name to Mosard. At least now she was in a position to warn him. It was with trembling fingers that she dialled his number back in the hotel room. It rang for a long time but there was no reply. She felt disappointed but not dejected, resolving to hire a car in the morning to drive to his address if there continued to be no reply on his phone. There wasn't but the hotel was very helpful and fixed her up with a car the next day.

Leaving early she caught the rush hour traffic, which delayed her, however it was just after ten by the time she arrived at the little village in Surrey. She soon found someone with knowledge of the road that was on the address she had been given. Driving close but not down it she pulled up by the side of the road and waited. This time she was determined that she would not compromise herself or her family and had kept a careful watch on her rear view mirror as she drove down from London. Although not noticing any vehicle following her, it was still better in her mind not to drive up to Al's door. A young boy of about ten with a fat dog in tow was walking up the street towards her. She called him across. As he approached she drew out of her pocket an envelope which contained a note that had been written before she had begun her journey. "How would you like to earn yourself a couple of pounds"? The young boy looked at her suspiciously. "Doing what exactly?" he asked, pulling his dog close to him. His mother had warned him about talking to strangers especially those who wore dark glasses such as this lady did, but he thought she sounded nice and of course there was the promise of money. Vi could see the troubled expression on the boy's face and realised it was a sign of the times they lived in. "Don't worry", she said, shoving him the envelope in her hand. "All I want you to do is deliver this letter to a house in the next road and two pounds is yours". He took it eagerly and studied the address. "Yes, o.k" he said. "I know this place, it's very close". She handed over the two pounds and watched him disappear up the road. She sat in the car for another half hour but there was no sign of Al. He either was not at home or the boy had failed to deliver the note. She reluctantly started the car and began the tedious drive back up to London.

She had already decided to stay two more days in the hope that Al would return and see her not, if not there was still the chance he may see it in time before someone got to him. But after the two days she knew that she must go home and back to her family. Her life was now with Greg and although at times he was a rather boring man he was always there when she needed him, whereas with Al if she had married him, it would be quite reasonable to assume their relationship would have been stormy, although no doubt also great fun making up after. At the time as well, her parents were very much against her seeing him, in fact she was sure that was one of the reasons why they had retuned to Israel sooner than had been planned. She and Al had met for the last time before her return at an English style pub and restaurant in the centre of Singapore on a hot and humid night, a night which would forever be in her memory, it was burned into her brain. The evening had begun well enough. They both sat at the bar sipping drinks, talking and laughing, promising each other to keep in touch. They were both a little drunk by the time they sat down to eat. It did not stop Al ordering a bottle of Chablis to go with the meal and it was empty by the time they finished. They sat and held hands across the table; it was a nice setting, lots of dark wood and polished horse brasses. There were just three other couples left sharing the room with them. "Al darling, it's nearly twelve, I have to go home. You know how strict my parents are", she had spoken softly to him. "Never mind your folks, you're eighteen years old, why don't you come back and stay the night with me?" She was surprised at this tone. Usually he was very understanding and they seldom had a row, maybe the drink had influenced him. She had replied. "Sweetheart, there is nothing in the world I would rather do, but you know what kind of reaction I would get when I got home, they are never going to let me forget it and I just don't want to live in that kind of atmosphere". He had been abrupt to her in his reply. "Alright, run on home to your mum and dad if it's more important to you". So saying he had removed his hand from hers. The tears had begun to roll down her cheeks. "You know that is just not true, it's so unfair". He had not replied to her but avoided her eyes and stared at the tablecloth. She had grabbed her purse and rushed out of the restaurant oblivious to the stares of the other diners. She had felt so wretched, so sad to leave him that way and had cried all the way home. They did not see each other again until the time in Geneva where they had been more like strangers to each other. Neither of them had mentioned their last night together in Singapore but they both knew it was in their thoughts. It was probably why he hadn't invited her back to his hotel that night for fear of spoiling the evening.

Looking back now as a married mother of two, she could see more clearly. No clouds of emotion blurred her vision as they had then, which made her feel at the time as though her world had ended. She had no doubt that they had both deeply loved each other but of course there was no turning the clock back. She just wished she could see him one more time before having to go home. She felt relieved at last turning into the road where her hotel was situated, the though of a cool shower after the hot and sticky drive was an impetus for her to quickly park the car and walk into the hotel lobby. "Key to room 315 please", she asked a rather harassed looking receptionist. "Ah Mrs Gelder, here you are, there is also a telegram for you". She thanked the woman, walked over and sank in one of the nearby seats. Her heart was thumping. She looked at the missive in her hand. It was a scrap of paper, so why was it she had the premonition it was bad news. She turned it over in her hands, slit it open and lay it upon her lap. She was right. It was bad news. It was a message from Greg. In it he said the children were ill and he wanted her to return home immediately. After all her expectations it seemed as though she never would meet Al again. She savagely crumpled the note in her hand and thrust it into her purse before beginning the lonely walk towards the elevator. It was time to pack her clothes.

Chapter 16

Al woke with a start. The sweat was pouring down his face and yet he could not seem to remember having a particularly bad dream. He threw back the bedclothes and got up. His mind was still foggy with sleep and a glance at his watch showed it coming up to six in the morning. Of course, the drone of the air conditioner had stopped. He fiddled with the controls but it seemed terminal. It didn't matter really; he could do with being up early. After a struggle he managed to open the long shut windows to let in the smells and odours of a tropical morning. It was time for a cool shower, cold was too much to hope for.

After an early breakfast of fruit and coffee he felt like a drive. It was far too early for JB to call him and he felt intrigued by the description of the beach given him by the girl last night. The cool breeze refreshed him and he made his way through the town and then picked up the coast road south. The sprawl of one and two storey houses in the outskirts gave way to clusters of palms and corrugated tin roofed wooden buildings surrounded by fields of rice and pineapple plantations interspersed with clusters of trees bearing bananas, mangoes and to a lesser extent rambutan. The road weaved and turned and then ran almost parallel with the shoreline, a sandy shoreline graced by the tall trunks and waving fronds of coconut trees. He passed through one or two villages either of which could have matched the description he had been given, so when he arrived at the next he resolved to stop. He turned off the road and pulled up just a few yards from the high water mark under the shade of two tall coconut trees. Taking his shoes off he walked across the white sand to the water's edge. The light blue sea was lapping with just a ripple. Offshore two fishing boats had raised their sails trying to catch the very light breeze. The early morning sun shimmered on the sea. He sat there with his feet in the water. The only sound to intrude on his thoughts was the gentle sighing as the sea tried to draw the sand back with it. A complete feeling of peace came over him. He wished it could be like this forever but he knew it could not be. Even now, his thoughts were dwelling on the task in front of him, an unpleasant task but one he must carry through if there were to be any future for Todd as well as himself. The mood was broken. The enormity of what he had planned almost made him want to abandon it but there was no turning back, of that he knew.

Walking towards him came a young boy of about twelve, carrying a basket that he could see contained various types of shellfish. He didn't have to speak the language that well to know that he wanted to sell whatever he could. Al looked over his wares before deciding on a large portion of mussels, not that he was very hungry, but they did look succulent and fresh and so very cheap. With the few words of Thai that he knew and the little English the boy could speak, they managed a sort of halting conversation. The boy mentioned it was unusual to see many 'farangs' down on his patch and he liked to practice the few words of English he knew. Whereas Al may have suspected his motives for being so friendly as a prelude to buying more of his stock, he seemed a good boy and sitting there on the beach in the sun took Al's mind off the pressing problems that lay ahead. He proudly told Al his mother spoke very good English as she used to have a good job in Bangkok, but now times were hard as bandits had killed his policeman father many years ago. Al was not sure that he believed him but he bought a little more of his stock, which made him very happy. He wore just a white t-shirt and dark shorts, which had seen better days, but they were clean. Al tried to explain to him that much as he enjoyed his company he must return to his hotel. The boy then said something that made the hairs stand up on the back of his neck. He pointed to a house not far away and said Al would be welcome to visit him and his mum if he ever came back this way, his mother's name was Anya.

Al thought about it as he drove back to the hotel. Surely it could not possibly be the girl he met and loved over a decade ago, although he had to admit she did say it was from a fishing village in this area that she originated, added to the fact her son had said she previously worked in Bangkok and spoke English. So why, even just to satisfy his curiosity had he not gone there and then to visit? Even as the thought arose he knew why. If by any chance it was her, meeting again after all these years would have thrown his mind in turmoil. He had to concentrate completely on the job in hand; he could not afford himself the luxury of dwelling on what might have been. It was sad but true and even if it were his Anya, no sooner before the echoes of greeting had died away than he would have to say his farewell and that would not be fair to her either. If there were to be a future after August 11th and he still had money in his pocket then he would return and if it were not she from whom he was driving away from, then so be it.

Arriving back at the hotel he made his way to the bar and ordered a beer. The shellfish had given him a thirst. Also he felt the need for a little sustenance before the anticipated call. He had sunk another beer and was about to make his way to the phone booth when he was paged to go to the lobby. Draining the glass he hurried across intrigued by the summons. There, standing in grey trousers and white shirt and wearing a bemused expression on his tanned face was J.B. He laughed at the surprise on Al's face. "Caught you in the bar again, tut, tut", he said wagging his finger. "I'm surprised at seeing you out of uniform and what are you doing here?" said Al. He gave a mock groan. "What kind of welcome is that after coming all the way down here to see you. In fact, I reckon you owe me a beer or maybe two after you hear what I have to say". "Come on", said Al, leading the way back to the bar. "I'll get you something to settle the dust and by the way it is great to see you".

It was small talk at first. He explained he had been granted leave for a few days, which meant he could see Al first before heading on up to Bangkok. Al told him that would suit him fine as they could travel up together before he headed off back to England. JB drew out of his pocket the piece of paper Al had given him at their last meeting on which he had written he basic route by which the Claymore mines should travel and laid it on the table in front of him. Al had chosen a discreetly lit corner of the hotel bar and kept an eye on the door in the corner. After Simon's startling revelations it would pay to be extra cautious. "Just what are you expecting to gain with your little plan Al"? he asked, knowing that Al was desperate to discover what he had arranged. "The lust for gold, well, paper money at least is my sole objective. I know you would expect me to say this and it is partly true, but I have another reason as well". "Which you are not going to tell me", said JB, with a questioning look. "I will tell you one day and I think you will understand but right now maybe it is better that you don't know". Al pointed at the paper in front of him. "How about telling me how you got on with the route. You know I am sitting on tender hooks". "Are you?" said JB, with a look of mock astonishment. "I had no idea it was so important". Al scowled at him at which he replied with a loud laugh and then continued in a more serious note. "Really, I was quite impressed with your route and as it turned out it was a lot easier to implement than I first thought. So, even as we sit here they are at present shipping the two Claymores up to Bangkok for you". Al waved at him to continue. If he had any questions he would put them to him at the end. JB went on to explain that they would be kept in Bangkok until flown out on a military transport to a U.S airbase just outside Madrid, there they would be transferred and loaded on a plane flying to the joint civil military airport at Las Palmas in the Canary Islands. The package would be addressed to a Captain Ramon Gonzales of the Spanish Civil Guard. Al had asked previously for JB to use the name. Todd was drawing up the false papers with which to gain access to the base at Las Palmas, which was not in any event very secure. Although the package was small, it would be heavy. JB had as he suggested put the customs declaration down as military training manuals. "Don't worry about this end", said JB, "as they will be dispatched without any problem, but when they arrive at Madrid I'm not so sure". "Don't fret about this", said Al, with more conviction than he actually felt. "You have done your part, but remember they are coming in on a military aircraft at a military airbase addressed to a member of the Spanish forces, that's why I feel it is highly unlikely to be spotted. They won't be inspected at Las Palmas as they will see the point of origin as Madrid, but will be left for this Captain Gonzales to collect". JB still looked a bit doubtful. "But you don't speak any Spanish do you?" he asked. "I don't have to, I've already thought of that. The papers along with a money enticement will be given to a local taxi driver to go in and collect it. That reduces the risk to me quite considerably". "Yeah" the American drawled with his east coast accent. "You seemed to have covered all the angles". "I hope so but tell me one thing, how did you manage to 'liberate' the two Claymores without any suspicions being raised?" A broad smile spread over JB's face. "That was the easy bit. I simply wrote off an extra two as being used on our operation against the commies". Al smiled with him knowing from past experience how easy it was to write off equipment after any kind of engagement.

Al toyed with the now empty glass on the table before putting the next question to JB. "Of course you have left out the most important piece of information that you know I need". JB looked puzzled at first before realising what Al was referring to. "I was just coming to that. Yes, the flight coming in to Las Palmas arrives at 10.30 in the evening of the 9th of August. I know that you asked for an earlier date but it was the best I was able to fix up". Al whistled through his teeth. The 9th.... and the Minister was arriving on the 11th. This gave him very little time to organise his reception from Todd and him. "That's o.k. JB you have done much more than I expected. I'll never forget it". "Hell, I owe you a favour", said JB, "only just make sure there is no comeback as I want to make sure I do forget it". "Point taken", said Al as he signalled the waiter to come over. JB held up his hands. "I have an early flight this afternoon up to the big city, so why don't you come along, maybe there is a spare seat". "You're right", said Al, standing up. "I think I've had enough to drink anyway".

Al was lucky there were several spare seats on the internal flight up to Bangkok. They arrived by late afternoon, which just provided him with enough time to book a flight out the next day to England. They parted company at the airport. JB was now married, with a government house on the outskirts of Bangkok. He asked Al to stay at his home for the night but this was not the time to intrude. However, Al took up the invitation to come over for dinner. This time he used a different hotel to the one he had used on the last visit. Although Simon had not mentioned anyone working with him there was always the possibility of the previous hotel being staked out, as he was pretty sure they were no aware that he knew he had been under surveillance. A hot and sticky afternoon progressed into a humid evening. Al tried to call Todd to inform him of their good fortune but there was no reply at his home. He dressed for the evening and called at the hotel bar downstairs where he was lucky enough to buy a bottle of reasonable champagne if at an extortionate price. He nursed his purchase carefully in the bumpy taxi ride out to JB's house.

It turned out to be a two-storey house with balconies outside the windows set in immaculate grounds. His whole family, his wife and two teenage daughters whom of course Al had never seen before, met him at the door. JB greeted him warmly. Al was struck by the way the girls and their mother looked at him. What had he been saying to them? Al broke the ice by saying, "Whatever John has been telling you about me count at the most as fifty per cent true and you might be getting nearer the truth". The girls giggled while his wife gave an infectious laugh saying she didn't believe her husband half the time anyway. A striking tall woman with curly blond hair and green eyes that sparkled whenever she smiled, which was a lot. Standing next to her daughters she could have been mistaken for a sister.

An appetising smell came from the kitchen making Al realise it was some time since he had enjoyed the benefits of home cooking. Before long they were all sitting at a large dining table. Al dutifully cracked open the bottle of champagne and poured it slowly into their glasses. The small talk died as JB stood up glass in hand. "Folks, I would like to propose a toast before we sit down to the great food that has been prepared by my ever inventive wife Kathy as I may not have been here if it had not been for the courage of one of us who is sitting amongst us today. He would tell you it was all down to luck as he tried to tell me but I know better than that. It was the thought of being invited here that finally convinced him to visit after a lapse of 17 years". They laughed at that. "So, to you Al and don't leave it so long next time". They all took a gulp of their drink and looked over expectantly at Al. He realised they wanted him to make some sort of reply. He wasn't prepared for this, nevertheless he rose slowly to his feet thoughts pounding, what could he say. "Thanks John. You have overstated the case of course but there is some truth in the saying being in the right place at the right time and I felt Lady Luck was a bit kind to me. I like to feel that my reward is in being able to help a friend, not just any friend but a special friend because there is no friendship on earth as deep as those forged in a baptism of fire. To men who have lived, worked and fought together there is a special affinity. I know it's hard for the man in the street to comprehend this. So, to you JB I raise my glass and may you always keep your powder dry". They all clinked their glasses together and Al felt warm towards this generous family, warmth that was not induced by any amount of alcohol. They unfolded their table napkins and surveyed the food spread upon the table. Kathy had indeed done well. There were fried king prawns and they really were king size, nestling on a fresh bed of lettuce leaves. Tureens of steaming hot vegetables to compliment the main dish surrounded these. Kathy's piece de resistance was a large grilled salmon. "Where did you get the salmon Kathy? You have certainly excelled yourself", said Al. At the other side of the table JB nodded in approval. She looked pleased at their appreciation. "It's no more than you boys deserve after your little adventure. You can help with the washing up later if you like". She suddenly jumped and rushed to the kitchen saying, "I've forgotten to bring the salad bowl through". JB laughed contentedly. "Don't worry Al she is only pulling your leg. The girls will do that little chore". He ignored them as his two daughters pulled faces at him and continued. "After the meal I have a nice surprise for us to partake in. I keep it for special occasions such as this. A bottle of bourbon, a vintage one, Jim Beams black label". They ate, drank and talked through an evening that was one of the most enjoyable Al had ever spent. Time sped by so fast; it was after midnight when he told them he must take his leave. He shook hands with them all there on the doorstep as they promised to each other that they must meet again and not before too long.

All too soon Al was back in the taxi travelling along the still busy roads towards the hotel. His thoughts dwelt on the happy hours he had just spent with the Brooks family. Why was it then throughout the evening there was something in the back of his mind, almost what can be described akin to a nagging toothache or a migraine that would not go away? The operative word of course was family. Since his wife and children had died that fateful day there had been something missing from his life. He still did not want to accept it and yet it was always there. Tonight brought it back so much more forcibly knowing that he was unable to entertain JB and his family in the same way should they ever come to England. It was on occasions such as this, seeing children so obviously happy within the security of their family that all the pain of that day returned. It was probably another reason why he had accepted the task that lay in front of him, for if he were to die what would it really matter, there would be no one to mourn him. But there was no point now in being negative. However, for whatever the future may bring there was still a life to be lived and nights like tonight he would cherish. He managed to reach Todd on his arrival back at the hotel. He sounded pleased with the news as Al expected, although not quite what he expected. He didn't think it was an insurmountable problem. Obviously they could not say too much on the phone, however they would have more time to talk tomorrow when Al returned home.

Al looked out of the small window of the Thai International 747 the next morning. The land below him gradually faded into the distance as the jet headed out over the Indian Ocean and he mentally waved goodbye. He hoped one day to return and if he did he would return again to the sleepy fishing village with the graceful coconut trees where he might possibly find a lost love but first there was a lot to do.

His arrival at Heathrow was greeted by a somewhat unusual hot British Summer's day, which he was grateful for as it made the transition easier after the heat of the Far East. Knowing what he did, he requested the taxi to stop some way from the apartment and used the back entrance. After the long journey he was glad to be able to put his feet up but first made a good cup of tea and settled down to read the accumulated mail. It was amazing how it piled up after just an absence of a few days. There was the usual sprinkling of unpopular bills and a large amount of junk mail, which always made his hackles rise up. It wasn't apparent from the envelopes what they contained. So it necessitated having to open them all before with a well-practised throw he dispatched them into the bin. He pulled one out of the pile, which seemed like another as it bore the legend of some London hotel. He had probably stayed there at some time and it was most likely an invite to make a return visit. He remembered staying at a Middle East hotel about 4 years ago and they still sent a card promptly each year on his birthday. But the strange thing about this letter was that it smelt slightly of perfume, an original idea he thought, to entice people. It was worth opening to see what they had to say.

It was incredulous, there staring at him on a sheet of hotel notepaper was a letter from Viola. His first thought was how on earth had she obtained his address, as he certainly had not given it to her. He read through the letter quickly and then slowly read it once more with the apprehension rising with each sentence until he finally laid it down on the table with a feeling of dread. Not only were Mossad aware of his existence as he already knew but now it transpired they also were aware of the assassination plot and date. He would have to tell Todd there was no point for him to risk his life unnecessarily as well as his own. In the letter Vi said she would be staying an extra day or so at the hotel and she would love it if he were to get a chance to meet up with her again. But first he rang Todd and arranged a meeting that afternoon. They would have to come to a decision whether or not to go ahead with their plan. He then rang the hotel where Vi was staying. To his surprise they were able to put him through. "Vi, it's Al. How on earth did you manage to find my address? It was wonderful to hear from you even if the news is bad. Anyway, why are you not out enjoying the sights of London?" The delight in her voice came over clear. "The only sign I want to see is your ugly face. Where have you been? I have to fly back out to Switzerland this afternoon". "Stay a day longer" suggested Al. Her voice was now tinged with sadness. "I would dearly love to but I've just received a message saying the kids are ill so I really should go home".

He knew in his heart he must try and see her, not just because of their past love but he had to find out what else she had given away. He also deserved an explanation as to why she had betrayed him. But that had to be tempered by the fact she had gone to some lengths to tell him that she was compromised. It did not seem to make sense. She mistook his silence as meaning that he did not wish to see her. "I can explain everything if I just sit down and talk to you for a while. I've still got a few hours before my plane leaves. Come on Al, make the effort", she pleaded. Despite his eagerness to see her he played it down. "Well, I did have another appointment, but I guess I can always delay it a little". "Please Al do that, more than anything I would like to see you before I go home". "I'll be there in a little over an hour, so while you are waiting why not order up some tea and sandwiches for us both". He did not replace the phone but dialled Todd's directly. He had to catch him before he left the house. He was in luck. He was just on the point of leaving. Al re-scheduled their meeting for later in the day.

It was with a mixture of anticipation and trepidation when Al walked into the lobby of the hotel Vi was staying in. Leaving the flat by the back entrance he had travelled up by train, observing all the time as to whether he was being followed. He was pretty certain that he wasn't but of course he could never be too sure. His desire to see Vi once more to find out just what she had divulged he felt outweighed the risk he took in going to see her. The voice was little higher than a whisper. "Al, follow me". Vi rose gracefully from a well-cushioned seat to the left of him and walked towards the lifts. He tucked in behind her, admiring the rear view. Despite bearing two children she seemed to have lost none of her shape. The long slim legs to the firm buttocks and a waist a twenty year old would have been proud of. He did not speak until the lift doors were firmly shut. "Still playing on the tennis courts". She turned towards him now wearing a half smile and threw her arms about his neck. "Just don't talk", she said, her voice a little husky. "I wanted to do this to you when I saw you walk in through the doors, but at least here there is nobody to see us". It was good to feel the warmth of her body against his. There was no point denying it, he still felt a strong desire for her even knowing it was a forbidden love. They clung together like that without speaking until the lift bell announced their arrival at the floor she was staying on. He followed her through to a comfortable room. Her suitcase lay half packed on the double bed, giving him a twinge of sadness knowing that it would not be long before they would have to say goodbye.

She kicked off her shoes and walked over to a small mini bar. "Join me in a glass of wine". "Of course", said Al. "You know I would never refuse an offer like that". She brought a brimful glass over which she gave to him without spilling a drop, moved the suitcase off the bed and sat down next to him. They raised their glasses together and drunk long and deep. "What can I say", she began. "I hate myself for what I had to do, but I was put in such a position that it was tearing me apart". "I'm a good listener", he said, and squeezed her hand. Her eyes were moist and it was easy to see that this girl, his girl from the past was going to tell him the truth. She explained how her husband had come home that night. The scene that followed and the reasons for it. Not knowing why he had requested the information in the first place it had seemed the wisest course to inform Mossad rather than jeopardise her whole family. From the way she described the situation, it was easy to see why she had chosen the course she had and he didn't blame her. In fact he felt angry with himself for putting her in the predicament in the first place. He really had no right to play on her emotions when it had been so long since they had been together. It was time to put that right. "Vi, I don't blame you in the slightest, if anything I should not have asked you". He put his arms around her to convey his sincerity. Her lips trembled and she leaned her head against his chest. She spoke almost in his ear. "But I feel that I have put you in grave danger. The man I spoke to had an air of menace that I have never seen before in a man. You must be very careful". She did not ask what he had planned and he respected her for that. Without a word being spoken they both knew it was best the subject was dropped. She spoke as though she was not sure of her ground, twisting a lock of hair round and round her finger.

"Remember our last night in Singapore together? I certainly do". "Yes", he said. "But I would rather not. If I remember correctly you stormed out when I asked you to spend the night with me. Still I guess I was pretty drunk at the time and young of course", he said as an after thought. "We were both so young", she said, staring dreamily into space. "Otherwise it may have turned out quite differently". "You're right", he said, giving her a kiss on the cheek. "I'm sorry I behaved like a fool but I'm glad I have this chance to tell you so.

I have often thought about it over the years. I even wondered whether or not we might have eventually married". She gave a delightful laugh, got up to refill their glasses and then joined him on the bed again. "Yes, I thought of it as well but I do know my parents would have been dead against it which would have made life hard. We shall never know but let us just keep the memories happy ones". Al drained his glass and put it down before replying. "You're so right, remember the night we spent on the beach in Johore". She came the closest thing to blushing since they met and slowly unbuttoned his shirt. "No", she said with a mischievous twinkle in her eye. "Are you able to demonstrate it in the little time that we have left?" He grabbed and pushed her back on the soft bed, putting his face right up close to hers. "Why, do you think I am past it?" She squirmed underneath him, trying but not very hard to escape. "All right", she said, gripping him in a tender spot. "Let me stand up and I will undress, you will see what you have been missing all these years". He watched her slowly peel off her clothes until she stood just in her knickers. "Come on, get undressed yourself and stop staring you idiot", she said, throwing a sock in his direction. They snuggled up close together in the bed, at first just exploring each other's body. She was very moist down below and her hands were manipulating him in a way she hadn't previously known when they first met. They moulded together as nature had intended with a fierce passion, both of them knowing that it was probably the last time they would ever see each other. The bed, not made of the stoutest construction squeaked in protest. They lay back after, ensconced together, each with their own private thoughts. It was Vi who first broke the trance. "Do you know that it is the first time I have been unfaithful to my husband since we married". "I'm sorry", said Al. "But try to not feel guilty about it". "That's the strange thing about it, I don't. After all you were my first love. I met you before my husband and my heart tells me that we won't meet again". "Besides", she said, climbing out of bed, "in a way it makes up for our disappointing farewell in Singapore". She glanced at her watch. "Al darling, I must hurry if I'm to catch that flight". He dressed quickly and helped her pack the few belongings that were scattered about the room. She stood by the door, suitcase at her feet. They embraced then looked each other in the eyes, neither wanting to be the first to say goodbye. Then she broke into a burst of laughter. "I'm glad to leave you with a smile on your face and not a tear, so share the joke with me", said Al. She laughed even more at that and then told him, "Your face was so serious and then I thought about our time in bed and the way the bed was rattling. I'm sorry but it just seemed so funny". He grinned back at her. They said their farewells once more and then he left first, not wanting to compromise her.

On the journey back home on the train Al stared out of the window at the countryside flashing past. He looked but saw nothing. His thoughts were all on the clandestine meeting he had just held, it was as if it had all been a dream but it wasn't. It was true he had been together with that wonderful woman. She had been so vibrant, it had evoked all the memories of those years past. But it was in the past; he had to accept that from now on. His future lay in a different direction. Hopefully he would find happiness with another woman because he knew that Vi although confessing she still loved him, her loyalties lay elsewhere and he would not try and change them. His mind had to be concentrated solely on the immediate future if there was to be one. He would find out pretty soon as it was nearly time to meet Todd.

After a change of clothes and a light snack he was ready to venture forth to meet up with his old pal. A meeting he did not relish as he could imagine his chagrin on discovering their whole plan had been blown. It seemed light years away since they had last met at the Riverside pub, when they had both been so full of enthusiasm for what seemed a meal ticket for life, but now he knew only too well if they proceeded they would be lucky to escape with their lives. As it was by now early evening he had chosen as their rendezvous a small out of the way Spanish restaurant renowned (to him anyway) for their superb chicken dishes although of course the food was a minor consideration but at least it may put Todd in a good frame of mind before he gave him the unwelcome news.

A reached the restaurant before him and ordered a good bottle of red wine he did not care for. However he remembered Todd having a weakness for it. The wall lights reflected dully off the brass ornaments, old flintlocks and other memorabilia from Spain while picture lights shone on paintings by obscure artists. Two elderly women sat in one corner picking over their meal, otherwise the place was empty. He did not have long to wait before a tired looking Todd squeezed himself into the chair opposite him. "You're looking well", he said, pouring himself a glass of wine and taking a quick gulp. "Ah, that's better, it settles the dust. So, had a good holiday did you?" "Yes, it was full of fun and peppered with lively chats plus a sojourn into the jungle which I am sure you would have loved, maybe you should have come with me". He knew Al was not being serious but sarcastic, rattling some coins in his pocket, an annoying habit of his he said. "No thanks, you know how much I hated the jungle and I'll be quite happy if I never see it again". "Hungry?" asked Al, picking up the menu. "Starved, what gastronomic feasts do they serve up here?" They settled on the chicken and ordered another bottle of wine as Todd had almost single handily demolished the first.

Although it was easy to see that there was no one within earshot, they sat through the meal discussing trivialities and it was only when the dishes had been cleared away that Al decided to let him in on the details that had emerged from his trip to Thailand. He listened throughout without interrupting, just giving the occasional nod whilst jotting down some notes. Al paused briefly while the waiter served coffee and cognac and then concluded by telling him about their unfortunate breach of security. At that he laughed. "Breach of security?" "I'd call it more of a bloody great hole. You mean to tell me that not only are Mossad aware of who we intend to knock off but the location as well?" he tailed off shaking his head.

"There's worse to come", said Al, reaching for the brandy. Todd had just put the coffee up to his lips. "Worse", he spluttered. "What on earth can be worse than what you have just told me?" "They know the date and my name". He thought it wise not to inform him about Viola giving the game away. "All I can think is that I must have been observed in Geneva and they were able to put two and two together". Todd looked stunned and glanced nervously about him. Al read his thoughts. "Don't worry I was not followed here. I made sure of that". He did not look very reassured and asked a question Al had been expecting. "The Minister is in Las Palmas for two days, so how would they know it was the 11th we were planning to hit them?" "We have to give them credit for being able to isolate the most obvious time", said Al, "that would have to be when he reviews the small arms demonstration. They would know that with the noise and location it would be ideal". Todd's face remained glum but he conceded the point. Al could see that he had taken it badly, whereas before it had been just a case of constructing the device and leaving it in a suitable location with a timer, now it was a whole different ball game. Perhaps it would be better if he helped him make up his mind. "Look Todd, I won't blame you one bit if you want to cry off. I know there is a hell of a risk to both of us, but you have more to lose than me. There is your wife and children to consider". He sat, eyebrows knotted together deep in thought. He had a great deal to consider. He may have thought also that he may be letting Al down if he pulled out. It might be better if he tried to make it easier for him. "You could still help me and I could give you an amount of money. After all I still need a detonator and the bomb being set up". Todd brightened up a little at that but still looked doubtful. "It would not be too difficult to set up as we will be working with two claymores, but of course we are unable to change their shape due to the hard plastic cover". He warmed to the subject. "I could give you the necessary instructions, what to do when you get hold of the mines. It's true but I think I would rather do it myself". "What exactly are you saying?" asked Al, not quite sure which way Todd had decided to go. "I'm saying", he spoke with a determined gleam in his eye. "That I will come with you to Las Palmas to set everything up. I really do need all the money you promised at the onset".

Al swirled the brandy around in the bottom of the glass and then raised it to him in salute. "Here's to us Todd. If we can get away with it we will be wealthy and deserve to be so. If we don't, it won't be for lack of trying". He raised a glass to Al and they clinked glasses both knowing they had struck a deal from which they may never return. "You know Al, for me the only real reward I want out of this is money, but what is your motivation, you seem so determined despite all the setbacks we've encountered and the risk is so great". Al laughed. "I thrive on adversity, no, that's not true. This Rubenstein when he was a young man he was a terrorist, although he would tell you different. He would have claimed that he was fighting for his homeland, his Israel. Just as the Palestinians who are called terrorists now will also tell you they are fighting for their homeland. Anyway, my father at that time was in the British Army in Palestine on security duties and therefore was one of those who stood between the Jews and their ultimate goal. He was killed by a group of terrorists amongst whose number was a certain Ben Rubenstein". "I'm sorry to hear that", said Todd. "I knew of course that your father had died just after the war, but I never liked to ask how". "And I did not wish to discuss it either", said Al. "But, that is all in the past now, let us hope that we have a future. First we have to get out of the country to Las Palmas as soon as possible. The longer we stay here the more chance there is of us being discovered". Todd nodded. "Which means you ought to come back to my house tonight. The wife will be pleased to see you and I will leave you the job of explaining to her why we are disappearing for a few days". Al laughed. "O.k., that's a small price to pay for her home cooking. I'll tell her that we are off to find a job". Al called the waiter over to ask for the bill. He had no need to return to the flat as he had everything he needed in a small bag knowing when he left it may be too dangerous for him to return. He then realised that if they were successful he would never see his flat again. He could never return, it would be lost forever, in fact there was a possibility that even returning to England could be out of the question. It was a sobering thought.

Chapter 17

Gran Canaria, the island upon which Las Palmas was the largest city and its capital was located in the north and was at present under a covering of grey cloud which was in complete contrast to the south of the island. A blazing sun burned down from a cloudless sky upon the volcanic landscape. The occasional splash of green dotting the hillsides showed where man had fought against the elements to plant small crops of hardy tomatoes and other vegetation.

Two men stood on the lip of one such valley intently studying the terrain that lay below them. Here there were two or three low roofed buildings halfway down the slope, otherwise there was no sign of man, no farmer ventured into this valley and for those who may forget, red warning flags flew from the surrounding peaks for it was the valley where the Spanish military carried out live firing exercises. The floor of the valley was strewn with boulders of all sizes and shapes, the largest jutting some twenty to thirty feet over what once used to be long cold lava trails. The smaller of the two men kicked with the toe of his shoe at the loose dry dust and turned to his companion. Beneath the khaki coloured forage cap and behind the dark shades the eyes of Mo shone intently. "You know, I think we have got the measure of this guy Jenkins. With our men positioned at all the vantage points well in advance we should be able to pick him off as soon as he makes an appearance". Harry Reynolds ran his fingers through the short grey-flecked hair and nodded slowly. "Let's hope that you are right or we are going to be looking at the biggest headlines since Munich". It was the 6th of August, giving them five days before the visit of the Minister to plan their security arrangements. Their immediate boss based in Israel had given them joint responsibility for this operation. It had been a shrewd move knowing as he did their antagonism towards each other and their ambition to succeed him when he retired. He thought it might bring out the best of them; also the Minister was a good friend and a contemporary of his. He would not like to see anything happen to him.

Mo decided not to try and run the show. They would have to co-operate together on this one if Reynolds would meet him half way. "What do you think Jenkins has planned?" he asked in a conciliatory tone. "Of course we are still not sure of Jenkins' motives in the first place when he asked for the Minister's itinerary. It may not have been a threat". "I agree Harry, but as you know we have to be prepared for any eventuality". Reynolds stared up at a light plane droning above before replying. "I would imagine the most obvious way would be to take a shot with a snipers rifle, there is a hundred hiding places where a man could take a bead on that dais below". "True, but don't forget we will be here before him and now that we have taken the precaution of informing the Spanish authorities to pick up Jenkins at any entry point as a security risk there is the possibility that if he feels he is under no threat he may well use his own passport". "Yes, that's true", Harry conceded. "That would be the end of it". "However, Mo said, gazing at the surrounding peaks, "we have to assume the man is not a complete fool, so first I think we ought to implement those ideas put forward in Geneva namely listening devices to completely encircle the valley with a twenty-four house watch being kept as from tomorrow". Reynolds gazed at the valley shimmering in the heat. "Also, the infra-red night scopes must be fully utilised but I don't think the heat detectors will be of much use. There will be too much heat retained in those rocks to give us an accurate reading of any intruder, a possible helicopter surveillance before the Minister arrives but during the demo we could not keep an aircraft aloft due to the danger of ricochets". Mo still wore a worried expression. "Why is it I still feel that somewhere along the line we have missed something, we have to make sure that every hole is plugged". Harry shook his head. "I think we have covered just about everything there is". Mo said nothing.

They sat down together in silence, deep in their own thoughts. It was a full three minutes before Mo suddenly smashed his clenched fist into the volcanic dust. "You know, we have been so preoccupied that Jenkins would use a rifle, we have not contemplated that he could decide to try and plant a bomb". Reynolds did not look impressed. "It had crossed my mind but he must know that we always search for devices at any location where there is an important meeting, so I think that will be the last method he will attempt". Mo was annoyed at the way Reynolds brushed his suggestion aside. "Yes, but don't you see that is the very reason why he may go for it. Knowing that it is the most obvious, he would reason we would also disregard it". Reynolds snorted. "Well, the area will be searched thoroughly as per normal procedures, that would be sufficient". Mo looked thoughtful, picking up and shifting small particles of rock through his hand.

Eventually he said. "If anything we must overestimate the man's capabilities, which means we must employ every device we have and there is one although relatively new which may just tip the tables". He went on to explain to a sceptical Harry Reynolds. Mo had nearly finished when Harry gripped his arm. "Act normal but study the terrain opposite on the skyline, I just saw a flash of light or a reflection amongst the rocks over there". Mo did as told but could see nothing. "Are you sure? There is nothing I can see". "Positive", replied Reynolds emphatically. "I am sure there is someone over there probably using glasses and I don't think it is a local otherwise they would not bother to hide". Mo thought quickly. "O.k., we had better check it out". He pulled out a two-way radio from his hip pocket and spoke urgently into it. (Snapping the antenna back as he replaced it). "Right, just in case you are correct, I have informed our driver down on the road to get up there and question whoever you saw. He should be able to take the man unawares". "And if it is Jenkins", Reynolds finished the sentence for him; "all our worries are over".

When Todd Rogers spat he was accurate, hitting the small lizard that had crawled up to within three feet of him squarely on the body, it scurried away. He lay in a prone position, sprawled on the hot ground not more than 600 yards opposite the two men on the valley ridge that faced him. He picked up the powerful field glasses once more to study their actions. The slightly more robust of the two wore a forage cap of some sort and was gesticulating with his arms in the general direction of the valley, sometimes even pointing towards him although he was positive he could not be seen. He felt troubled. Had these the faceless men of Mossad come like him to survey where their defence Minister would be reviewing a small arms demonstration in a few days? Perhaps Al had been wise to send him out in advance using the argument that they knew nothing of Todd and therefore it was better kept that way and would enable him to carry out a through reconnaissance of the area where the bomb was to be placed. Al had remained in England until such time as when he had acquired new documents to travel. He finely adjusted the binoculars until the men's faces swam into view. No clues there but he may just be able to recognise them if he were to see them again which would be helpful. The smaller of the two was smoking. Todd eased himself back from the skyline into dead ground. It was time to reflect on what he had seen and more importantly the significance of the two men. His first objective had been to plan the position of the bomb, but now that just was not feasible if the valley was under surveillance. What should have been a pretty hard task was now turning into an impossible one. Todd's original plan had been to site one or possibly both claymores approximately 50 feet from the viewing dais as there would have been a good chance of them being undetected with just a light covering of earth on them. From them he would have run a wire to a powerful battery at 150 yards distance. He could have lain in wait there behind some large rocks before choosing the exact moment to detonate them. But of course that was before he learnt that they had been compromised. Mossard had justifiably earned a reputation for being very efficient and it was more than likely that the two men he had just seen were involved in the security apparatus. He was already handicapped by the mines not arriving until the 9th, so that precluded him from positioning them earlier but now it was almost suicidal to approach closer than 200 yards. There could be no doubt the immediate area to the viewing stand would be thoroughly searched.

Down to the front of him he heard a few pebbles rattling down the slope but thought no more of it, probably one of the local goats foraging about. He had reason to kick himself a few moments later. His blood froze when a shadow fell across him. He looked up to see a brawny built man with greying hair and a moustache to match. He was of middle-eastern appearance with an unusual feature, extremely long earlobes. Even more unusual was the fact that he wore a light jacket with an ominous bulge under the left armpit. "Que Pasar", he enquired in a menacing tone. It was time to bluff it out Todd thought quickly. "Tourista", he blustered, getting up and going to walk past the man. A hairy well-muscled arm barred his way. "You come with me, someone wants to talk to you", he said in a heavy accent. The man was perspiring heavily and still a little out of breath after his climb up the hill. If Todd had a chance of getting away it would have to be now. Al had warned him about being too complacent and that they were up against the most ruthless people he was liable to come across. Now not only had he put himself in danger but it could mean that he had left his family and Al down. The realisation sent a surge of anger through him. He aimed a kick at the man's balls and was successful. The man doubled over with a grunt of pain. Todd took his chance and began running down the hill leaping from boulder to boulder. There was a shout from behind him but he did not bother to look round. There was a vicious crack, fragments of rock erupted from a nearby outcropping. He began running in a zigzag fashion hoping to put the man off his aim. There were two more shots and then nothing other than the beat of his heart against his ribs. He risked a look behind to see that his pursuer had holstered his gun and was running hard after him. Working in an office for the last few years had not kept Todd as fit as he used to be. Now it was the fear that drove his legs even if he knew he was being overhauled. His car at the bottom of the valley beckoned invitingly but it still seemed a long way off. There was another heart stopping crack as the man behind stopped to take another shot at him. Luckily his aim was off, but more important it gave Todd his chance to increase his lead.

Leaping into the car he prayed it would start first time. It did. Putting it into gear he slammed his foot down sending clouds of dust and gravel flying out after him. He bounced over the rough track leading to the main road and turned left. As yet he could see no sign of pursuit in his rear view mirror but that was not to say he was not being followed. He diverted down a small track leading to the sea. It was then that he saw it. A large black powerful saloon car bearing down. His friend with the long earlobes was in the driving seat. The road was deteriorating. They drove closer to the sea, the rough surface giving way to small and large potholes dotting the surface causing the car to buck and rear. He desperately swerved trying to avoid the larger ones. The track ended in sand, the whole foreshore was covered in gently sloping sand dunes. He changed down in low gear and drove more slowly across. If he had not, it was almost certain he would have been stuck within a few yards. He watched in his mirror as the car behind roared up after him to hit the sand hard, it slowed but was still gaining.

He was by now driving along the sea's edge hoping to find more hard packed sand to increase his speed. He watched the speedometer begin to rise and put his foot down hard as he picked up a small trail leading away towards higher ground. The bullet when it pierced through the rear window would have missed him but it continued to glance off the car's interior to cut a furrow above his right eye. Blood sputtered over the windscreen, it was only then that Todd realised he had been shot, almost stupidly coming to the conclusion that the blood was his. He fought desperately to keep control of the wheel as blood streamed into his eye obscuring his vision. He felt himself sliding into a red mist of pain and although his left eye was clear his vision was blurring. Todd was sinking into unconsciousness but knew there was nothing he could do. His hands slid from the wheel. The path he was following had by now risen which meant there was a ten-foot drop on the seaward side. The hired Seat car careered over the edge to drop in a sheet of spray onto the water below. Slowly it began to sink, the cold Atlantic water rushed in. The shock of it more than anything as it crept slowly up his body brought Todd back to consciousness. The water was by now up to his neck and rising quickly. He took a deep breath as the car slid under and wound down the window propelling himself through it he swam not straight up but as far as he could away from it before lungs bursting, he surfaced cautiously.

Taking a deep almost delicious gasp of air he sank down again. In the brief glimpse he took as he surfaced he was able to see his adversary standing next to the lip of the small cliff, staring down at the bubbles rising from the sunken Seat. He kept swimming underwater away from the scene and closer in to the beach until his feet touched soft sand. Risking a quick glance he saw the man still standing there. Ducking down again, Todd put more distance between them before risking another look. He saw the back of the man, walking towards his car and heard the engine fire. It was after several seconds of listening to the running engine that Todd had the ominous premonition the man was not in fact in the car but creeping back to the cliff edge to take another look. Sinking under the small waves the cold water had the effect of anaesthetising his wound, but it still throbbed with pain. He surfaced to hear the sound of the car driving away. Waiting until the sound had completely died away before emerging dripping water, he staggered up onto the dry sand. Sinking to his knees, chest heaving he took in great gulps of air.

It was time to take stock of his situation and the most pressing was his wound. Immersion in the cold water had to a certain extent stemmed the flow of blood but now it was beginning to stream down his face. He took his shirt off and wrung the water from it before tearing a strip from the bottom. Taking care, he bound the cloth about his head. Making sure to keep a good distance from the track he walked half a mile inland where he sat down behind a large grassy knoll. He found some money although wet still in his pocket. He spread it on the grass to dry. After a half hour he was reasonably dry himself and decided to make the long trek back to the road. He wasn't really surprised after two taxis had sped past without stopping. He must look quite a sight with his crumpled clothes and rough bloodstained bandage. Although not his first choice, the rough battered truck with its cargo of tomatoes, which drew up in response to his wave, was more than welcome. He was in luck; the man was going to Las Palmas and waved aside his proffered pesetas. After his initial attempt at saying a few words in Spanish explaining he had been the victim of an accident, the journey continued smoothly in silence for which Todd was grateful. He had a lot on his mind but what he could not shut out was his rising anger at his close escape from death. Now the shock was wearing off, it was being replaced by a desire for revenge. What had been at first purely a mercenary mission was now a feeling from the guts to see it through.

By the time his helpful driver dropped him off in the centre of Las Palmas he had a new idea forming in his mind on how they could deal with the Minister's visit. In some strange and unreal way 'Earlobes' had done his masters a disservice, although he would never know. "He's been away a long time". Harry Reynolds spoke to Mo as they stood by the side of the road, which ran through the valley. They watched as the car sped towards them leaving a cloud of dust in its wake. "The question is, why?" Mo replied. Their driver was one of their Spanish operatives who worked for them on a freelance basis and he knew from his file that the man was inclined to be overenthusiastic which wasn't always for the best. They stepped back as the car screeched to a halt. It was an air-conditioned car. They did not wait for an invitation but clambered in quickly to escape the heat. Harry Reynolds was the first to speak. "We heard shots. Was that anything to do with you?" The driver sounded almost nonchalant. "You don't have to worry about him anymore, he's feeding the fishes". Mo and Harry looked at each other in astonishment. Mo spoke with a firmness that was intended. "I think you had better explain exactly what happened". The driver looked a little nervous but spoke with conviction. "Well, I went up there to check on this guy just at you asked and you were right, he was sitting just below the skyline with a large pair of binoculars around his neck, which seemed pretty suspicious to me, especially when I discovered he was not Spanish". "You spoke to him", Harry interrupted. "Yeah, that's right. I told him someone wanted to speak to him. That's when he attacked me and ran off down the hill, so I fired a couple of shots in order to make him stop but of course I aimed to miss him". "Of course", Harry chimed in sarcastically. The driver ignored the interruption. "So this fellow who ran like a hare made it to his car and drove off. So I figured this has to be our man. He drove like a maniac right down to the sea with me following him closely. Anyway as he got close to the edge he lost control of his car and it plunged over". "And he did not get out I take it", Mo said solemnly. "That's right", replied the man, nodding his head. Mo pointed with his finger towards the sea. "Take us to the exact spot and on the way describe exactly what this man looked like". They both listened intently during the drive.

By the time they arrived they had both come to the same conclusion. "I don't think it was Jenkins, going by that description". Mo stared out over the sparking sea; the soft murmur came up to him from the shore below as waves ended their long journey. The hot air over the land behind him was rising, causing a cooling breeze to sweep in from the sea. He thought if a man had died here it wasn't such a bad place. He looked to Harry for a reply. "No, it wasn't him but in that case who was it?" Harry looked troubled. Mo turned to the driver. "Were there any witnesses?" "None". The driver said as he shifted his weight from foot to foot. Mo took his cap off and ran his fingers through what was left of his hair, before replacing it. "There is reason to believe that Jenkins had an accomplice in England. Now, it may have been him." Harry shrugged his shoulders. "We will never know". "That's right", said Mo with a sign. "But I don't think we ought to drop our guard. If there's one thing I have learnt in this business it's that never to take any breaks for granted". "But you don't think", Harry insisted with a gesture towards the spot where the car went down. "That if and we are almost certain that it was Jenkins' partner in crime, we may have completely disrupted his plan?" "We just can't take that chance. We will implement our scheme just as if this had never happened. We know that it wasn't Jenkins, so as far as I'm concerned the threat is still there". "I suppose you're right", Harry conceded. "Still, if they pick Jenkins up at the airport we can wrap it all up and go home". "I hope so". Mo turned away from the glittering sea and strode back to the car, adding over his shoulder. "If they don't, we still have some sweating to do". The driver had said nothing during the conversation; instead his eyes were riveted on a spot further up the beach. There seemed to be a set of footprints in the sand leading away from the beach, but oddly enough none leading to it. He called the other two men across.

Chapter 18

Al Jenkins stared up at the steel sides of the Russian cruise liner as it towered above him from his position on the dockside at Tilbury, London. Within a short time he would be boarding after already having completed immigration formalities. The officer who checked his passport had not even asked for it, but merely on seeing the cover waved him through as he stood in a long line of impatient passengers. For his part he knew he had plenty of time to digest the news that Todd had phoned through the previous afternoon. The ship would not dock in Las Palmas until the afternoon of the 9th August, but when he arrived he would have to act fast to secure the claymores. That was his first objective. Then, he could sit down and discuss with Todd which options were left open to them. He shifted the weight of the bag on his shoulders and began climbing up the gangway. After being shown his quarters he took a stroll up on deck. There was a blast from the ship's horn. Looking over the handrail he watched the mooring lines being cast off, saw the upturned faces of friends, lovers, or families waving as the gap between ship and shore increased. He could almost feel the warmth coming from those people radiating up to him, some continued waving until they were mere dots in the distance. He had noticed this disparity before between farewells at an airport and those going by sea. Was it because at the airport after a brief hug and kisses the departing person walked through into departures to disappear? The plane was seldom if ever seen. You were already stuck in a traffic jam trying to get out of the airport. In contrast to an aircraft's noisy departure, ships were inclined by their very nature to move slowly away, almost in deference to the passengers' wishes before picking up their full speed. He listened now to the reassuring thump of the engines deep in the ship's bowels as they drove him ever closer to his destination and his date with destiny.

The estuary was widening as he watched the land slipping away. Sea breezes had already replaced the smell of land but his thoughts were on what lay ahead. After listening to Todd on the phone yesterday, a feeling of horror had crept over him, almost numbness. That it was going to be an impossible situation that lay ahead if they were to continue. He told Todd that if he had second thoughts he would not think any less of him as a man. Therefore, it had come as a complete surprise to hear that after the ordeal he had just been through Todd's voice had taken on a new tone of determination that had not been there before. "Pull out, no way Al, those bastards think they killed me. Well, they are soon going to find out how wrong they were". He had almost shouted down the phone. "Besides", he added. "If they assume I'm dead don't you think the element of surprise has shifted back in our favour?" "Let's hope so", Al had replied. "So, I'll see you on the 9th. Get some sangria cold and senoritas warm!" Todd had given a less than polite reply and signed off. Al turned to join the throng of happy holidaymakers strolling along the deck. He really should feel some sort of shame it occurred to him. Todd was in the firing line at present and yet he was the one with weak knees.

Al was so wrapped up in his thoughts that he failed to notice the woman in front of him had stopped to look at a passing warship. "I'm very sorry", he said as she turned to face him. "I walked right into the back of you". "Dinada" she replied in Spanish. Then realising he was English, said "that's o.k." He was about to walk on when she spoke again. "That ship, is it English?" He said it was "Why then does it fly a white flag?" she said, looking puzzled.

"At this distance it may look white, but it has a Union Jack in the corner". He went on to explain about the White Ensign, the Blue Ensign and the Red one. She seemed genuinely interested. She was an easy person to talk to and maybe it would not have happened on a street in London, but here on a cruise liner there was a certain rapport, a camaraderie that ocean voyages seem to foster. She was a woman in her mid-thirties, more plain than good looking, but the clothes she wore were elegant and expensive and they could not conceal how well she kept herself in shape. The wind blew her shoulder length black hair away from a serious looking face, but her dark brown eyes were alive with a vitality that he had noticed in few other women. She said she was travelling alone, so he suggested that after settling in why not meet up in the bar later that night. She did not hesitate very long before agreeing. Her name was Christina.

He found a seat that looked out over the sea, although by the time that he arrived it was already growing dark outside. Amidst the potted plants in a corner, a pianist was playing some popular melodies. There was a sprinkling of people, a few of whom seemed to be serious drinkers but the majority were having pre-dinner drinks. He had passed on dinner this evening, having settled for a bar snack earlier. The thought of having a sit down three-course meal was in direct contrast to what his stomach felt. It was as though it had knotted itself into a hard ball, not with apprehension at meeting Christina but the knowledge that with every turn of the huge ship's propellers he was getting closer to his destination. The enormity of what he had undertaken had struck home during the short time he was in his cabin. It had been one thing to agree to the project on the phone but completely another to realise that now he was committed to what lay ahead at the end of this journey. It was the reason why he had invited the Spanish woman tonight. Perhaps spending some time with her would take his mind off thinking about the consequences should Todd and he fail. So a chance to find a little happiness over the next day or so was not something to pass up.

"Hello Al". Her pleasant voice broke into his thoughts. He looked up to see her standing there. She had put her hair up. Coiled elegantly, it showed off her fine neck. Wisps of hair curled about her ears and her stunning black dress looked as though it would have cost a week's wages. There was just enough cleavage showing to indicate what a fine bust she possessed. He must have sat there with his mouth hanging open because she spoke again to him. "May I join you"? He stood up and indicated the seat opposite. "Of course. Excuse me, but you almost look like a different woman from the one I met up on deck. Muy bonito". "Thank you. It's amazing what a little make up and a different dress can do but I know that I am not so attractive". "I disagree". Al flattered. "You must be the best looking lady on the ship". Only the ship?" she laughed, a friendly seductive laugh.

The conversation flowed easily, interrupted only by the arrival of drinks. She drank white wine while Al chose a vodka cocktail. "Salute", he said and raised his glass to hers. "Here's to a happy and safe voyage". She was eager to talk about herself. She told him it was a good chance to practise some of her English, although as she continued he had the impression that her life had been quite lonely. Raised by wealthy parents on the island of Tenerife, her upbringing had been strict with the emphasis on education. Up until the age of 18 she had been required to be home by ten each evening. She explained how that was followed by years in University studying law; years she said when her constant companions were volumes of boring law books. There had not been a great deal of time to socialise. Now of course she was qualified and free to lead her life how she chose, but due to her profession her words were that it brought her into contact with rather boring people. She had been in London for the past six weeks to improve her English and had decided to go home on this ship. It made a nice break after studying and an even better option than flying on overcrowded planes.

Al found himself beginning to unwind as he listened to her easy chat. He watched as her gold earrings bobbed about as she emphasised a point, even the tragic consequences surrounding the death of his wife and children no longer impinged on his thoughts. It was in the past now and he had to look to his future. Previously, when meeting people for the first time he invariably had spoken about the death of his wife. He now felt there was no longer any need to do so, rather than state he was a widower which always meant the next question was "What happened?" He would simply say he was single. "You're single?" she said, unable to keep the surprise out of her voice. "I would have thought you were married by now". He explained that due to the nature of his work, which necessitated him spending half his life on offshore oil platforms, he perhaps had not had too many chances in establishing a lasting relationship. She seemed happy with that and he was surprised when she reached across and squeezed his hand saying, "I'm very glad to meet someone like you, listening to all my boring stories. So tell me an interesting story about yourself". "I will, but first let us refill our glasses. All this talking is thirsty work". She laughed. "O.k., but this time I pay".

As she had just been learning English, he told her about the time when he had wanted to improve his command of the Malay language. He undertook a trip into the jungle to visit a small Kampong. There, nobody spoke any English, so if he were to get by he would have to speak their language. She nodded. "That's a good idea, so you learn to think in the language as well". "I had made friends with a girl there and told her in Malay it would be nice if we were friends. This seemed to cause a lot of excitement on her part and she insisted we go to see her parents. I received a wonderful welcome from them and we all ended up sitting on the floor together drinking rice wine and listening to Malay music coming from a battered transistor. Anyway, after a time the room started to fill up with other relatives of hers who came over to shake my hand. I had this terrible feeling that went right down to the bottom of my stomach that something was terribly wrong. Have you ever known that?" Christina slowly nodded her head. "Yes, I think I have. In one of the first court cases I undertook I was about to deliver my summing up when I realised a vital piece of evidence had not been presented". "Yes, that would be similar", said Al. "Well anyway, I spoke again to my new friend to ask what all the commotion was about and as she tried to explain, it suddenly dawned on me what had happened". "Come on then", she said, "I'm dying to know". Al sipped his drink as she glared across the table at him. "When I had used the Malay word 'kawan' she had thought I had said 'kawin' and that means to get married instead of 'friend'". Christina put her hand to her mouth as her face split into a broad grin. "It wasn't funny at the time, in fact things began to look nasty as if I had deliberately led the girl on. But, later I think they decided it had been a mistake so we ended up having a party".

The bar began to fill up as more people returned from the restaurants. The noise level rose while the pianist gamely competed for his share of attention. All this meant nothing to Christina and Al. They were enjoying themselves, exploring each other's lives, laughing, commiserating or agreeing on different stories. But now the crush of people was beginning to encroach upon their own little domain. They were joined by others in their corner, several brightly dressed middle aged women talking loudly on the merits of their last ocean cruise and what their offspring were doing or attempting to do. Al leaned over to talk to Christina so she could hear him above the hubbub and chatter. "Why don't we go up on deck for a stroll"? "Good idea", she replied. "I think I need some fresh air". They elbowed their way out. Several people seemed to be the worse for drink by now. Al protectively guided her through the throng to emerge out onto the open deck.

They climbed a set of steep steps to gain a better vantage point. He grasped her hand to help her up. They stood at the handrail, gazing out. He realised he had not relinquished her hand but she made no attempt to pull it away and to him it seemed the most natural thing to do. They were content to stand there and say nothing. From below the muted sounds of a band came up into the night air. They were steaming through the busy English Channel, around them on all sides at varying distances ships were passing in the night, their lights glittering and reflecting off the dark deep waters. Christina was the first to break the silence between them. "It's beautiful and so peaceful. I feel really relaxed after the hustle and bustle of London and of course the bar downstairs was getting so crowded". "You're so right", Al responded, giving her hand a squeeze. "Made even better in my case by being in the company of a beautiful woman". "You're very kind", she said simply. The moon appeared from behind a dark cloud to throw a sparking trail across a benign sea but even so there was a chill in the light wind. He saw her shiver. "You're getting cold. I think it would be wise to take you back to your cabin. It is nearly midnight". "Maybe, although I have enjoyed our evening out together, especially as it was so unexpected". He escorted her back down the stairs, back into the warmth of the ship along the passageways until they arrived at her door. He did not ask her to invite him in, as he knew it would have made it awkward for her to refuse him. The night had been so perfect he had no wish to spoil it now. He kissed her tenderly on both cheeks. "Thank you Al for such a nice time". He looked into her deep brown eyes as she rested a long well manicured hand upon his shoulder. "So, why don't we meet up again tomorrow night? We could have our dinner together and then perhaps go to the ship's dance. They have a good band there I hear". Her eyes shone with anticipation. "That would be wonderful, but I'm afraid I am not a very good dancer". "Don't worry, neither am I, so we can make a mess of it together". She laughed and he blew her a kiss as she retreated into her room.

He was sure that he was not unique amongst humans, feeling that your whole being is lifted after that first encounter with a person whom you find is very attractive, to discover that the feelings are mutual. He walked back to his cabin feeling almost light headed and most importantly the evening had removed the doubts and worries that had been in the back of his mind when he had first boarded. It was with anticipation the next evening that he waited in the restaurant for Christina to appear. He was quite looking forward to a good meal to boot at the appetising smells that drifted out of the galley. But during the day he had come to the conclusion it would be unfair to initiate an affair with her, as he knew that after they docked in Las Palmas it was highly unlikely that they would meet again. Moreover, he had no way of knowing if he would be alive in a week's time.

At the sight of her gracefully threading her way through the dinner tables his negative thoughts seemed to evaporate. What she lacked in looks was more than made up by the style in which she dressed. Several heads turned to watch her as she came to sit next to him. With good reason too as tonight her complete outfit was a brilliant red, from the tight fitting dress that emphasised her trim figure down to the stiletto shoes and matching handbag, there was a flash of light reflected from the small but beautiful brooch she wore. On some women it may have looked out of place, but on her you could see that it belonged. "You look even more attractive tonight than yesterday. You must be eating the right sort of pills". She gave him a blank look at first and then a stunning smile. "I'm not sure that I understand all your English jokes but thank you for the compliment". She smoothed her dress down her legs a little but there was still a great deal of smooth, trim and shapely thigh showing. His earlier resolve not to try to seduce her was under a distinct threat. He remarked on the beauty of the brooch while they studied the menu together. "I'm lucky in having a doting father who enjoys buying me these sort of gifts". "So any potential husband for you has a lot to live up to, to keep you in the style you are accustomed". She objected strongly. "That's not true. I'm not looking for a rich man, just one that loves me. But you are right, I think it scares many off." "Well, I'm not rich but how about a bottle of champagne. It's our night on board together and who knows what the future will bring". Her eyes sparkled mischievously. "I think that is a wonderful idea. We can drink to both our futures". He signalled the hovering wine waiter to take their order.

It was a very special time that night. They laughed and joked as they chose the food and talked some more as they ate it. The champagne was having its effect on her by the time they reached the dance floor. After a couple of fast dances they only chose the slow ones. She snuggled up close to him with her arms about his neck. "You awaken feelings in me that I did not know I had", she whispered. "You consume my mind". "You came to me just when I needed you most", he replied softly. She pressed her body close against him and kissed him on the lips. "I want to hold you all night". "Give me all the sweet talk when we're leaving", he said, which earned him a poke in the ribs. "Then I'll know you are serious". "Don't joke at a time like this Al". "O.k. let's go up on deck where we can find a place to ourselves". They found a spot that was secluded and out of the wind on a bench seat that looked out over the sea. In contrast to last night there was not a ship or a light to be seen in any direction, it was as if they were completely alone in the world with just the pale moon and stars shining down upon them. He put his arm around Christina's shoulders while she dovetailed her head against his neck. "I like it this way", she said, putting her arm around him. "Just the two of us together, you know I could come to love you". "You're a wonderful woman Chris but you cant' know me after just two days and nights". She stopped him talking further by placing her moist tender lips against his. He responded and drew her close up against him. He felt her body yield. Their embrace grew harder. He moved his free hand up over her body until it came to rest on her left breast. Through the thin fabric of her dress he felt her nipple hardening, she was wearing no bra. She whispered his name and said something in Spanish. He did not understand but it sounded nice. They lay entwined in each other's arms but the seat was proving uncomfortable. "Shall we go where it is a little more soft", he suggested. She nodded and rose to her feet. No words were needed.

He led her down to her cabin. She gave him the key to open it leaning heavily against him. She was tired but also just a little drunk. "I think it would be better if you had a nice coffee", he said, guiding her over to the single bunk. He then realised there were no facilities available. "I'll be back in five minutes with something warm for you to pep you up". He saw her give him a feeble wave as he closed the door. It was closer to ten minutes by the time he put the key in the door once again. She lay on her back with her feet hanging over the side of the bunk. She was fast asleep. Putting the coffee down he gently slid off her shoes and lifted her legs up onto the bed. She gave a moan but did not awaken. He pulled the blankets up to cover her. Bending down he brushed a wisp of hair away from her eyes and kissed her softly. She looked so peaceful he could not bring himself to wake her before he left but spoke softly as he gazed at her incumbent form. "What sweet surprise in meeting one so fair, so trusting. You don't know how close you have come to touching my heart. It is so sad that our lives have to part as I must go far from here, but I am richer for meeting you". Leaving her key on the bedside table he switched off the light and closed the door behind him.

Back in his cabin he reflected on the past few hours. Wonderful happy hours that nearly culminated in them spending the night together, but this way had turned out for the best. He knew it would have hurt her deeply on telling her that there would be only the slightest chance they would meet again. But he knew there could be no hiding from the truth, after the 11th he must leave the islands forever. Moreover, even going back to England would be out of the question, at least for the immediate future. A glance at his watch showed two in the morning. It was the 9th of August. His heart quickened a beat but the sound of the water rushing by outside the shuttle window soon lulled him into a deep sleep.

He couldn't seem to remember how he had been caught but he was. The two soldiers in their khaki uniforms frogmarched him towards the wooden stake driven into the hard packed brown dirt, binding him securely to it. Behind him he had noticed the wall was pockmarked with bullet holes. The two soldiers had joined up with the rest of the firing squad and in unison on a word of command had raised their rifles to aim at him. On one side the officer had his sword held high in the air while on the other a soldier with a single side drum was beginning to tap out a monotonous beat. He knew when the drumming stopped the officer's sword would come down and the men would open fire. He stared hard at each one of the men facing him even as the sweat rolled into his eyes. He stared into their very souls with a fixed gaze. One by one they lowered their rifles. The drumming stopped as the officer gave a command and the same two men who had bound him came back in his direction. Were they going to free him? It was not to be. They tied a blindfold over his eyes. He heard the drumming start up again and knew once more he was in their sights. This time he knew it would be the end unless he did something. He fought frantically to free himself from his bonds before the insistent tap of the drum stopped. He awoke pulling the sheet from over his eyes where it had fallen and sat up with a start. Someone was knocking on the door.

Quickly wrapping a towel around himself he went over to open it. Partly due to his relief at waking from a nightmare but also on seeing it was Christina he put his arms about her, kissed her and invited her in. "I'm surprised", she said as they walked over to sit on his unmade bed. "That you are so happy to see me. I thought that after falling asleep on you last night you may be a little angry and many men would be". He cradled her hand in his. "After the wonderful evening we had together I could never be angry with you". Her dark hair framed her face. She cast her eyes down to look at their hands together and spoke with a tinge of sadness in her voice. "Why can't you come back to see me after your business is completed? You didn't quite explain that when we talked last night. We could have many more wonderful nights together. Why deprive yourself of that? I'm sure you could get some time off when you come back from the oil field". He did not like the way the conversation was going and at the same time he did not want to hurt her. "If I get a chance I'll come over to see you in Tenerife before leaving, how is that?" She sighed wistfully. "That sounds like a maybe but we are still together now". "You're right", he said. "Perhaps we should make the most of it".

He could not admire her slender long legs, which contrasted against her tight white shorts without feelings of desire rising within him. With deft hands she slipped the towel from around his waist. "I'll always want to remember you and remember you in the best way", she spoke softly in his ear. She stood up and began peeling off her clothes while Al admired her hourglass figure. "You know it's just as well I didn't make the bed", he murmured as he drew her naked body against his. She pressed close and hard against him and gave a low moan. Slowly he guided and lowered her onto the bed covering her body in kisses. She wrapped her arms around him and whispered, "I dreamt of us being together last night, it seemed so natural, I want you now". He entered her deeply as her nails dug into his back. They swept along with the gentle rocking of the ship. There were just them in the World. Christina was the first to rise. She slipped into the shower. On her return Al was by now sitting on the bed. He looked at her with a loving look. "Well, you had better let me get shaved and cleaned up". "Need my help sweetheart?" she replied, fiddling with his toothbrush. "Believe it or not it is something I have done many years unaided. I'll meet you in half an hour for a late breakfast". Putting her arm about his waist she leaved over and kissed him softly. "Don't be late", she whispered, "As I'll have your breakfast ordered".

She had as well by the time he showed up. They talked through the meal discussing everything except when they might meet up again. They were both leaving the ship at Las Palmas and she knew it might be the last time they saw each other. That being so, she put on a brave face. Al knew that she thought a lot of him and it was true she was making rapid advances into that part of his brain, which contained the emotional section. They exchanged addresses and went for their last stroll on deck, arm in arm, each with their own thoughts. She became excited at the first glimpse of Mount Teide on Tenerife in the far distance. The sea sparkled as the sun shone down from an almost cloudless sky. It was not so much the excitement as apprehension as Al stared at the distant mountain. This voyage had been a slice of heaven in between a sandwich of hell. It had seemed almost unreal. There, in the far distance lay the real world, a world of hate, deception and greed. It was a world that Todd and he had agreed to enter when they accepted the task that lay ahead of them.

Christina stopped to lean on the handrail to watch the land grow larger as they approached. He felt his heart warm to her. So versed in law and yet so naïve in love. This girl was an uncut diamond just waiting to be found. Yet, like a doddering old prospector he was letting it slip through his hands. As though reading his thoughts, she gripped his arm tightly and spoke. "Al, you know that I've fallen in love with you and I'm sure that your feelings are much the same about me. You can't disguise that by the way you have treated me but there is something holding you back from making any sort of commitment. Tell me you don't have a wife hidden away somewhere". He gave a chuckle. "Not guilty. You can rest assured about that. At the moment I'm not in a position to make a commitment to any woman no matter how beguiling and it would not be fair to you". He turned to face her, placing his arms about her shoulders. "Listen, in my heyday I thought the world belonged to me but now I know it is not true". With her fingers she traced an imaginary line down his face. "I'm not sure that I understand you but if you are trying to say that you're past it, nothing could be further from the truth. So don't put yourself down". They both watched a seagull swoop down to glide effortlessly alongside them, the sharp eyes watchful for any scraps of food thrown overboard.

There was an unspoken agreement that neither of them wanted to row during their last couple of hours together. They clung to each other watching the land grow ever larger until the busy city of Las Palmas could be distinguished, some parts historic and attractive while others seemed dirty and uncared for, interspersed with an occasional gleaming new block. Tall, ocean-going yachts passed them with pyramids of sail set to catch the gentle breeze bound for exotic destinations. It was time to go below to prepare for disembarkation. She gazed wistfully at the horizon and talked almost with resignation in her voice. "When I look at the world I see just what a wonderful place it is. I thank God for that and also my privileged lifestyle, my fortunate upbringing and my success as a lawyer. But you must know that it all seems so empty unless you have that special someone to share it with". "I shall come over to see you in Tenerife before I leave", he said simply. Her dejected face lit up with pleasure. They kissed long and hard and said their farewells. He watched her disappear below decks to her cabin thinking at the same time it was a promise he would keep unless events determined otherwise.

Through the window of the taxi he looked back at the ship as they pulled away. It had been such a perfect crossing it was almost like a dream, but good for him in more ways than one. When he thought back to his arrival on the ship he had been a ball of nerves, almost to the point of not being able to think straight. Now he felt composed, almost calm as he surveyed his new surroundings. Las Palmas was waking up after the afternoon siesta. Bars and restaurants were beginning to fill up as the taxi sped along through the narrow streets. He could imagine Todd sitting in the small guesthouse biting his fingernails as to whether he would show up on time. They pulled up with a jerk outside an anonymous looking building in a small side street just off the centre. He checked the address that Todd had given him. It was correct.

He paid off the taxi driver and walked with his bags into a small lobby. One or two faded prints decorated the wall while in one corner a large cheese plant looked as though it could do with some water. Behind a narrow desk stood a short middle-aged pot bellied man with an oval face and long side burns. His face wore an expression almost of suspicion. "Buenos Tardes", Al said, hoping the man spoke a little English. "Senor Rogers, is he staying at this hotel?" "Ahh! Si, Mr Rogers he stay here a few days ago". In his broken English he went on to explain that Todd had booked a room for him next to his. Al signed the register and carried his bags upstairs to find his room. He dumped his bags down. A brief look round showed a single bed dominating the centre of the room with an adjacent cracked hand washbasin. The only other furniture was a small wardrobe and single chair, still it was ridiculously cheap and he was not going to be staying long. He went and knocked on Todd's door. There was no sound of movement within; maybe he was having an extended siesta. He knocked harder and waited, only to be met by silence. Annoyed but not alarmed he locked his room and went in search of the receptionist. He found him watching T.V in a small adjoining room to the lobby. "Donde este Senor Rogers, por favor", he asked pointing upstairs. He looked puzzled. "He go out this morning, quite early". He has not returned since then". Al persisted, while at the same time he experienced a sinking feeling in his gut. Todd should have been here to meet him. The man spread his hands in a gesture of defeat. "No, he don't come back". Al tried not to think of the worst as he climbed back up the dust-covered stairs but by his not being here it would have to be extremely important or a case of enemy action. At the moment he had no way of knowing.

Chapter 19

Todd walked towards his hotel still sporting the bloody bandage around his head and wearing what remained of his shirt following his unscheduled swim earlier in the day, when he had become parted from his car. For once he was grateful for having booked this out of the way, down at heel hostel although he had cursed it on arrival for its lack of facilities. He was aware that as long as his room was paid for each day his appearance was of little concern to those who ran it. He even managed a grin at the thought of the consternation he could have caused if he had been booked in at the classy five-star Hotel Royale down on the seafront. But here all he received was a raised eyebrow and a longer stare than normal. He explained about having an accident and were there any clinics nearby where he could receive treatment. The man gave him a couple of addresses in the vicinity. After cleaning himself up he found a doctor at one of the clinics who was prepared to treat him for a price. The doctor cleaned the wound and then put several stitches in. He explained that the injury would require a fresh dressing for the next few days. Todd recalled making it back to the hotel through a red mist of searing pain.

He gulped down some of the painkillers he had been given and stretched out on the bed. He went out like a light.

Over the next two days most of his time was spent holed up in the hotel room, nursing himself back to health but also giving him time to finalise his plans for the bomb. By the morning of the 9th he had a pretty clear idea of how it was going to be carried out. He had set off using a vehicle from a different hire firm, the previous company with whom he had hired a car were not over eager to lend him another after his 'accident'. After his observations of the killing ground in the valley on the 6th he had come to the conclusion to attempt to conceal a device in the vicinity of the viewing dais was just so much wishful thinking. The people they were up against were thorough. He had a nasty reminder above his right eye as proof. He left the environs of Las Palmas heading south, passing through many new holiday developments, as they pressed hard by the highway, the density highest at Playa del Ingles. He then turned inland, passing charming villages and a terraced landscape of tomato plantations, here and there a larger splash of green revealed a stretch of banana trees. He soon spotted what he was after. A beat up pickup truck used for transporting tomatoes. It was important the grower's name was on the door panel to lend authenticity to what he proposed. Unfortunately a quick stroll around the vehicle revealed it had no engine, no point progressing any further there.

Todd drove off to continue his search, moving from village to village. Those trucks, which suited his requirements, were unavailable for one reason or another but mainly their owners had no wish to part with them even when he offered slightly above the market value. He was starting to feel a little desperate knowing that Al was due to arrive soon. However, it was less important to be at the hotel on time than to achieve his objective. He cursed to himself as he drove down yet another dusty trail. This was supposed to be the easy bit and yet it was proving to be a headache in more ways than one. His wound was beginning to throb with the heat and constant movement as the car rattled along. He suddenly applied the brakes. Out of the corner of his eye he noticed what appeared to be a small pickup parked to one side of a house that had several trees surrounding it. He put the car into reverse and backed up alongside it. A small-wizened old lady dressed all in black answered his knock on the door. She spoke no English but through the few words of Spanish he knew and some improvised sign language he managed to convey that he wished to view her truck. She accompanied him on his tour of inspection making a clucking noise to the effect the van was inoperative. In that she was correct. One tyre was flat, the battery was missing and the exterior showed a general lack of maintenance. However, the engine seemed to be in good repair and in all other aspects it suited him down to the ground. If he could get someone from the local garage to come round to check it out and it was possible to fix up, would she be interested in selling he asked. It seemed she did not comprehend what he was proposing but made clear he must wait for her husband to return from the fields in order to discuss with him what he had in mind.

He sat outside under the shade of a tall jacaranda tree staring out at the dusty landscape willing the man to return. He had by now already missed the deadline to meet Al at the hotel. Still, he was out here sweating while his partner could always console himself with a cold San Miguel. He saw the man coming towards him up a small track from the fields, his footsteps raising a little puff of dust with each step he took and sensed his hostility towards him, which he could understand. What was this tourist doing sitting in his backyard as though he owned the place miles off the beaten tourist track? When Todd made his intentions known the man's attitude visibly softened. To him it was a chance of making some money on the truck he had more or less abandoned. The man who seemed to be of a similar age to his wife agreed to Todd's proposal that they invite a mechanic from the local garage to assess if the truck could run without major repairs. After a further wait, the farmer's wife bought him a glass of warm red wine, which, although welcome, did nothing for his palate. A battered pick up truck arrived to disgorge a sweating fat man dressed in greasy overalls. He viewed the ancient pickup with an air of disdain but could not hide his professional interest in a new challenge. Giving Todd a Spanish version, if it were a horse it would have to be shot. But the upshot was he thought it could be repaired although he could not guarantee it ready before tomorrow afternoon. Todd knew he had to take that chance. The possibility of finding another vehicle today seemed remote. He paid the farmer of who seemed more than pleased with the afternoon's business and left a deposit with the mechanic to encourage him to make an early start on the work.

It was time to 'burn rubber' if that were at all possible on these country roads, before arriving at the main highway. Already, the sun was beginning to set below the volcanic mountains to the west, throwing long shadows across the land. You could almost feel the temperature dropping under the clear skies. He knew Al would be worried by his absence. He resolved to stop at the first roadside telephone booth to inform him that matters were under control. Unfortunately, the first one he stopped at was out of order, but a few miles further on he found one that seemed to be reliable. The receptionist came on the phone. Had an English man come to see him that afternoon, Todd asked. The answer was affirmative but he would not be able to speak with him as he had just left the hotel minutes before Todd called. He put the phone back in its cradle and looked out of the booth at a couple of swallows diving and weaving in the evening air as they sought insects rising from the land. It meant Al had already left for the airport to collect the two claymores. He prayed that events would go smoothly. He drove hard and fast as he swept down the four-lane expressway into Las Palmas, even so it was eight thirty by the time he arrived. There was nothing for him to do except wait with crossed fingers. He lay on his bed after a cold shower, letting the dull ache in his head gradually subside, and his mind busy. Almost without realising he drifted off into a deep sleep and did not awaken until there was a loud knock on his door. He slid his feet into a pair of sandals and shuffled across. "Who is it?" he called out, his voice little better than a croak. The unmistakable voice of Al came through the thin panelling. "Just open the bloody door or do I need an invitation?" Todd turned the key.

It had been far easier than Al thought. His original plan was to approach a taxi driver at the airport taxi rank who was familiar with the area to proceed to the military side of the airfield and pick up the package. However, that had proved unnecessary. During the journey to the airport, in conversation with the driver of the cab he had hailed it proved that the man had made several trips to the military airfield. Would he be prepared to make a visit to pick up a package for a friend of his, Al had asked. His response was why not go together whereby Al explained that he had no pass and there was other business for him to attend to at the airport. He swung it by paying the driver up front and arranging to meet back over at the arrivals lounge. Al sat for the next half an hour slumped down behind a seat where he would observe the door unobtrusively, watching carefully to see that when he arrived, he wasn't accompanied by a posse of policemen. It was with some relief that when the driver did show up he was alone. Al waited a couple of minutes before showing himself to make sure the driver was not followed. Under his arm he carried a large bulky object. Al asked him on the way back to drop him off several streets away from where the hotel was located. There was no point in advertising where he stayed.

He was greeted more warmly at the hotel this time and informed that his friend had arrived back. It was news Al most wanted to hear. When Todd opened his door he was shocked by his appearance. His face was a deathly pale, the eyes were bloodshot and he seemed unsteady on his feet. When it spoke it seemed he had almost lost his voice. "What a sight for sore eyes. It's bloody good to see you Al". He extended his hand towards Al who shook it warmly and gave him a slap on the back. "You look a mess. Looks like we are going to have to get you in shape for the big day". Todd waved his hands. "I'm fine really, just fell asleep after spending all day hunting down a pickup truck in the south of the island". Al was puzzled. "A pickup truck? We will need faster transport than that. Admittedly it would blend in well." A thought crossed his mind. He put it into words. "At the moment Todd I am concerned about you.

Have you had anything to eat today on your travels?" He shook his head. A quick glance at his watch told him it was nearly midnight, but still young for the Las Palmas nightlife. "Right, get your gear on, we are going out to get a slap up meal. I haven't eaten since breakfast either, so it will do us both good". "Maybe you're right", admitted Todd grudgingly. "Let me just splash some water over my face and we will head on out".

The streets were full and bustling with foreign tourists, hawkers and the occasional hooker. Music blared from disco doorways. They walked to the seafront, selecting a steak restaurant that looked out over the beach. The smell of frying steaks hit them as they entered and chose a table, sending saliva glands into overdrive. Todd selected an expensive wine, a Château Latour. He certainly deserved it. "Thanks Todd for hanging in there when all you had to do was catch the next flight back to the U.K. As you know I would have perfectly understood. Do you feel like talking about it now?" Al watched him place his glass on the table, the liquid sparkling as the light caught it. The same light giving a gleam to his eyes, his voice was low, barely concealing his suppressed rage as he recalled the events that so nearly led to his death. Al had never seen him this way before. "Let's hope, he said, keeping his voice low, "that the man who tried to kill me will be there on the 11th because I would like to get a crack at him. I would like to see the bastard wasted". They spoke of other subjects as the chef arrived to cook their steaks 'à la flambé' on his trolley next to their table. It was something that Al had always enjoyed watching as the chef deftly added the herbs and spices with wine and a dash of Spanish brandy, mixing and then igniting the contents with a 'whoosh' of blue flame. He could see Todd visibly relaxing in the restaurant's cosy atmosphere; the wine was working and bringing some colour back to his cheeks. They talked little during the meal, more intent on devouring the succulent steaks and fresh salad that accompanied; reluctant to disturb each other's enjoyment until the plates were cleared away and a large glass of Courvoisier brandy had been placed in front of each of them.

Todd leaned over the table towards Al. "Trying to place a bomb in the vicinity of the viewing dais at the valley is completely out of the question". He looked at him as though expecting a swift protest but it was obvious he was about to explain why. Al had to agree with him as most of the risk would be on his shoulders. "Ever since they took a shot at me I'm sure that the valley has been under twenty-four hour surveillance". He stopped to swirl the amber liquid around his glass, had a sip and continued. "Even with a good sniper's rifle which we don't have, I would not give much for our chances". Al was not downhearted; his feeling told him Todd still had a trick up his sleeve. It was like him to leave the best news for last. He let him continue. "It came to me as I returned from my narrow escape on the beach. I had hitched a lift on one of those trucks transporting tomatoes down to the city. Yes of course I was frightened but I was also very angry. The idea was quite simple but I believe it has the best chance of succeeding". Al was beginning to get impatient. "O.k. Todd, tell me about it". That drew a wry smile from him. "If the firing range is not feasible to plant a bomb, where's the next best spot?" "The road in I should think", Al replied, as he thought about it. "However, he could fly in by chopper". Todd looked pleased with himself. "No that's just it. I studied the valley very carefully before I was discovered. There is no helicopter landing pad or even an area suitable. The valley floor is covered with large rocks". Al took a sip of the brandy, felt the fiery liquid burn its way down his throat. Todd followed his example before continuing. "There is only one road leading in, a lonely road with very little traffic. A car parked alongside would raise suspicion, but a pickup truck with a load of tomatoes on the back with the name of a local grower emblazoned on the side would merit no more than a passing glance I would think". "That's true", Al conceded. "So what I propose is this. I intend to plant amongst the tomatoes the two claymores. They will be positioned to cover 180 degrees facing the road. The pickup to be parked a few feet off the road and immobilised, so if any of our friends come sniffing around they will assume it's been left there due to a breakdown". Although he was happy to leave the explosive side of the operation in Todd's capable hands, there was something troubling Al. He knew claymores were normally detonated by wire. Al voiced his fears that if someone did take a look over the truck they would soon spot the wires leading from it. "You're quite right", he said. "It's what I have been working on these past few days. Luckily Las Palmas is awash with shops full of electronic goods. I have been able to construct a device whereby I will be in a position to detonate the mines remotely". Al was impressed. It was the reason he had chosen Todd in the first instance, his ability to improvise. But even he continued to be surprised by his inventiveness. "There is one drawback though", he said, as if he sensed Al's elation. "I will have to be within

200 feet of the pickup. Further away I could not guarantee the remote signal being strong enough to detonate the mines". Todd noticed the look of concern on Al's face. "Don't worry, I think the risk is small. There is good cover off the road".

The soft music had stopped and the lights were turned up. There were few people left in the restaurant. It was time to go. "Come on Todd, drink up, I think we both need a good night's kip. We don't know what problems we may come up against tomorrow". Al watched Todd drain his glass and then gingerly feeling his wound above the eye. "You're right. They say that each new dawn you see is a victory, well in my case if I see a new dawn in a week's time I will have won the war". They walked out into the night air, their stomachs full, their thirsts satisfied. It was an enjoyable stroll. Before turning into their street there was a disco that had yet to close its doors and through them came the sound of the 60's Beach Boys hit 'God only knows'. It was a song that Viola and Al had danced to on many occasions out in Singapore. They both found it a haunting melody. The lyrics were so apt to their situation at the time. Al thought it strange that he should think of her at this moment. 'God only knows'. They had laughed to hide

their sorrow 'because if He knows, he wasn't
telling them'.

Chapter 20

More than a thousand miles away Vi was sleeping peacefully in her bed, alongside her husband whose breathing was deep and even. Outside the moon shone briefly upon the city of Geneva before being obscured by swiftly moving black clouds. There was a series of knocks on her apartment door. Vi stirred and then sat up, unsure what had disturbed her sleep. There it was again, an insistent tapping on her front door. She leant over and shook her husband. "Greg, there is someone knocking on our front door". He moaned before replying. "Are you sure? It must be two or three in the morning". As if in answer the knocking was repeated, only louder this time and carrying with it a sense of urgency. Greg slipped on a dressing gown, went down to the door and asked who it was without opening it. Vi listened to the muffled voices from the bedroom and heard Greg open the door to their late night visitor. "It's o.k. honey, it's Mo from the Mission. He says he wants a quick chat to you". She couldn't think of anyone she disliked more than having to talk to than this man in the early hours. They both looked at her as she walked in to take a seat, facing them. Greg was aware of her feelings. He stood up. "I'll go and make us all a cup of coffee", he said, as he disappeared into the kitchen.

Vi was left to stare at Mo's ugly red face. He tried to sound apologetic. "I'm sorry to wake you up so late at night Mrs Gelder, but I am afraid we have a small crisis on our hands". She felt her throat go dry, wondered if once again she had been spotted with Al in London, but that meeting was several days ago. Surely they would have approached her before now. Mo continued talking. "As you are aware the Defence Minister will be in the Canaries on the 11th. Unfortunately his normal secretary has suddenly been taken ill, so you may take it as a compliment that you have been chosen to replace her". She realised her mouth was agape but made no attempt to close it. "Therefore, he continued, "you have been booked on the first flight from Geneva in the morning, that is, in about four hours time. You will travel to Tel Aviv where you will be met by our people and assigned to the Minister's staff".

He stopped speaking as Greg returned with three steaming cups of coffee and then addressed himself to both of them. "Greg, I was just telling your wife she has been chosen to accompany Ben Rubenstein on his trip to the Canaries". Greg was enthusiastic. "That's great, that's a wonderful promotion", he said, as he turned towards Vi, placing an arm about her shoulders. Mo was quick to point out the position was only temporary. It only applied to the Las Palmas visit while Rubenstein's regular secretary was unwell. Greg was not put off. "It's still a great opportunity, don't you think so darling?" Vi just nodded her head. She knew that Mo's reason for sending her had nothing to do with giving her a chance to advance in the Diplomatic section of the mission. It was far more sinister. Her fears were founded as she listened to the Mossard man explain in greater detail exactly what her assignment was. As well as completing any paperwork he needed done, she was to accompany him in his car on all official visits and stand close to him at any function. Mo certainly did not want to leave anything to chance she thought bitterly. If there was an attempt on the minister's life and Al was involved in some way, no doubt Mo was counting on her presence to forestall it. Greg sensed she was not overjoyed by the prospect of the trip. "What's troubling you Vi, you don't look too happy". She put on a brave face. "I'm fine thanks Greg. I never look my best at this time in the morning". Mo stood up. "Yes, I'm sorry for disturbing you like this. I must let you get back to sleep for a couple of hours".

Vi left her seat to open the door for him. He smiled as he left. "By the way, I shall be coming over with you". "I wouldn't want it any other way", she retorted. It was difficult for her to get back to sleep. Her mind was too busy, thoughts crowding in upon her, visions of Al being stymied by her appearance on the scene.

It came as a surprise to find Greg shaking her roughly by the arm. "Darling wake up. You have to get to the airport on time". It was not a dream as she somehow hoped it might have been. It was a reality and she felt like death. She would not have made it to the airport on time had it not been for Greg bustling about getting her some food to eat, helping pack her suitcase. It was at times like this she really appreciated his concern. As he dropped her at the airport terminal she made her thanks obvious, giving him a long lingering kiss. It surprised and delighted him. She knew that she was guilty of treating him with a certain coolness since Al had reappeared in her life. She saw Mo coming towards her out of the corner of her eye. "You had better go home Greg before the children wake up". They embraced and he was gone.

She spoke little to Mo on the flight to Tel Aviv. She had no wish to although it was understandable that men like him did what they had to in safeguarding the nation's security. It did not mean she had to agree with the methods they employed, in fact she detested him. It seemed he had little to say to her regarding the trip other than repeating the necessity of remaining close to the minister at all times. At Tel Aviv they made a brief stop over to join up with he minister's party, before continuing their journey in a plane provided especially for them. She met him shortly before boarding the aircraft. A slight wizened figure of a man looking the 73 years that he was, with a distinct stoop and a shock of white hair, his face was a leathery brown but the eyes were bright and blue. Looking at him it was hard to imagine that he had killed people during the turbulent years when Israel became a nation. He had spoken kindly to her, thanking her for making the trip at such short notice. She saw no more of him then during the flight, he being surrounded by aides and the ever-present hovering figure of Mo. It gave her time to reflect on her own situation. What would she do if she came face to face with Al in the Canaries? Betray him? She still could not be sure of his intentions. He was devious but she had never seen him as a killer. More than anything she feared for his life. He surely had no idea of the people he was up against, how ruthless and professional they were.

The sun was setting as they flew in over the islands. By this time tomorrow they would all be flying back or would they? There was a low-key reception for them on their arrival at the airport before being whisked away in a convoy of black saloons. She gained the impression the Spanish wished to play down the visit as though it were better if the world did not realise they may purchase Israeli arms. There was a great deal of Arab money invested in Spain. They were driven at high speed before sweeping through a large archway into a courtyard of an imposing villa on the outskirts of Las Palmas; this was to be their home for the next day or so.

She was shown her room by a Spanish assistant but had hardly begun unpacking her clothes before there was a knock on her door. It was Mo. He gave her a mocking bow. "I hope that you are pleased with your accommodation. You are not required tonight. The Minister will be having a private dinner reception. If you want anything to eat call a steward". Vi nodded and spoke with a resigned tone. "What's happening in the morning?" "You will receive a call, quite early I imagine. One other thing, you are not permitted to leave the villa tonight or make any outside phone calls". He closed the door in her face before she had a chance to object. Through her windows she could see the courtyard outside. It was lit by bright arc lights. At the gate were two armed guards. She knew that she was a guest here but felt as though it was some sort of luxurious prison. If you were told to stay in you did not move out, the hidden menace was there. In her heart she was pleased she had no duties tonight, being exhausted following the traumatic events of the past twenty-four hours, she desperately needed a good night's sleep before facing tomorrow. But first she would take up the offer of food. Pressing the button beside her bed she waited only a few moments before her summons was answered. The steward was efficient and courteous, taking her order on a notepad before turning to leave. As he did so Vi was able to observe the other side of his face, which he had kept from her view, when he first entered the room. Two vivid red scars ran from ear to chin while the eye was an opaque colour. He was blind in one eye, no wonder he had kept his head turned away from her. She stood staring at the now closed door and felt a chill run down her spine, but why? She was being silly. It was perfectly safe here, there was no point in letting her emotions overcome common sense. She ate well, washed away some of the travel dirt and climbed into a deep soft bed. There were butterflies in her stomach at the thought of tomorrow but exhaustion triumphed and she soon fell into a deep sleep.

Her psychological clock awoke her long before there was any knock on her door. She was glad of it for when the summons came she was as mentally prepared for it, as she ever would be. They had breakfast together, her, Mo and half a dozen of the Minister's aides and military attachés. It was a bright airy room dominated by the long dining table, the early morning sun streaming through the windows. Her dining companions spoke little to her but cast several sideways glances as she ate listening to them talk on the various merits of different weapon systems. The stewards cleared away the dishes leaving them alone. A man whom he addressed as Harry joined Mo at the head of the table. Mo raised his hand to draw their attention. The talking stopped as they looked expectantly towards him.

"Gentlemen and Mrs Gelder, as you know the reason for our visit to this delightful island is to put on a show for the Spanish to induce them to purchase Israeli small arms. As you further know, this demonstration at the firing rang was due to begin at 12 noon. However, it has now been re-scheduled for 11 a.m. this morning". A red-faced bull of a man wearing Colonel's rank voiced his surprise. "Why weren't we told of this sooner?" The Mossard man looked at him. "In the interest of State Security nobody was told. We believe there is a plot to assassinate the Defence Minister during his visit here and we have to take it seriously". He stopped, as there was a quick buzz of conversation around the table. He continued. "I have been assigned as case officer with assistance from my associate here, Harry Reynolds. The motorcade when it leaves here will now be at 10 instead of 11 and order of persons travelling have been changed. Harry is now going to detail how it affects you and which car you will be travelling in". Harry smoothed out a sheet of paper in front of him and read out the list of names of the people seated around the table who were then allocated to a particular car. When he finished, he asked if there were any questions. Viola raised her hand. "You say I am to travel in the last car, but who is going to travel with me?" Harry did not need to look at the paper in front of him. He was well aware of the details. "Yes, that is part of the deception. The car in the lead bearing our flag would have contained the Minister but he will be travelling in the rear car with you Mrs Gelder and of course you will have a competent driver". It did not come as much of a surprise to her. It was the reason why she had been chosen for the trip. "I am sure you will be quite safe but you must realise my uppermost concern at the moment is for the safety of the Minister". Reynolds looked around the table. "Any more questions?" he asked, although implying by his tone he did not expect any. Vi felt like replying "my children's uppermost concern is their mother".

They filed out into the courtyard where the four official cars stood, their drivers stood in a huddle, smoking Spanish cigarettes and chatting amongst themselves. They reluctantly ground their butts out and positioned themselves next to their respective cars. Vi likewise stood next to the last one. Protocol demanded she waited for the Minister before taking her seat. She watched Mo and the man called Harry enter the first car with another man carrying some electronic gadgetry. Her driver was standing with the door open waiting for the Minister. She noticed the man had unusually long earlobes. "I believe you are travelling with me Mrs Gelder". She turned to see Ben Rubenstein standing just behind her, looking frail in the harsh examination of the sun, his jacket sagged on the thin shoulders. "That's right Sir, I believe we are all ready to move off". He indicated for her to take her seat first. Their driver spoke on his radio to the lead car. Within two minutes the four cars were moving slowly out of the courtyard.

"It makes a change sitting with a pretty woman. Normally I have to endure my journeys with a couple of beefy security men". It was unusual he reflected to replace his regular secretary with this lovely nervous woman, although he had to accept that Mossard's fears were usually well founded but they did not always go to the lengths they were employing on this occasion. Would the presence of a female by his side deter any potential assassin he wondered. A determined Arab terrorist would give it no more than a passing thought as they had demonstrated only too well in the past. This time his advisers had insisted it was a different ball game. They seemed sure that the threat was going to come from Europeans but could not provide a motive, whether it was purely for a financial reward or some unknown grudge harboured over the years. He looked out now at the passing countryside, the tourist buses mingling with the local traffic until they turned off the main highway on to a secondary road.

Here life was quieter, rocky slopes gave way to patches of brilliant green farmed plots, sleepy villages straggled the route. Elderly men walked with stooped backs, a legacy of years of toil in the harsh climate. The women wore mainly black, something he could never understand in a hot country, but in other ways the terrain reminded him of his home in Israel. His Israel, the country he loved but did not see until as a youth his parents had sent him in 1937 to live with an uncle in Palestine, as it was then called. The family jewellery business in Munich had by this time been attacked twice by rampaging mobs of Hitler youth but they insisted on staying to salvage what they could before leaving to join him. But, they had left it too late. According to a family friend who escaped later, his hardworking lovable and loyal mother and father had been arrested in 1940 by the Gestapo and sent to Belsen. Nobody could shed any light on their fate. His head told him there was no doubt Belsen was where their lives ended, but for many years after the war his heart ached at the thought they could be alive possibly somewhere. The ultimate sacrifice made by them was constantly with him in the early years of Israel's emergence as a new nation. The thought that if by chance they should be found alive and brought back to their new homeland, they would find a son to be proud of. With this thought uppermost in Ben's mind, he had joined the newly formed army to fight to form the Jewish State against the Arabs who had no wish for it and the British who were reluctant to grant it independence and who sought to stem the flow of Jewish settlers from war ravaged Europe.

He volunteered for the most hazardous operations and became adept in the art of laying ambushes. He became renowned for his indomitable will. As a junior officer one dark and windswept night he was in charge of securing a perimeter around a small bay where Jewish immigrants were to land. Along the road leading to it a British jeep with three men aboard had approached. Although not wishing to kill the occupants, as the tyres were shot out the vehicle had overturned to crash down a steep bank and all three had been killed. It saddened him despite the remark from his second in command who sneered, "If the British are not part of the solution, they are part of the problem". He seemed to have heard that said somewhere before in a different context. What if it were the son of one of those dead British soldiers who had come back to haunt him. Time magazine had run a profile of his life when he was appointed Defence Minister a year ago. As well as mentioning the highlights of his career such as the leading role he undertook in the Yom Kipper war they had printed his involvement in that fatal ambush, something he did not thank them for.

He was surprised at how calm he felt at the thought of confrontation or even sudden death. Apart from his childhood, life had been good to him. He met and married a wonderful woman who bore him two sons, both now with families of their own. His wife Beth sadly passed away two years ago with angina, so if he were to pass from his life to the next he may meet up with her again. He strongly believed there was more to life than just one existence, even so, he shivered as dark racing clouds swept in from the Atlantic. He should have been enjoying his retirement by now. It had been offered but he decided to stay on for these last couple of years as though reluctant to relinquish the power he held with the present Government despite knowing the State was in safe hands. But the thought of being put out to grass in his perception was completely alien.

He turned to look at his companion. She sat straight-backed, staring straight ahead. It had been no untruth when he earlier told her she was pretty. She was very attractive, fresh faced and with an engaging smile that reminded him of his Beth when she was young. His life was nearly spent while hers was in its prime. He desperately wanted her to come through alive. He had seen enough of the bloodletting, the tear stretched faces of widows clutching children to them in support at several of the funerals he had attended since becoming Minister.

He watched as the lead car turned off the gravelled road to follow a dusty trail towards the firing range, the driver sounding his horn at the slow moving, battered pick-up truck that preceded, watched as the truck pulled over to let the car pass. Then, as the lead car drew level, gasped in horror as a great white sheet of flame erupted from the side of the truck. A microsecond later they heard the sound of the explosion, a deep ear-splitting blast of noise that swept over them. Vi was stunned into mute silence by the sheer violence of the explosion. She looked in horror at the scene that lay in front of them, a cloud of black smoke rising over the two vehicles. Rubenstein was the first to react, "It's an ambush, turn the car round and get out of here", he screamed at the driver. 'Earlobes' seemed not to hear at first, both hands gripping the wheel so hard, the veins stood out. He then slammed the car into reverse, the wheels spinning, throwing up great clouds of dust and grit before gripping. The driver had underestimated the speed at which the car sped back. With a bone jarring thump the back wheels dropped into a deep culvert that ran alongside the road. He swore and banged his fist against the dash when the car refused to budge. He turned to look at the two of them sitting at the back. "I'll take a look to see if I can shift it. If not, I'll call over one of the other cars". The Minister was impatient. "Just get a move on, for God's sake", the normally staid voice breaking into a harsh command. They both watched the driver jump out to disappear round the back of the car, then turned their attention back to the conflagration taking place further up the road.

There was a further explosion as the car's fuel tank erupted in a ball of flame, even inside their car with the windows closed it did not prevent them from hearing the chilling scream of a man in agony. Suddenly, their view was eclipsed as a black Seat saloon pulled up hard in front of them, scattering loose chippings from the road, some of which rattled against their windows. There was something vaguely familiar about the black clad figure that leapt out of the front seat and ran towards them. Her heart surged with joy when she realised it was none other than Al, but almost immediately her emotions changed to one of dread. In his right hand the light glinted dully from the black barrel of an automatic pistol. Their driver looked up, startled to see the man running towards them. Swearing, he dropped professionally to his knees, pulling out a gun from his shoulder holster in one swift movement. He never had a chance to use it, the weapon in Al's hand spat fire twice. From where she sat immobilised by fear, Vi felt the impact as the rounds slammed into 'earlobes' broad chest. She watched as the man's blood, coming from his mouth, toppled slowly backwards into the ditch. She felt transfixed as though she were witnessing events in a bad dream as the car door was opened and the still smoking barrel of Al's gun was aimed at the frail figure beside her. But feeling the man tense up made her realise only too clearly she was about to see the man killed. "Please God, no Al", she heard herself screaming in a voice she did not recognise as her own.

Chapter 21

They were roused out of bed earlier than they wished. Twice before nine in the morning the chambermaid knocked on their door asking if they wished to go down for breakfast, although Al suspected it was more a case of her wanting to clean the room early. He looked over at his dozing partner. Todd lay flat on his back with his mouth half open, the stillness of the room broken only by the rasping breathing. "Todd, wake up, you lazy bugger. We've got a job to do". The eyes blinked open. "You're right. I'm finding it hard to sleep since we were woken earlier". He raised himself up on one elbow to look across at Al. "In fact, she must be about due to knock on our door again, so, are you game for a paella and black coffee breakfast?"

After breakfast Todd set to work on the remote detonating device. Even though he would not admit it, he still had doubts about whether it would detonate the explosives at the range he envisaged. It was soon time for them to trek up into the hills to the garage where hopefully they would find Todd's truck in working order. The same fat mechanic in greasy overalls, who had taken on the task, greeted them. He wore a broad grin as they approached. "The motor, she work good, just like new", he said in a tobacco stained voice full of enthusiasm. "I doubt that very much", replied Al dryly, "but turn the motor over and we'll see if you are right Senor". The engine was slow in starting but settled down to a steady if noisy rhythm after a few moments, which was the signal for the mechanic to stick out a grubby hand to ask for the remainder of the money he was owed.

The sun was way past its strength and beginning to dip towards the far horizon when Todd drove back down the track in the battered truck, leaving a plume of dust in their wake. Todd was looking quite pleased with himself. "Don't worry, I'm sure that this old lady will make it on time tomorrow". Al was not sure he held the same view but thought better than to voice his fears. Instead, there were other things on his mind. "We still have to locate and load some tomatoes on board before we're finished today. What's your peseta position?" Todd shook his head. "I'm not sure, but don't forget all we need are tomatoes that have missed the market. They should be cheap". Their task turned out easier than expected. The first village they came upon were able to provide ample produce that was in various stages of decay.

Parking the wagon up, they immobilised it by removing the rotor arm and caught a bus back to Las Palmas. Al was pleased. The one thing he had been fighting all along since the inception of his plan was Father time and now it looked as though it was one battle they had won. One battle, but the war was yet to come. Tomorrow would lay bare all their hopes and aspirations. By this time in the coming day, it would be known just how they had fared. He felt the tension building up deep inside as he gazed at the countryside flashing past. Todd sat in silence next to him, also seeming absorbed by the vista of Gran Canaria, but it was obvious his mind was elsewhere and busy. "Al", he said slowly, after several minutes had elapsed. "I want you to promise me one thing. If anything should happen to me, promise me that you will take care of Tracy". "Don't worry about a thing, you know that goes without saying, but let's be positive and say that nothing is going to happen to either of us". Up until now it was something that had not been discussed. It was something that had always been there in the subconscious, but both were loathe to bring it out. The thought of dying was too morbid but at the same time when playing for big stakes they knew the cost of failure could be precisely that.

Once back at the hotel they went once more over their plans for the morrow. Todd was happy with the device he had constructed and if he had any doubts about whether it would detonate the claymores, he kept them to himself. They would leave early in the morning, conceal the explosives amongst the tomatoes on the truck and leave it parked just off the road leading to the rifle range. Todd would detonate it from a safe distance as the Minister drove by. Al would then pick him up, drive off and make good their escape. It all sounded too simple, too logical almost to work, but it was the one with the best chance of succeeding. They toasted each other with a glass of cheap Spanish brandy before turning in for their last night in the hotel. It was still reasonably early, but tomorrow would be a long day.

Al woke first and beat Todd to the shower, washing first in warm water and then switching it to cold, letting the water cascade over him until he was almost shivering. Stepping out to towel himself down he felt invigorated, his mind sharp and his body refreshed. While Todd was taking his shower, Al carefully packed his clothes but not before taking out a slim package which had been concealed in the bottom of the case. It was another reason why he had chosen to travel by ship, knowing that there would be no X-ray scanner to pinpoint the Walther PPK he now turned over in his hands. Carefully stripping it down he cleaned each moving part, lightly oiling each component piece before reassembling and inserting a full clip of 9 mm rounds. He put a further two clips into his jacket pocket and tucked the gun into his waistband. They both had a light breakfast before checking out. Neither felt like eating but it made sense to get something into their stomachs.

By 9.30 a.m they were watching the taxi which had deposited them by the side of the road disappear back towards Las Palmas. Across the road from them stood the garage where they had arranged to pick up the hire car. Quickly completing the formalities they drove off to where they had parked the truck the day before. They were both relieved to see it was just as it had been left, nothing seemed to have been touched. It was a lonely spot that was not overlooked by any habitation. Todd set to work installing the claymore mines, positioning them so they faced away from the truck. Al kept watch while his partner made sure the mines were completely concealed, but not overdoing it on the amount of tomatoes placed over them. When they detonated he wanted to make sure that they achieved the maximum effect. Al peered down the road they had travelled to reach this spot. Nothing stirred except for the slight breeze, which rustled the leaves of a nearby tree. It was a perfect morning. The only noise that reached his ears was the distant drone of an aircraft coming in to land at Las Palmas airport. The tap on the shoulder from Todd almost startled him. "Well, that's all set up and I do think it is going to work. How much time do we have?" Al glanced at his wrist. "We will leave in ten minutes. That should put us at the entrance to the rifle range at about 10.15 a.m, which is not too early but at the same time you will still be able to park up off the road and get in a position to detonate the mines". Al noticed the flicker of doubt or was it anxiety cross the man's eyes. "If we had parked the pick up some time earlier there was a good chance of Mossard investigating and discovering the mines. This way it will only be a matter of thirty minutes or so before the Minister's car passes that point". "You are probably right", Todd replied, shuffling from one foot to the other, a nervous habit he had never managed to cure. Al continued, "I know we have covered this ground before but don't forget once you have pressed the button, get the hell out of there, don't wait to see what damage you have done, just get back to me where I will be waiting in the car". Todd gave a slow smile. "Believe me, I will be back to that car before the echoes have died away". It was time to go. They both clasped hands in a firm handshake. There was no need for a show of continental emotion, it was not their way, and the handshake said it all.

Al breathed a sigh of relief as the pick up started, then jumped into his own car to follow at a safe distance of 200 yards. They drove along the narrow twisting roads at a leisurely pace, only increasing their speed when they joined the main highway heading South. There was surely still plenty of time when Todd arrived at the dusty road leading up to the rifle range. Al slowed down looking for a place to park. As he did so, he was overtaken in rapid succession by four shining black saloons. He only managed a fleeting glimpse of the occupants but it was enough to make him press his foot back down on the accelerator. When he saw the cars in front indicate, they were turning up the road that Todd had just taken. It confirmed his worst fears. The Minister had arrived early. It would be impossible for Todd to implement his plan. Al felt almost dizzy with disbelief, his head swam at the thought of all their carefully laid plans coming to nothing and all for the want of arriving just an hour earlier. He swore loud and long as he watched the lead car in front of him begin to overtake Todd, the car wore the flag of Israel.

If Mo Johnston was concerned about the Minister's safety, there was not a sign of it on his face as he climbed into the car to sit beside Harry Reynolds. If anything, his thoughts were more about his own. He knew that there was a chance it was far more likely their own car could be subject to attack, rather than the one containing the Minister. Still, swapping cars and re-arranging the time schedule was his idea and he did not give Jenkins much chance of a hit, in fact he almost felt contemptuous of the man. There was also the added bonus of getting the long sought after promotion he yearned for at the conclusion of this successful mission. He and Harry spoke little on the journey to the road leading to the rifle range. They were both too professional for that, each observing their own areas of observation, scanning both the cars in front and behind.

As they approached the road leading up to the range, Harry was the first to notice the dilapidated pick up truck moving slowly along. "I don't remember seeing any tomato fields up that way", he said suspiciously. Mo sounded almost bored when he replied. "There could be in the valleys beyond". Mo continued. "But keep your weapon at the ready as we pass". The car turned into the bumpy dusty road. "O.k. Harry, time to turn on our box of tricks". His colleague snapped open the black leather briefcase that lay on the seat between them. It revealed a sophisticated radio signalling scanning device, which sent out powerful beams along preset frequencies at a very rapid rate, although relatively new it had performed well on tests and was once responsible for detonating a device, which had been concealed in a culvert on the West Bank. With the rise in the number of remote controlled bombs that terrorists were now using, Mossard had developed an effective tool in pre-empting them.

Harry switched it on just prior to them overtaking the pick up. He stared at the cab of the other vehicle. There was something wrong, the man's face was in shadow but his arm resting on the window frame was pale. Of course, that was it. If it were a genuine local tomato worker it would have been a dark swarthy brown. Despite Mo sitting next to him, he found himself screaming a warning as at the same time he reached with one hand to switch off the scanner while the other was already opening the door nearest to him. The hospital told him later that it was this last action that had saved him, the force of the explosion had blown open the door and him through it, while Mo had shielded him to a large extent being on the side closest to the pick up. Dozens of red-hot ball bearings had thudded into the car and Mo's body, but he was lying several feet away when the car caught fire and exploded. He had not come through unscathed however. He was concussed and there were three steel balls lodged in him, one in the shoulder and two in his legs. He was fast losing consciousness while in the distance he thought he heard gunfire. Before he finally blacked out he was to remember the prophetic words of the instructor when they were first introduced to the scanner. "Don't ever forget, this device can be a double edged weapon".

Chapter 22

Al had no clear idea of what choice of action he could undertake when he set off in pursuit of the four shining limos, other than a desire to retrieve the situation no matter how hopeless it looked. He had to admit with a sense of grudging admiration that Mossad always seemed to be one step ahead of them; whichever way they turned they were outguessed.

He felt the adrenalin pumping as he closed up on the rear car. He watched the leading car begin to overtake Todd when the devastating explosion occurred. The force ripped away the cab from the ageing pick up in a maelstrom of flying debris. There was no doubt that in the violence of the blast, Todd's life had ended. He slowed down as he watched the fiercely burning vehicles and felt a terrible rage build up inside him. They had been through so much together that it almost seemed cruel that Todd's life should end this way. Although it was possible that he had taken the Minister's life with his own, he felt someone must pay for the death of his friend.

The rear car had stopped, reversed and stuck in a ditch. The driver matched the description of Todd's earlier attacker. He was convicted and sentenced in Al's mind, even as he came shuddering to a halt. He ran over and caught him reaching for a gun. Two bullets into his chest put him on his back while out of the corner of his eye; Al noticed the two pale staring faces in the rear seats of the car. The sudden realisation of who they were brought an audible gasp to his throat. Viola?! Sitting next to Rubenstein whom he thought had been caught in the explosion up the road. Still, now was the chance to finish him off once and for all. He had the means in his hand. He opened the door and brought his weapon up to aim straight at the man's heart. He found he could not bring himself to look into the man's eyes as he slowly squeezed the trigger. Viola's heart rendering cry caused him to involuntarily snatch the gun up sending the bullet to tear through the thin fabric and metal of the roof. He looked at her and saw the anguish on her face, a face in torment as he saw the conflicting emotions battle within. On the one side was the love she had for him, while on the other was her revulsion that she may witness the death of the man sitting next to her. This side proved the stronger. "Just leave Al, please", she implored. Al switched his gaze to his quarry who stared impassively back without uttering a word. It was as if the noise of the gun in the confined space of the car had deafened him. In the distance Al could hear the crackling noise coming from the two burning vehicles, but more ominously close to him came the sound of running feet, followed closely by the crack of an automatic pistol. A bullet ricocheted off the dusty ground close beside him. He fired off a quick shot in their direction, he didn't expect to hit them, more to spoil their aim and ran for his car. Ducking and swearing he slammed the door closed just as the first rounds hit the car. Two round neat holes appeared on the windscreen and exited through the back. Al spun the car round and roared off down the bumpy trail back towards the main highway. He watched in his rear view mirror the two figures who had been taking a shot at him, run back to their car. He knew they were not about to give up on him just yet. Al watched with some satisfaction the dust cloud he was creating, with a little luck his pursuers would not know which way he turned when he hit the main road. His instinct almost made him turn the wheel in the direction of the relative safety towards the urban sprawl of Las Palmas, which was just what the people behind him would also guess, so instead he turned the car South and quickly built up the revs to increase the distance between him and those whose feelings towards him could not be called friendly.

The well-travelled route into the south of the island took him past San Augustin with its black volcanic sand and into the concrete playground of Playa Del Ingles. In the distance the sun sparkled on a blue sea. People lay prostate in the sun, with maybe the only thought in their minds was over which type of food to choose for their lunch. Al knew his life hung on a knife's edge. If only he could exchange with one of those contented suntan oil covered bodies, he wouldn't hesitate for a moment. The road narrowed as he left the urban area of holidaymakers' dreams to head along a more winding route which followed the coastline. Like the car, his mind was racing. How could he escape from the island without being detected even if he managed to elude those following him. On one of the rare long stretches of road he had glimpsed what looked suspiciously like one of the Mossad cars in the distance. After a few more miles his worst fears were confirmed. It was one of their cars and it was gaining on him. He was approaching what was once a picturesque village that hugged the coastline but had since grown into another tourist trap with modern villas sprawling up the sides of the valley that enclosed it. Ahead he could see the roads were narrow and congested and at an intersection there was a police car parked up. He knew it would be folly to keep heading in that direction. Down on his left he caught a glimpse of yachts riding at anchor in a sheltered marina. An idea of what course of action he could take was already forming in his mind.

Taking the first turning left, he knew there could be no turning back. Those following him would soon realise he had left the main road, but at least this way it gave him several precious minutes to try and execute his plan. Adjacent to the marina there was a large car park. It was fortunate as he could park his car amongst the others, which would give him more breathing space before it was noticed. He backed it in between two others, locked it up and began walking slowly towards the sound of water, the slender masts of the boats outlined against a clear blue sky. Running at this stage would only draw attention to himself. He passed lithe young sunburned bodies and more elderly men sporting a variety of hats with accents of Northern Europe predominant.

Down on the wooden pier against which several boats were moored, he paced slowly along glancing at each in turn, the second from the last in line was what he was looking for. The owner had carelessly left the keys in the ignition. Al swiftly glanced about him to make sure that he was not being observed, bent down to quickly unfasten the boat's moorings, slid them over

the side where they splashed softly in the water and stepped quickly onto the wooden deck of the boat. He pondered before switching on the engine on whether it would fire, could there be a fuel stopcock or other switch to be thrown before it would work. He turned the key, nothing, then tried again with the same result. The gap between the dock and the boat was growing wider. If he didn't get it started soon there was no doubt it would draw attention to himself. Slowly he eased forward the control throttles and tried the ignition once more. With a great sense of relief he felt the engine throb into life below his feet. Increasing the power he steered the vessel towards the harbour's entrance. So far so good, he was expecting to hear at any moment shouts and howls of outrage from behind him on the dock, but he was not tempted to look back. The yacht was gliding easily over the water towards the open sea. He reached the entrance passing on the starboard side, the breakwater of massive concrete blocks while to port where the harbour wall ran out it was surmounted by a small control tower. He peered at it as he sailed by, looking for signs of activity to suggest his theft had been discovered but the only signs of life were two elderly looking fishermen casting their lines into the sluggish current. He was out.

With each passing metre of sea that the sleek vessel sailed over Al could feel some of the tension easing away, but at the same time he knew that there were still several hours of daylight left in which he stood a good change of being caught. He stole a look over his shoulder at the coastline behind him. It was receding but not fast enough for his liking. It was time to think where he could head. At the moment he was just steering away from land, it was time to find a chart, at least he knew how to read a compass. He lashed down the wheel and went forward into the cockpit quickly finding a chart of the area. After looking over it for a short time he knew exactly which course he could set. It just surprised him that he had not thought of it sooner. Distance was a limiting factor as at the moment the boat was still underway on its motor, until he thought he could master the sails.

Just to the Northeast past the island of Fuerteventura lay Tenerife the island where Kristina lived. He had promised to give her a call, although it was to have been under rather different circumstances. He mentally congratulated himself but on looking over the side at the swirling water surging past, it brought home to him how much he still had to do. The wind was coming from a favourable direction for where he was heading, so he went forward to raise the foresail, then slowly winding on the windlasses he raised the main sail, keeping it firmly reefed against the wind. He would rather lose way than take the chance of losing the mast or even capsizing her. But she was a fine vessel, built in Holland and with the sails raised she steered herself through the water cutting down on the uneasy motion that he had been experiencing previously, which was giving him a sense of nausea. Killing the engine, he stared ahead into the distance where the hazy shape of Fuerteventura could just be seen hugging the horizon.

The adrenaline had stopped pounding in his brain. He drew in deep draughts of the moist laden ocean air and turned to look at the island he was leaving behind. He could still make out the faint smidgen of smoke that rose from the two burning vehicles. It marked the funeral pyre of his trusting, loyal and devoted family man that he was, but unlucky pal Todd. Al felt his eyes stinging and it was not from the occasional sea spray that whipped over the bows. He resolved then and there that every penny that was left in the Swiss bank account would be transferred to Todd's joint account that he held with his wife. If she were sensible she would not go short. As for himself, he cursed loudly at his hesitation at not blowing away Rubenstein when he had the chance. There would be no pay-day for him but just a life of constantly looking over his shoulder, wondering if a Mossad thug was on his tail.

His stomach was growling. He realised it was hours since he had anything to eat. There must be food on the boat somewhere. Going through the cockpit he then entered the forward cabin, the highly varnished wood contrasting with the untidy scene that greeted his eyes. The mess table in the centre was covered with dirty plates and cups. There were also several dirty wine glasses, clothes were scattered on the deck in profusion, the whole cabin stank of alcohol. He reached behind him to latch the door open before going further into the dim interior when he saw something that caused him to gasp. Lying on one of two bunk beds was the form of a woman. A young, attractive woman, completely naked except for the empty wine bottle clutched to her bosom.

Chapter 23

It had been an hour since the two Mosard agents had located Jenkins car where he had left it in the car park. It was time to report in. Reluctantly the taller of the two reached for the handset of the radio. There was nothing to report, they had drawn a blank. They had searched thoroughly around the car park and the immediate vicinity but there had been no sign or sightings of Jenkins, the guy had just vanished. He was told to enlist the help of the local police and to keep on searching.

There was one other bit of news to pass on as well, they had just received notification from the hospital that Mo Reynolds had died from the injuries he had received, but Harry was expected to recover quickly. The Defence Minister was badly shaken up but otherwise was unharmed. He replaced the mike of the car radio with a puzzled expression on his face as his colleague wandered up. "So what news do they have for us. Is it bad?" he said, leaning against the side of the car, pulling a pack of cigarettes from his pocket. The tall man, Simon Levy, took his time in answering. He had been assigned as Ben Rubenstein's personal bodyguard for some four years now and nobody had ever been that close to killing the Minister, but what puzzled him was he could have been killed according to the information he had just received but wasn't. He became aware of his pal looking at him with a questioning gaze. "The news is bad and good. First, Mo Reynolds is dead and the driver of Ben's car was also killed but for some strange reason the assassin did not kill the Minister". His pal sucked on his cigarette and then said with a hint of sadness in his voice. "So, they got old Mo. I knew he would take one risk too many, that was a man who was never going to pick up his pension. Still, Rubenstein is still with us. I guess the bastard who killed his driver panicked before he had time to shoot him as well".

Simon was just about to make his reply when the sound of raised voices from the direction of the Marina intruded. He ought to investigate. With a signal to the other man they walked swiftly towards the sound of the commotion. As they approached they saw a small knot of people at the centre of which was a deeply tanned broad-chested blonde haired man who was talking loudly to a police officer and gesticulating towards the open sea. People were crowding around listening. The two Mossad agents joined the throng. The agitated man was speaking in English, which to Simon's ears sounded like a Dutch accent. "I tell you I do not lie, my yacht has been stolen from the Marina and my girlfriend is still asleep on it. You must do something quickly". He shouted loudly. The policeman did not appear to be too concerned but he did speak into his radio and then tried to reassure the raging Dutchman in his broken English that a search would be made as soon as possible.

Simon turned to his colleague. "You know what that means. Our man has pinched a boat and is out there in the open sea somewhere". The other man just spread his hands in a gesture of finality. "No wonder we could not find him. Still it should not be long before he is picked up by the Police". Simon looked doubtful. "Somehow I don't think we have heard the last of Jenkins and I would not be surprised if he gets away". They both walked slowly back towards their car. Already the temperature was dropping as the shadows lengthened; the day was drawing to a close.

Far out over the water the wind was being kind to Jenkins, staying in the same quarter and pushing the sailboat onwards towards the distant shores of Tenerife. He stood transfixed, staring at the female form that lay on the bunk bed. She was a fine specimen of woman with an hourglass figure and a tan that showed the benefit of many days of lying in the sun. But his first thoughts were that he had stumbled in on a corpse until he noticed the gentle rise and fall of her perfectly formed breasts, given the fact that the cabin also stank of alcohol it was fair to assume that the lady had been on a bender the night before.

As though she became conscious of his gaze, her eyelids suddenly fluttered open and her eyes met those of Jenkins, she gave a high-pitched scream and threw the bottle she had been clutching in the general direction of Jenkins. Al ducked the missile, which landed with a crash behind him, picked up a discarded bed sheet and threw it over to the hysterical woman. His action quickly dispelled her fears causing her to stop screaming as she clasped the sheet to her bosom. "Who the hell are you, get out of here", she raved at him. Al did as he was told, there seemed no point in antagonising her at this stage, he had enough on his hands sailing the boat. As he closed the door behind him something heavy hit it with a thud. He would have to face her later but more urgent matters demanded his attention. As he came on deck the wind had changed enough to leave the sails flapping, the boat had lost its way. He set about resetting the sails until once more the bows of the vessel cut cleanly towards the distant island of Tenerife. The deep blue of the sea had changed to a more sinister grey with the onset of nightfall but of that he was grateful. The police would now be out in force looking for him and the woman below decks. The cover of darkness was just what he needed to try to remain undetected. His original plan had been to sail to Tenerife and lie low for a couple of days with Christina, but now the more he thought about it there was a good chance he may get caught plus it would also implicate Christina. There had to be another way. He thought long and hard and in doing so staring out to sea he failed to notice the nimble woman crawling up the steps from the cabin. If he had he would have noticed that in her right hand she held a long curved knife and her face wore an expression of hate and determination. The sound of the sea rushing by masked her approach until he saw her suddenly rise up and lunge at him with the knife. He instinctively ducked but was not quick enough to avoid the blade, which slashed through the top of his left arm. She drew her arm back again aiming for his midriff. Years of training in the Marines came to his rescue, he instinctively parried with his left and then followed through with a straight arm palm first to her face, it was more effective than a punch, the idea to off balance the attacker. It did. She fell backwards with a cry and landed heavily on the deck, the knife flying from her hand to splash harmlessly in the sea. He knelt down beside her and raised her head gently, she gave a groan, the fight had gone out of her. It was obvious when she spoke softly. "Look, if you are going to kill me get it over with, don't play with me". Al was surprised to hear that the woman was in fear of her life. "You have got it all wrong, it's true I stole this boat but I had no idea that there was anyone on board. I did not set out to kidnap you", he said reassuringly. She did not look totally convinced as he helped her to her feet but allowed him to guide her down the steps back into the cabin with his arm around her waist.

She sat on her bed wearing shorts and a blouse, watching Jenkins as he cast about looking for something to eat, the original reason for going below. "So, why did you steal the boat? You must know that you won't get very far", she said in a voice that was close to normal. Al retrieved some bread and cheese from the back of a cupboard before replying. "Someone wants me dead back in Las Palmas, it became expedient for me to leave by the first available means which happened to be your boat". She looked hard at him. "So it was not the Police who were really after you originally". "That's right", he said, as he cut some slices off the loaf, changing the subject he went on, "Would you like some of this?", proffering the bread towards her. She did not have to think long. "After last night I could eat anything". He cut and buttered a few more slices, arranged them on a plate with cheese and carried them over to where she sat on the bed. They both ate ravenously for several minutes in total silence before she turned to him. "Well, that has filled a hole, all I need now is a refreshing shower after which I will expect you to tell me exactly when you plan to let me get off". Al nodded vaguely, gave her arm a reassuring squeeze and made his way up on deck to check the vessel's position.

They were making good progress up the western coast of Tenerife Island which was now only discernable as a black smudge interspersed with twinkling lights. He thought he heard the sound of a helicopter in the distance at one stage, but it soon faded away to leave them alone on the glittering sea. He intended to sail between the islands of Lanzarote and Tenerife and head east towards the coast of Africa. When still in sight of the islands he would launch the boat's dinghy with the girl in it, once the authorities discovered her, it may take some off the heat off him. Lashing the wheel once more he decided it was time to inform her of her intended departure, he caught her just as she stepped out of the shower donning a robe to cover her nakedness. She put her fingers to her nose as he moved closer. "I think it is about time you took a shower as well, you stink", she said with disdain. Al laughed. "Maybe I will take your advice, then I'll tell you how you are going to get off this boat".

He quickly stripped his clothes off in the corner of the cabin, conscious she was observing him out of the corner of her eye. Wrapping a towel about his waist he stepped over to the shower, but before closing the plastic curtains he looked over to where she sat on the bunk drying her long blonde hair. "Don't get any ideas about using the radio, I've immobilised it". She smiled mysteriously. "Don't worry, I have no idea where we are, if I did use it." He showered quickly, deciding it would not be wise to leave her to her own devices for long. When he emerged she was still on the bed but now had adopted a reclining position, in her right hand she held a whisky glass. She raised it to her lips giving it a swirl as she saw him.

Al distinctly heard the rattle of ice, it was a sound he liked. She pointed a well manicured finger towards a cabinet at the forward end of the cabin. "Help yourself, there's quite a selection". "At the moment any drink will do" Al replied as he surveyed the rows of bottles before deciding to choose a blue label Smirnoff. He gave himself a generous portion before moving over to join her on the bunk. "Well, you and I will be parting company before long if the wind holds up". She sat up and moved closer to him, he had her attention now. "Are you going to make me walk the plank?" she said with a mocking smile. Al told her his plans for her intended departure. She took it well. "As long as I get my feet back on dry land tonight I won't hate you too much. What a holiday! Being kidnapped and then set upon the empty sea in a small boat! She rose, went to fix herself another drink and then came back to where he sat.

The naked flesh of her smooth shoulder touched his own as she settled herself on the bed, it was if there were an electric current running through her. Al felt the tingle and it went all the way to his groin. He picked up the hair brush she left on the bed and ran it through her hair with a couple of strokes. She turned her head to peer into his eyes. "and just what do you think your game is." She said slowly but without a hint of malice. His face split into a broad grin. "We must have you looking your best when you step ashore." He continued using the brush with long slow strokes, with his free hand he gently held her head to counteract the brushing, she raised no objection, her eyes looked dreamy.

She let herself lean against him while with her left hand stroked the fine hairs on his upper thigh that was as sensual as it was gentle. Al abandoned the brush in favour of using his hand to glide through the blond locks and down onto the nape of her smooth neck. She gave out an almost inaudible sigh and slowly, teasingly slid her hand further up his leg until it made contact with his now erect manhood. Her long slim fingers delicately playing and exploring that part of his anatomy she had never seen. He let his hand glide down to cup the perfectly formed breast while at the same time pressing his lips to hers, he felt her tongue darting in and out. Slowly peeling the robe off her she allowed him to push her back onto the bed, she wore nothing underneath. Dropping the towel, Al gently eased himself on her, she gave a stifled cry as he penetrated her moist flesh. They moved and rocked slowly together in time to the boats motion. The sound of water lapping against the hull seemed to stir a basic emotion from the time they were both in the womb. It was not long before their movement far outstripped that of the boats, she writhed under him the long fingernails leaving red streaks done his back. Her eyes opened wide suddenly. "You bastard, you're raping me and I'm loving it don't stop." It was the signal for him to arch his naked body hard against her, they both groaned in the final fusion. She shouted something in Dutch and then said in a more normal tone. "God, that was good, you bastard." He gave her an affectionate kiss although they both knew that their love making was not so much due to love and affection. But more as a result of the danger and trepidation that they both found themselves in. It added that spark, that extra element of fear of the unknown as they sailed through the dark night towards an uncertain fate. Al felt the wooden deck beneath his feet tilt over at sharper angle than it had previously which served to remind him that it was time to check their position. They were still standing well out to sea from the island but the wind had freshened, he took in some of the sail as there was always the chance of being caught out in a sudden squall. Unlashing the wheel he began steering the vessel towards the distant north point of the island of Tenerife.

Maybe it was the darkness that made the distance appear far greater than it was as within two hours they were approaching the northern tip of Tenerife. It would be soon time for his sailing companion to depart.

"Hey, you down there below decks." He called out. The door at the bottom of the steps leading to the cabin opened. She stood there, silhouetted against the light streaming out behind her, illuminating the golden tresses that fell in a cascade to her shoulders. "Time for me to walk the plank, I suppose." She muttered. He nodded in return. "In half an hour we will be very close to shore, and the tide is coming in so you won't have any problems."No, but you will when they catch you." He turned his face from her to watch the approaching coastline and spoke quietly almost to himself. "I don't have a lot to live for, so in a way I don't really care." The water slapped and gurgled along the boats side, the wind moaned softly through the rigging and when he turned to look at her again she had already gone inside. When she emerged some time later it was with two holdall bags and wearing her waterproof clothing that did not quite manage to disguise the curves of her body. They worked in silence getting the rubber dingy ready and loading it up before gently lowering it over the side. He helped her clamber into the fragile craft, kissed her softly on the lips and pushed the boat away. He shouted across the widening gap of water between the two boats."Maybe you will think twice before lying in after a skinfull next time." She laughed. "I doubt it, look after the boat even if it is insured, farewell my love." " He called back "And safe passage to my fair one." She shipped out her oars and began pulling towards the shore. Before long she was lost to view in the darkness.

But he still stood there gripping the handrails tightly staring towards the distant twinkling lights on the shore. But there would be no escape for him that way, wearily he pointed the bow towards the open sea, towards the east knowing full well the next landfall in that direction was the coast of west Africa. But it was the only option open to him. His previous plan of going ashore in Tenerife to lie low with Christina would have stood had it not been complicated by finding the woman aboard. Her presence meant the police were looking for a kidnapper and not just some boat thief, it meant that they would be much more diligent. But with a fair wind he could be over the horizon by dawn, he had told his shipmate that he was heading for Lanzerote so they would look there first. Although it was possible that he could be picked up on radar he suddenly realized. Walking over to the mainmast he lowered the radar reflector on its lanyard, it might just help his chances of escaping detection. It was now time to clear his mind, after the distraction of the girl on board, to plan what he could do next it was strange but he realized that he did not even know the girl's name, he looked back over his shoulder to the now distant island as though the answer might be provided.

Now that he had left the islands behind the swells out on the open ocean were much higher and the wind was increasing in strength. The yacht was tilting over at a much sharper angle but he was loath to take in sail. He needed to make as much speed as was possible despite every now and then huge waves breaking over the bows. He clung to the bucking wheel to maintain his course. He needed to summon his reserves of energy as the night crept on and the weather closed in. By now his eyes were stinging with salt and the deck was awash. He knew that he would have to bring the sails down or there was a very real danger the vessel would capsize. He had just begun to turn into the wind when it happened. With a tremendous crack the mainsail split from top to bottom. He dropped the tattered sail, and then brought the yacht back on course with great difficulty with the foresail to push him on out of danger. He gripped the wheel and thought of the bleak future that lay before him. There was some money left in the Swiss account but he had already decided that if he were to get out of this alive he would send the bulk of the remaining funds to Simon Todds widow. It was the very least he could do. The thought of his friend lying dead back on the island did nothing to cheer him up. Todd must have seen the saloon car with its flag passing him and pressed the detonate button which would have exploded both mines. That depressed Al even further as Todd would not have been aware the Minister was not in that car. Al thought that if his life were to end out here amid the storm tossed waves, perhaps he would welcome it.

He sensed it first before seeing it and when he did it was as though his heart missed a beat and his legs turned to jelly. Coming directly towards his port quarter no more than 300 metres away was a wall of blackness even darker than the night surrounding it, at the base of which was a seething mass of white water. He recognised it at once for what it was, a massive supertanker which obviously was not aware of his presence for as it surged towards him there was no reduction of speed or variation in course. He frantically threw the tiller over but with limited sail the boat was slow to answer the helm. With terrifying speed the huge vessel was eating up the distance between them, then just as he was about to draw clear the wind was taken from the sails by the sheer size of the crude carrier bearing down on him. The sickly smell of crude oil permeated the air, while the heavy thump of the engines carried across the water to him despite the roar of the gale. There were no alternatives left open, with his life vest on he stepped up onto the side of the doomed yacht and threw himself into the churning seas.

Chapter 24

Second Officer Jim Riley was fed up, extremely fed up, he should have been home in Newcastle, N. E. England with the wife and kids and not standing watch on the bridge of the V.L.C.C. Global Trader in the middle of the night as they sailed south off the coast of Morocco. He should have left the ship when it docked in Rotterdam with a cargo of crude from Das Island in Abu Dhabi, only to be told that his relief was in hospital after a car accident. So he had reluctantly agreed to stay on board. They were making good time doing some 17 knots despite the gale that had blown up over the last couple of hours which brought home to him the overriding reason for his present depression. Although it had been faint he was convinced that within the last 30 seconds they had hit something, it wasn't just another large wave but something more solid. His sense of duty overcame his desire to ignore it, he rang down to the engine room to stop all engines and then reached for the phone to the Captain's cabin reluctantly. The Dutch captain picked it up on the third ring, his voice was heavy with sleep and tinged with slight annoyance after Jim explained why he was stopping the ship."O.K. O.K. bring the ship round and head back, I'll be up on the bridge in ten minutes." In fact it was closer to fifteen by the time he walked through the bridge door accompanied by a blast of cold air. "What have we got Jim, seen anything yet." He demanded brusquely as was his way. Jim lowered the binoculars from his eyes."Nothing to report yet, but there is still some way to go before we reach the position." The skipper Case Bolwerk, muttered to himself and then spoke out loud. " I just hope we have not hit one of the local fishing boats or we will never get to Cape Town." Then as an afterthought added. "We will make one sweep and if there is nothing seen continue on our course." Jim nodded his head."Suit's me Skipper." In the raging gale that was now engulfing them both men thought there was little likelihood of seeing anything. Which is why when the shout came from the starboard lookout that he had sighted something it came as a surprise. The skipper just beat Jim out of the door onto the exposed bridge wing, the wind tore at their clothes. "There, over there." Shouted the lookout and shone a searchlight on a spot about 200 meters away in the blackness. At first none of them could see anything until rising on one of the heavy swells the sea gave forth its secret, a mishmash of broken scattered wood. On some there was no mistaking the bright paintwork of the seas latest victim. The Captain shouted to make himself heard above the gale. "Looks like you were right Jim, maybe a sailing boat. Bring the ship round to put the wreckage on our lee side and we will see if we can spot any survivors ." The huge ship responded slowly but after a while it came round until the wreckage lay on the sheltered side of the vessel. Although it did little to diminish the long sweeping swells. They swept the seas with probing searchlights looking for any sign of life but after a good half an hour there was still nothing to show for their efforts."I'm sorry Jim." Captain Bolwerk said with genuine regret in his voice. "But it looks as though we will have to call it off, I think that anyone who was on that boat will have drowned by now." They were standing on the bridge and even on a ship of its size it was rolling heavily, for anyone out there on the open sea it would have been horrific conditions, no one could possibly last long. Jim was inclined to agree but felt it was worth one last shot."You know Skipper maybe we have been concentrating too much on the leeward side let's make a final sweep on the weather side and if we find nothing we get under way again." The skipper nodded reluctantly. Jim rushed outside before the Captain had time to change his mind and barked orders at the men to sweep the seas on the weather side. The searchlights cut great swathes through the inky night to dance upon the white crests of the rolling swells. Suddenly there was a shout. Jim rushed over to the man and followed his pointing finger, he felt his pulse quicken, there, not more than a few crest tops away the light reflected back from what could only be a lifejacket and more importantly it contained a man's head. They lost him for a few seconds as the man disappeared into the trough but they could confirm it

was defiantly a man when he rose up on the next swell. Jim rapped his orders into the hand held radio and watched as the crew put into effect the drill they had practiced so many times for rescuing a man overboard. The ship's boat was soon launched and brought round to where the man floated. With their skill and dedication two stocky crewmen lifted him slowly dripping from the savage sea.   The man's head dropped down with his chin resting against the life jacket, his arms hung limply from his sides. The eyes were closed there seemed to be no life in the body, as Jim observed the shrivelled skin, he feared the worst. As the boat came along side there was a waiting stretcher .They slowly laid his body in it, the men lifting it having difficulty keeping their feet as the deck moved under them. But they knew there was no time to waste out here on the open deck and swiftly bore their casualty inside to the brightly lit cabin that served as a sick bay. Laying the unconscious man on a bunk Jim Riley felt the man's pulse, he could feel a very faint flicker of life, but bending down over him he could see the man had stopped breathing. If they were to save him they had to move very fast and that meant getting air into the mans lungs before any damage was done to his oxygen starved brain."Quickly." He shouted to one of the seaman standing by."Bring me the oxygen." He gently applied the mask over the man's face and turned on the valve.

Chapter 25

As Al dived over the side from the Dutch yacht he knew his only chance of living was to try to get out of the path of the huge ship that was nearly upon him. Even here in the tropics the water felt icy as it closed over his head, but the life vest soon brought him bobbing to the top. He struck out strongly away from the onrushing vessel driven by that primeval desire to survive. The huge black hull loomed high above him, seconds later there came a terrible splintering crash as the boat was stove in. What had been a graceful yacht was reduced to so much driftwood and swept along the ship's side. He kept pumping with his arms trying to put distance between him and the ship behind. It was one thing to drown but the thought of being sucked into the giant revolving propellers terrified him, his body responded with a massive dose of adrenalin. Suddenly he knew he had survived because although he could not see it due to the salt water blinding his eyes the sound of the ship's engine was receding. He had survived but for how long. The waves were increasing in size, constantly submerging him. His situation was desperate, out here alone in the middle of the Atlantic, miles from anywhere. It was with a feeling of dread at the thought that beneath his kicking feet lay a thousand feet of ocean. But he knew he must try to survive, he owed that much to Todd's widow and children. After an hour he knew it was time to give up trying to keep his head above the rolling waves, he was exhausted. Feeling suddenly very sad that his life should end this way he closed his eyes against the salt spray and let his head rest against the life vest. With the cold and wind he began slipping into unconsciousness when suddenly there seemed to be a bright light. So maybe he was heading into hell, was his last thought before he blacked out.

He came out of the coma with a start, ripping the facemask off he bent over the side of the bunk and emptied the contents of his stomach on the floor. He felt like death but his brain was telling him that wasn't the case. A weather beaten but kindly looking face swam into view and he spoke in English. "We had almost given up on you there for a minute". "I am glad you didn't", Al managed to croak back. "Don't talk now", he spoke softly. "We've got to get you out of these wet clothes and into a nice warm bunk". Al felt helpless as they removed his sodden clothing quickly and efficiently before kitting him up with warm undergarments. They supported him, a man on either side out into a narrow corridor. It was almost as if he were dreaming as they led him into a small cabin and into an inviting bunk in the corner. After a few mouthfuls of hot invigorating soup sleep swept over him, the sleep of the exhausted. There were to be no dreams.

He awoke very slowly, letting his eyes gently take in his new surroundings. Through his single porthole, on the horizon, the sun was slowly sinking into the sea. It did not surprise him as he realized that he had been asleep for nearly ten hours. He still felt groggy but also very hungry so that had to be a good sign, against all the odds he had somehow survived. However, his sudden elation was tempered when he thought over the events of the last twenty-four hours. It had been within his grasp to kill Rubenstein, an extra million dollars to set himself up for life. But with Viola there he just couldn't do it. It just wasn't possible to be a killer with a conscience. He suddenly felt good about himself but the future looked bleak. It was time to take stock of the situation he now found himself in. He was travelling on a ship to God knows where, but still he was alive. His rescuers would have kept his passport and money belt, sodden but intact. Plus his pursuers would be looking for the yacht in which he left harbour on but they would draw a blank there considering it was now on the bottom of the sea. But where did that leave him? He looked out of the small porthole at the sea rushing past, the sea that had let him escape, could it provide inspiration. There was just the possibility it could, in the back of his mind a faint plan was beginning to take shape.

The soft knock on the door interrupted his thoughts. Around the corner of the door popped the head of the officer who had treated him earlier. "How are you feeling now", he enquired. "A bit groggy but glad to be alive", replied Al. The officer pulled up a chair and introduced himself as Jim Reilly, Second Officer on the oil tanker Global Trade en route to dry dock in Japan. He sounded apologetic as he spoke. "I've spoken to the Captain as to whether we could drop you off at Cape Town, but in this game time is money and he is not prepared to do that". He watched Al's face for a reaction, seeing none, he continued. "But we will be stopping at Singapore, you can leave the ship there". "That's fine", said Al, "I am in no hurry". "When we ran you down where were you bound", asked Jim. "Heading for Tenerife, but I was blown off course". The lie came easily to Al. "I don't know how we didn't see you, did your boat carry a radar reflector?". "It did, but don't worry it was fully insured". "You don't sound too angry considering you have lost your boat", said Jim, running a hand through his salt-flecked hair. Al stared out of the porthole before turning to face Jim. "You saved my life, what more could I ask?".

Inwardly he thought he hadn't lost a boat but he had lost his best friend just two days previously, was it just two days, it seemed an age. An age in which so much had happened, so much had past. But would the pain ever past, he thought not. With time the wound may heal but forever there would always be the mental scar.

Over the next few days good food, lots of rest and bracing walks around the decks brought Al back to full health. It was during these walks he would make his way to the bows of the ship. Grasping the handrails he stared toward the distant horizon in solitude while all around lay the changing face of the sea. The horizon was always empty but his thoughts were not, he knew there had to be something at the end of the voyage. But there was no way of knowing what. There could be no going home, no welcoming arms to enfold him. All he had was the clothes he stood up in although it would be possible to draw money from the bank in Singapore before consigning the rest to Todd's widow. But each day brought him closer to landfall; he had watched Table Top Mountain in the distance as they rounded the Cape. A vicious storm had slowed the ship a little; huge green waves breaking over the forecastle had kept him in his cabin for two or three days.

Then as suddenly as the storm arose it past them by leaving its legacy of long undulating swells. Al ventured back on deck to look around, nothing had changed, the vast expanse of the Indian Ocean stretched in all directions. But having studied the charts that morning on the bridge he was aware that several hundred miles North of their present route lay the Island of Mauritius.

It brought back memories of a fantastic two weeks he had once spent there on holiday, a time when he had absolutely no worries. The images came flooding back, an island embraced by a spectacular coral reef transforming the ocean into coastal lagoons, which were laced with golden powder soft coral beaches. He had also explored the interior, going down roads lying through the bougainvillea and flame trees, driving through villages hidden in lush coastal vegetation, plateau towns with charming old colonial houses. Flowers and trees provided a riot of colour and everywhere the green and golden mantel of sugar cane. His fondest memories though were reserved for the unique and diverse peoples of the Island. Beautiful people with soft features, infectious smiles and disarming personalities.

"Hey Al", the shout came from behind him. It was Jim Reilly, they had become firm friends. "Time to eat". Within a few days the Indonesian Islands had been reached, Al was back on deck studying the distant jungle with interest. As it was on one of these islands, Borneo, he had very nearly lost his life. It had been a long time ago but he could still recall it as if it were yesterday.

Chapter 26

It was time to hit back, for months the Indonesian Army had been mounting raids across the Borneo border. Malaysia had asked Britain for help and they were part of it.

They were 42 Commando Royal Marines and their Company was dug in a fortified position just across the border in Sarawak. The Indonesians had been launching attacks from their side of the border and then scuttling back to their base. Lieutenant Nobby Clark and Al had been given the task of finding and devising a way to attack it. They were helped in their task by two Ibans, local tribesmen who were excellent trackers and could smell a cigarette at 200 yards in the jungle. For days the four of them trekked deep into the impenetrable jungle searching for signs and tracks. They were all on tenderhooks not knowing when or if they would bump into the enemy. Then they had their lucky break, some bored Indonesian soldier had scratched his name on a tree trunk. They searched around and soon picked up a trail. By now they were extra cautious as they closed in on the enemy camp. They found it, but stayed out of sight, well hidden. They waited for the rain, as they knew it would every late afternoon. There was a very good reason for this, when the torrential rain arrived it created a fearsome din on the jungle canopy and all the Indonesian soldiers would dash for cover. That would give them the perfect chance to creep right up close to the enemy positions and so it proved to be the case. Nobby and Al crawled to within feet of their objective noting all the details, they could even see the shoulder flashes on the enemy troops. It told them they were up against the 201st Silliwangi Division. They withdrew silently and began their march back to base where they would be debriefed. They had gained a great deal of information but at what cost to their nervous mental state.

Based on their observations, further up the chain of command the orders came down that they were to mount an attack on the enemy base which was over the border and was therefore classified and codenamed Claret. There were to be two companies involved, Al would lead Lima company and Lt. Clark Mike company, in total about 300 Marines. They left in daylight in single file but by the time they crossed the border it had grown dark. Al really had to strain to follow the trail due to the darkness behind him each man had to maintain contact with the one in front by means of a small luminous patch at the rear of each mans jungle hat. They moved very slowly through the forbidding jungle, with each step praying that they would not come up against a trip wire. Even though the night air was cool Al was drenched in sweat. Lt. Clark led his company to attack the enemy camp at the base of the hill while Al led his men to the top positions. They slowly crawled forward on their bellies and even occupied some empty enemy trenches. It was then a case of waiting for the signal to attack which would be just before dawn. As they did so one of the Indonesian sentries strolled over and relieved himself right next to the man on Al"s right, he tried to press his body even further into the damp earth, his heart in his mouth. There could be no mistake about the signal when it came, a huge booming blast of sound preceded by a brilliant flash of white light coming from the lower camp. Its what Nobby and Al had devised after their recce. They had seen that the enemy huts were sandbagged around the base but the roofs were made of wood and rattan leaves, it was their weak point. So they had tied claymore mines to the end of long bamboo poles and laid them gently in position on the roof. It was the sound of these mines detonating, each one sending 700 ballbearings into the sleeping occupants below that they heard now.

They opened fire with everything they had, rifles, machine guns and grenade launchers in a deafening burst of sound, advancing slowly up the hill, the morning gloom lit by a hundred muzzle flashes. The enemy position in front of them erupted into a maelstrom of flying shrapnel and wood splinters .Despite the damage they were inflicting some of the enemy were still firing back, more so when the machine gun next to Al jammed, he quickly flicked his M16 onto automatic to regain the firefight. But not before one of his men went down with a bullet in the leg, he felt a tug on his sleeve a quick look showed a neat round bullet hole, it showed how close he had been to being hit. The noise was deafening but above it orders were shouted to withdraw and regroup. They were a long way from base and they had casualties to take care of. Slowly back down the hill they went watching the whole time to see if the enemy were going to launch a counter attack, it did not come. They retraced their steps for about a mile until they came to a fairly open area. Quickly cutting down the few trees there were they called in a helicopter to lift their casualties. While behind them artillery and mortar fire was called in on the Indonesian positions. It would keep them busy during the medivac. One of the men was missing, they later found out that he had been cut off, refused to

351

surrender, and consequently been shot dead. Other than that they had three wounded, one seriously and that was his friend and mentor Lt. Clark, he had been shot in the stomach .The chopper landed safely and they gently loaded the wounded men in only to hear later that it was not soon enough for Lt. Nobby Clark, who died on the flight. As the Troop Sergeant aptly put it, "You can't chop wood without getting splinters". We were later to find out that the Indonesians had suffered 22 fatalities. Nobby and Al were awarded the same , a Mention in Dispatches but of course Nobby never collected his.

The sun was setting on the distant horizon, a chill wind blew up from the sea. Tomorrow they would dock at Singapore, he shivered and it was not only due to the cold. Next day in his cabin Al suddenly felt the ships engines change in tone, they were slowing down. A glance at his watch showed nearly midday, they had to be approaching Singapore. A quick walk out on deck confirmed it. In the distance the tall serried ranks of Singapore's skyscrapers could be seen, light reflecting off the glass towers. While closer to hand they had been joined by other vessels of various sizes. He could smell the land after all the days at sea, a strange heady mixture almost of decay and rotting vegetation. The water rushing past the ships side had changed from a deep blue to a muddy brown, It was time to go and thank the people who had saved his life and treated him with such kindness, because from now on he was on his own.

The immigration authorities were not pleased at Al's explanation as to how he ended up on the dockside, but with Jim Riley supporting his story they grudgingly gave him a two week visitors visa. The ship was staying overnight while taking on bunkers, giving Jim the chance of enjoying a few hours of well earned shore leave. Al was very glad of the company even if it were just for a limited time. They emerged from the cool customs building into the blinding glare of a hot Singapore afternoon, the humidity was close to ninety percent. Within minutes the sweat was pouring off them, Al waved down a passing yellow and black cab. It screeched to a halt, the two of them jumped quickly into the air –conditioned interior. "Where to, Jonny" the Chinese taxi driver smiled at them. Jim and Al exchanged glances and then spoke almost in unison. "A nice bar, that has plenty of cool beer". After fifteen minutes of hair raising driving through busy streets they pulled up outside a garishly painted building in a quiet street just off Orchard Road. The large neon sign above the entrance spelt "Dragons Bar". Jim laughed. "I hope that does not refer to the women who work here." Al chuckled. "It would not surprise me." The contrast between the bright hot day and inside the bar was total. It was cool and it was dark. It took several minutes for their eyes to get accustomed to the gloom. There were few customers in the dimly lit bar so finding a vacant table was pretty easy.

A bored looking Chinese girl clad in a bright red cheongsam slid gracefully off her bar stool and headed purposely in their direction. They both ordered Tiger tops, a combination of local beer topped up with lemonade. Gulping down the first pint they reordered, The same girl brought them their drinks, then swiftly pulled out a chair to sit between them. "You buy me a drink". She said softly, fluttering her eyelashes. Jim and Al exchanged glances. It was Jim who spoke first. "Why the hell not, we've been starved of female company for quite a while." Jim snorted when he saw the bill. "That's bloody expensive, what are you drinking." He asked noting that her glass was already empty. "Champagne." She replied matter of factly. "Can I have one more." Al was surprised when Jim said yes. They both carried on with their banter while a waiter brought over another drink for the girl. But this time Jim was watching her out of the corner of his eye. Watching as she pressed the glass to her lips. Watching as she brought the glass down to expertly tip the contents into the nearby potted plant. He pretended surprise to see her glass empty. "You must be very thirsty, would you like another drink." Her face split into a broad smile. "Ohh yes, it's a very nice drink thank you." Jim waved aside Al's objections and gave him a wink. The drink was brought over and placed in front of her. Without paying Jim stretched over the table, grasped the drink in his hand and slowly poured it over her head. The liquid cascaded onto her, down her face and into her cheongsam . Standing up Jim muttered "If you don't want to drink it, you can wear it." At first the girl's face was a mixture of shock and disbelief, she then let out a piercing scream. Al jumped up. "Come on Jim, I think we have outstayed our welcome."They both made it through the bar swing doors chased by two angry looking waiters armed with sticks. Quickly hailing a passing cab Jim and Al piled in the back, they sped off without a backward glance. It was then they both convulsed with laughter.

"Did you see that girl's face. Jim chortled, it was well worth the price of those drinks." Al let out a big bellow of laughter. "I've always wanted to do that but never had the guts." Al stopped the taxi at a nearby hotel, he had to stay somewhere for the night. After checking in with a pleasantly smiling receptionist it was time for a farewell drink with Jim in the hotel bar. They made themselves comfortable in a couple of easy chairs and ordered Singapore slings. The drinks were swiftly brought over, they both raised their glasses in salute before taking a deep draw. It was Al who spoke first "Jim there is a saying that there is no rehearsal for life, we have one shot at it, and we have to make the best of it." He paused, watching wistfully as a couple walked by hand in hand. "and when I saw your ship bearing down on me that day I thought I'd had my crack at it and now it's over." He leaned closer over the table towards Jim. "But thanks mainly due to you I have my life back, I don't know what it holds in store but I'm going to make the most of it."

If anything, Jim looked slightly embarrassed. He spoke slowly, carefully choosing his words. "What I did was not unusual, it's the rule of the sea to help a fellow mariner in distress, I just kept to those guidelines." Al laughed, "You and me both know you did a great deal more than that but hey who am I to argue." He turned in his seat to call the waiter over. "Let's get down to some serious drinking, I owe you that at least."

Chapter 27

Al groaned as he turned over on the starched hotel sheets to stare at the bedside digital clock. It was just after 10 in the morning and it felt as though a man with a jackhammer had been let loose in his skull. His mouth was dry and furry, there was only one thing for it he needed to drink gallons of water with some aspirin. As he sat on the side of the bed gulping down water it all came back to him, the events of last night. A smile slowly spread over his face as he recalled their time in the Dragon Bar, he then let out a low chuckle as he remembered Jim later in the hotel bar. The poor guy had risen from his seat to go back to his ship only to totter a few steps across the floor before collapsing in a heap. With help from a couple of waiters they had managed to pour him into the back of a taxi, he made sure the taxi driver knew where to take him. His mood changed to one of sadness at the thought of never seeing Jim again, of never going home again. Perhaps never gazing out of an aircraft window down at the green fields of England on a Heathrow approach. His sombre mood persisted as he took a wash and dressed. But as he turned the key in the lock of his hotel room and headed for the nearby elevator he knew that it was time to banish all negative thoughts. By the time he walked through the revolving doors onto the busy street outside he was back to his normal happy self. Helped in no small part by the beaming smile the petite attractive receptionist had flashed at him. But his main priority was to sort out his finances, thank god that his passport had not been lost, at least he could prove to the bank authorities who he was. It took time, too much time but by three in the afternoon it had all been resolved, a cheque for the bulk of the money from the account would go to Todd's widow, It left him with nearly 10,000 dollars to use. He withdrew a couple of grand, it was time to make plans but not before he had a little fun first. Taking a cab to Orchard road he went shopping for a complete new outfit of clothes and shoes.

Arriving back at the hotel he noticed the same receptionist was on duty, he walked slowly over to claim his key. She gave him the same beaming smile she had earlier. Her name tag bore the legend "Jessica Lim" "You still working Jessica" he said softy, "I am but I finish in half an hour." The way she said it sounded like an invitation to Al. What was there to lose. "Tell you what," He tried to sound casual despite his pulse quickening.

"Why don't you let me take you out for dinner tonight." She glanced around before replying. "I don't see the harm in it, it would be nice but don't tell anyone in the hotel here." She spoke very quietly as if afraid she would be overheard. "We are not supposed to date the guests." Al laughed, "Don't worry, your secret will be safe with me." She lent over the desk and scribbled something on a piece of paper, pushing it over to him she whispered. "Meet me at eight at this address." Al smiled, gave her a nod and headed for the elevator.

Al whistled and hummed to himself as he took a shower and dressed in his new clothes, he felt as if he was reborn. What was the saying "Where there is life there is hope." had a real meaning to him. He had been plucked from the sea to live a new life and he meant to make the most of it. Although a glance in the mirror before leaving the room showed a few flecks of grey hair where there had been none before.

"The Mandarin Hotel, Orchard road." He read off the note to the taxi driver. It took barely 10 minutes to reach his destination. He entered the lobby, it was massive and imposing, its centrepiece a huge sparkling chanderlier. There were several well dressed people scattered around reclining in luxurious easy chairs. One of them now rose and began walking towards him. He barely recognised her at first, it was Jessica. But hardly the Jessica he last saw in the hotel. She was transformed into a vision, tall for a Chinese girl she walked with an easy grace in a slinky white evening dress that showed a lot of bosom, against the white dress the flowing glossy black hair made the perfect contrast. There was genuine warmth in the almond eyes as she came up close to him and whispered "You know I don't even know your name." Al laughed "You are so right, well it's Al, Al Jenkins." She guided him towards one of the lifts. "We're going to a restaurant that's at the very top of the hotel, I hope that you will like it." The lift doors closed with a swish behind them, they were alone. He took her soft hand in his and raised it to his lips, she didn't pull away. " You know, you are the most beautiful girl in this hotel." She gave a low laugh. "Only the hotel, I'm disappointed, but you look pretty good and that is a deep tan where did you get it.." Al wasn't about to tell her it came from long days staring over a ship's rail. "Maybe too much leisure time."

The lift came to a smooth stop at the 30th floor, they stepped out directly into the restaurant, Al was impressed. Wide sweeping windows circled the whole eating area, it was a revolving restaurant, affording a wonderful panoramic view of Singapore by night. They were quickly shown a table by one of the windows. Taking a seat Al stared across at his date the light of a flickering candle reflected in her dark eyes, eyes that were full of warmth. "Chose whatever you like on the menu, let's make this a night to remember." He whispered across to her. And it was such a night, two and a half hours spent eating, drinking and indulging in small talk and jokes as the restaurant revolved giving them unrivalled views over the city. All too soon for him they were in a cab taking Jessica back to her home. She lived in a poorer part of the city with her Mum and Dad, the taxi pulled up at a large apartment block. Although it was close to midnight it was still fairly busy, street hawkers by the side of the road doing a brisk trade. The clatter of woks and the smell of spicy foods came to them through the open taxi windows. She turned to him taking his hands in hers, "It's been a wonderful evening but I'm afraid I can't ask you in, it's my parents, they are a bit old fashioned." She paused before saying, "I'm sorry Al." "Don't be" he replied. "You've given me such a great time." He drew her in against his chest, holding her tightly, they kissed deeply and passionately. She broke away."I must go, I'm working tomorrow, but I will see you then." "You bet you will," he called after her as she walked away.

He waited till midday before calling Jessica, he was in luck she was working on the desk downstairs. "How about me taking you somewhere tonight, do you feel up for it ?" " I could not think for anything better, what have you got in mind." She replied. "I've got you in mind." He joked. "No, I noticed last night the Shangri-La hotel has a nightclub, shall we give it whirl." She paused slightly before replying. "That sounds great, you know I can't wait until I get away from here, see you there in the coffee shop at eight." He beat her to it this time arriving some time before her, his wasn't the only head to turn as she walked in. She wore figure hugging blue jeans which led to a bare midriff with just a skimpy crop top which was well filled with her ample bosom. Sliding into the seat beside him she gave him a quick peck on the cheek. "Hope I didn't keep you waiting too long." She whispered. "You know I would wait for you all night, you look fabulous." They sat and chatted happy in each other's company before he took her hand and led the way into "Barbarella's" the hotel nightclub. They found a secluded corner with soft plush seats and ordered drinks. Al found it hard to keep his eyes off her, not only was she beautiful but more importantly she had a shy and modest way about her. They had a couple of quick dances together before the DJ played some soft music. Al held her in his arms while she entwined hers around his neck moulding her soft pliant body into his. He spoke softly in her ear. "After this you don't have to go straight home you know. She spoke with a husky voice. "Where would you like to go." "Before you arrived here tonight, I took the liberty to book a room upstairs, I also ordered a good bottle of champagne, it should be nicely chilled by now." It was several seconds before she replied. "You've got some cheek but this dancing is thirsty business." He gave her a squeeze and led her off the dance floor. Ten minutes later Al turned the key in the lock of room 409 and ushered Jessica into the interior. He kicked the door shut behind him, drew Jessica into his arms and kissed her long and hard. She broke away and said in mock indignation. " Hey, where's that drink you promised me." "Of course." Al said spreading his arms wide." How forgetful of me." He reached over to a small coffee table upon which stood a silver ice bucket with a bottle of Moet and Chandon protruding from the top. They sat close together on the bed and raised their chilled glasses to each other."Here's to us." Al said. "I've been a lucky guy meeting you, you are so good for me, you just don't realise." Jessica slid her free arm around his waist and whispered. "Do you think you care enough about me to love me." "No doubt about that I am falling in love with you." He responded. He drew her down on the bed letting his lips explore the soft nape of her neck, ears and down to her swelling bosom. Easing off the crop top he let the tip of his tongue excite the erect nipples. She moaned softly before swinging her feet off the bed and quickly discarded the remainder of her clothes. Just before she reached over to switch off the bedside light Al got a glimpse of her beautiful naked body before she disappeared under the sheets. He shed his clothes in seconds and joined her in the soft bed. It was as though an electric current passed though them as they touched, they fused together as one. The ice in the bucket had melted long before they finally fell asleep entwined in each other's arms.

The insistant ringing of the phone finally brought him out of his deep sleep, a quick glance at his watch showed it was 6 a.m. the time he had asked to be called. He gently shook Jessica awake."Come on Sweetheart, time I took you home. "What time is it." She said rubbing sleep from her eyes. When he told her she sat bolt upright, "God, my Dad isn't going to be happy." They both dressed quickly and made their way downstairs. Al paid the bill and hailed a waiting cab, they hardly spoke on the journey to her home. He held her tightly, while she rested her head on his shoulder. It was if all their emotions had been spent during during the night. She whispered into his ear. "You know Al, I think I've fallen in love with you, you are very special to me. " "I've got you babe." He said "in the words of the song that's all that I need, I love you too." The cab pulled in next to her apartment building. " Call me later today darling." She said, kissed him and eased her graceful body from the car. She turned abruptly."By the way I forgot to tell you, earlier today at the hotel there was a man who called to ask if you were staying there, but did not leave a name."

He said goodbye, but wasn't thinking of her, a terrible feeling of dread seemed to come over him. Who was the stranger? And why was he looking for him? There was no knowing, there was no one with any knowledge that he was staying in Singapore apart from the ship's crew he had just left. But there was a nagging doubt in the back of his mind, what if Mossard had discovered his whereabouts. He couldn't leave anything to chance there was only one thing for it, he had to get out of Singapore and fast. Arriving back at his hotel room the first thing he did after packing up his few possessions was to write a short letter to Jessica, he would leave it at reception. He checked out and left the hotel on foot. It would be easier to establish if there was anyone following. After two blocks he was positive there wasn't , quickly hailing a passing cab he was at Singapore central train station in ten minutes. He was in luck, there was a train departing in fifteen minutes for Bangkok, that would have to do. It would put him a thousand miles from the Lion city. He bought a ticket for a sleeping berth, because sleep was the one thing that that he needed right now. He found himself suspiciously eyeing his fellow passengers but none seemed to show any interest in him. Settling into a window seat he watched the urban jungle of Singapore pass by until the train rumbled over the causeway and into Malaysia. He gazed at the receding shoreline of Singapore with a mixture of relief and sadness. Glad to be away from any prying eyes but deeply upset at the thought of not knowing when he would hold the warm and wonderful person that was Jessica. Each turn of the wheels below him was taking him further away from her, and into a very uncertain future.

Chapter 28

The gentle rocking of the train soon induced sleep to a weary Al, he was oblivious for several hours as the train rolled through the scenic Malaysian countryside with its pretty villages and forested hills. When he awoke he felt groggy and hungry, it was soon resolved by a visit to the restaurant car where he ordered a large plate of nasi goreng. The Malaysian special fried rice with an egg on top was one of his favourite meals. He washed it down with a pint of cold tiger beer and soon began to feel a lot chirpier. It was time to take stock and consider the options open to him when he arrived at Bangkok. All of a sudden it came to him, in fact he wondered why the thought had not crossed his mind earlier. The big aussie Simon Richards had implored him to come and visit when he had a chance, who knows with his connections maybe he could just find a job and settle in Australia, His mind began buzzing with ideas, but deep down he realized it was far too soon to resurface in Australia. Now was the time to lie low for at least a year. Before the train had reached the border with Thailand he had more or less decided where he would spend it. There had been plenty of time on the long journey north to think over his life and where it was heading now. There were so many maybe's or if's but one thing he could never have changed was the fateful day that both his wife and children died at the bottom of a cliff. He had clawed at the walls and cried floods of tears but there was no relief. It was at that moment his life had lost it's direction, its purpose. It was the reason why he was on this train now, for had his Wife been alive today he would never have even considered the hit on Rubenstein. Yes there had been good times, very good times, and it was those he must remember, there was no point being being bitter, that would just eat away inside. He watched the passing landscape and observed women bent double harvesting rice in the muddy paddy fields. What life did they have, working each day from dawn to dusk to put a little food on the table. Everything was relative, he had been fortunate in so many ways, much more so than many people. By the time the train had pulled in to Bangkok station he had almost convinced himself that he was a lucky guy.

It was time to find some transport, for where he intended to go it was a must. He mingled easily with the throngs of people scurrying about their business on the packed streets until he became upon a garage that sold 4 by 4's. He haggled with the owner over the price of a second hand land cruiser that had seen better days until they both came to a compromise. He was well aware that what little money he had was diminishing too fast for his liking. He picked up a road map and then slowly began driving through Bangkok's busy streets towards the south. But he was in no hurry despite having a great distance to travel, after all he intended to stay about a year. After a couple of hours he picked up the main highway heading south, heading towards his ultimate destination, Pattani. He had thought long and hard coming up on the train as to what his next move could be. He needed to rent a small but inexpensive house far from the big cities and tourist resorts, and he knew just the place. It had to be the beautiful little village he had discovered on the coast near Pattani.

Night started drawing in before he had barely covered half the distance, it was time to find somewhere to rest his weary head before commencing his journey on the morrow. Arriving at a sleepy little town he spotted what passed for a small hotel. Although the place was run down the staff were welcoming and friendly, they were quick to tell him very few farangs stayed at their place. The room was basic but Al did not care too much as it came so cheap and more importantly had a phone. He knew that he must call Jessica, she was working tonight and had only the letter which said that he was being urgently called away on business. He was lucky, she picked up the phone first time. "Al" she said in that low tone he loved. "You should not really call me at work."Her voice became almost became a whisper. "Even though I love you so much." He felt his heart melting. "So sorry to have to have left so soon, but I am sure that it won't be for long." He lied. " That makes me so happy." She said with a wistful tone. "Oh, that man phoned again for you, said that his name was Jim Riley, and something about his ship being delayed." Al felt a surge of relief sweep through him, of course Mossad were clever but not that clever to discover that he was staying at a hotel in Singapore. He had become too paranoid, he was in the clear although he must not let his guard slip. "Are you still there." Her voice rose a little. "Sure, I was thinking of our time last night." "Don't make me blush, I've got people at the desk darling, here is my home phone number, call me soon."

His last thought before falling asleep under the creaking fan was one of peace. At least here surely there could be no threat to him, the trail had gone cold for Mossard in the Canaries.

He woke with a start, sitting bolt upright not knowing where he was until it all came back to him and he visibly relaxed. He knew it would take some time before the feeling of apprehension he had each time he awoke would pass. He had a Thai breakfast of rice and soup which was spiced up with chillies, it certainly made him fully awake before hitting the road once more. He pulled away from the hotel and began the final leg of his journey to what he hoped would be a refuge from the trials and tribulations of the last few weeks. As he approached the outskirts of Pattani a feeling of guilt overcame his other emotions, after all he had escaped from the Canaries whereas Todd had not. He knew he had to find out if Todd's widow was at least a lot richer, it was time to call the bank in Switzerland. He would feel a great deal happier if the transfer had gone through. Pulling up at the local post office he first bought several phone cards and found an empty booth.

The call went through without any trouble."Ah, Mr Jenkins," the voice on the other end of the line came through remarkably clear."We can confirm that the money was transferred as you requested." The bank official replied. A wave of relief swept over Al. "That's wonderful, but I don't suppose that leaves a great deal in my account." "On the contrary Mr Jenkins." The bank official politely replied." Just over a week ago the sum of one million dollars was lodged in your account." He paused, Al could hear him tapping on his computer keys. "Ah yes, it came from the Bank of the Middle East." Al gripped the receiver hard, his head swimming, trying to take in what he had just heard. "Would there be anything else Sir." The voice was insistent in his ear."Er, no, that's great." Al said absentmindedly. He put the phone down very gently as if afraid he had heard wrong. There was only one thing for it, he must call Yousef, surely he must know that Ben Rubenstein was still alive, it would mean of course that he could recall the money. There was the problem of course of not having Yousef's number. He could however ask the operator to put him in touch with the Sheik's household. After what seemed an interminable time a soft female voice came through asking what business department he required. Al explained slowly who he needed to speak to, and that it was very urgent. She wasn't too impressed but said she would try. He watched as his credits on the phone card slowly ebbed away, he knew it would be very hard to make the connection again. He almost jumped at the sound of Yousef 's voice. He sounded brusque and none too happy."This is not a secure line to call on you know." "There shouldn't be a problem, I'm calling from a phone box outside Europe." Yousef replied in a more relaxed tone. "Perhaps your right, but why are you calling, I've kept my side of the deal as you have properly already found out." "Yes you have." Al's voice tailed away not quite sure what to say next. "Anyway," Yousef continued. "It was quite brilliant, how you managed it I don't want to know but the fact that he died of a heart attack is widely known." "A heart attack." Al faltered then quickly went on. "Mind you, a dear friend of mine also died out there." "Sorry to hear that but of course you were playing for high stakes." Yousef replied matter- of- factly. "You won't hear from me again." The line went dead, Yousef had put down the phone.

Al walked from the phone booth out into the free fresh air, his feet felt light as a feather, he felt as if he were in a dream as the enormity of what he had just heard began to sink in. So the old bastard Rubenstein had shuffled off his mortal coil. It was quite likely that the heart attack had been brought on by the events in the Canaries, in particular when he had looked down the barrel of Al's gun. So that was why the Sheik had paid up, it all made sense. They had put it all down to him which in a way was quite justified. He punched the air in delight, he didn't care who was looking, he had one million dollars in the bank. All of a sudden the future looked bright, he would still stay in Thailand for a year but now he could stay in comfort. After that, well maybe

Australia he could go into business with Simon Richards, there were plenty of possibilities. It was time to check out the area around the sleepy little village on the coast for a house which he could rent, nothing out of the ordinary. He knew that to attract attention was not a good idea.

It had been raining during his time in the post office but now as he made his way to the battered looking land cruiser the dark rain clouds were slowly clearing. The sun was breaking though by the time he approached the coast, making the roads steam with heat but giving a freshly washed look to the World. With the knowledge that he was now a wealthy man all the colours seemed much brighter, more vibrant. He pulled up close to the spot where he had first alighted just a few weeks ago, was it just that recently, it seemed eons ago. He had hardly sat down on the warm sand when the boy he had seen on his previous visit approached with a basket full of seafood. Al was in a benevolent mood and paid over the odds for a small portion. It occurred to him that the boy may know someone who knew of houses for rent. Hadn't he said his mother was named Anya and spoke good english. "Yes, you come to my house, I'm sure my mother can help you, not far." The boy said pointing in the direction of a nearby clump of tall coconut trees. Al followed with not a little trepidation, what if it were the Anya he knew from 16 years ago. He picked his way through the fallen coconut husks, there were also banana and papaya trees with ripening fruit when he saw the house at the end of a short lane. He was surprised to see the house was fairly substantial and mostly brick built with a small veranda to the front. It was on this veranda that a woman leaned against the wooden handrail staring in his direction. Al gazed back as he slowly came closer he could see the recognition in her dark eyes. She walked down the couple of steps and came towards him, despite the years, she still retained the beauty, the charm he had fallen in love with, it was Anya.

"Somchai," she almost whispered, the name she called him by when they were in Bangkok."Is it really you, never in my wildest dreams did I ever expect to see you again." Al drew her close against him, she lay her head upon his chest. "Anya." he breathed. "I have found you, and I have found peace." They stood together, arms locked around each other not speaking for several seconds. Al was almost glad she wasn't looking at his face, for the tears that welled up and rolled down his cheeks he had no control over. She stood apart and looked him up and down."You look good, the years have been kind to you but I think you are tired." "Always the perceptive Anya." He laughed. She looked earnest and wiping a tear from her eyes said. " I have a surprise for you." Turning her head towards the house she called loudly. "Suwanee." A girl in her teens came to the doorway. Anya beckoned her over to where they stood. She was tall for a Thai and her hair and skin was lighter than her mothers. As she came towards them Al studied her closely, the hairs on the back of his neck stood up, there was something about this beautiful girl he couldn't fathom out, the penetrating eyes were so unlike her mother's. As she joined them Anya spoke. "Suwanee, I want you to meet your father." She looked almost startled at first, then threw her arms around Al's neck. "Khun Paw." She cried. Al gripped her hard as he blinked back the tears. She had used the thai words for father, words he expected never to hear again.

Printed in Great Britain
by Amazon